DREAMS COME TRUE AT PRIMROSE HALL

JILL STEEPLES

Boldwood

First published in Great Britain in 2023 by Boldwood Books Ltd.

Copyright © Jill Steeples, 2023

Cover Design by Debbie Clement Design

Cover Photography: iStock & Shutterstock

Every effort has been made to obtain the necessary permissions with reference to copyright material, both illustrative and quoted. We apologise for any omissions in this respect and will be pleased to make the appropriate acknowledgements in any future edition.

A CIP catalogue record for this book is available from the British Library.

Paperback ISBN 978-1-80280-713-4

Large Print ISBN 978-1-80280-712-7

Hardback ISBN 978-1-80280-711-0

Ebook ISBN 978-1-80280-715-8

Kindle ISBN 978-1-80280-714-1

Audio CD ISBN 978-1-80280-706-6

MP3 CD ISBN 978-1-80280-707-3

Digital audio download ISBN 978-1-80280-709-7

Boldwood Books Ltd
23 Bowerdean Street
London SW6 3TN
www.boldwoodbooks.com

To Dearest Darling Ellie

1

Pia Temple emerged from the Wildflower Trail in Primrose Woods, clipped Bertie, the Dalmatian, onto his lead, patting his head for his uncharacteristically good behaviour today, and took the path that led towards home. She paused outside the entrance to the visitors' centre and Treetops Cafe to read the notices in the window, as she always did, interested to see what was going on in the local area. Most of them she'd seen before and her eyes skittered over those, before her gaze alighted on a new postcard that immediately drew her interest.

Man/Girl Friday required!

Personal assistant required to work for the MD of a private company within a busy household environment. Duties to include admin work, personal organisation, animal care and so much more. Enthusiasm and a willingness to learn more important than experience. This is a full-time live-in position with a good salary for the right applicant. Please apply to JM Enterprises on the following email address.

Pia pulled out her phone and took a snap of the advert. She'd fire off an application as soon as she got home. If there was one thing Pia was in desperate need of right now, it was a job. And if there was one thing she needed even more than a job, it was a place to live. She scanned the words again, in search of anything that might preclude her from applying. Admin work? That would be a doddle, and organisation was her middle name – she'd spent the last few years organising all sorts of things: doctors' visits, hospital appointments, bed pans – surely some of those skills would be transferable. As for animals, she absolutely loved them. Dogs, cats, budgerigars – you name it, Pia had an affinity with them. It was what she'd always wanted to do after leaving school, train in animal management, but life had got in the way of that particular dream, even if her love for animals hadn't diminished in the meantime. And while she knew that at twenty-eight she didn't have much, or indeed any experience, in an office environment, she had plenty of enthusiasm and willingness to do almost anything, within reason.

As she walked home with Bertie, a kernel of excitement ran through her veins. The job would suit her perfectly. She knew better, though, than to get her hopes up. She'd applied for enough jobs in recent months to know that a lot of employers didn't even bother to reply, and in the few interviews she had attended, she'd lost out to other more experienced applicants. There were no details on the ad as to where the job would be based, but it would have to be locally or why else would it be advertised in Primrose Woods?

'It's only us!' Pia called out, a little while later, as she let herself in through the back door of her neighbour, Wendy's, house. She immediately grabbed the towel from the cupboard to wipe down Bertie's muddy paws. 'Will you keep still,' she gently scolded him as he danced around on his tiptoes, eager to be freed so that he could go and greet his mum. With paws cleaned as well as possible with a wriggly, unhelpful Dalmatian, Pia unclipped his lead and he went bouncing off into the living room. Pia heard Wendy's laughter ring out as she made a fuss of her beloved dog's return, while Pia flicked the kettle on and pulled two mugs out from the corner cabinet. She pottered around the kitchen, putting away the crockery on the draining board and running a cloth across the surfaces. She liked to help out where she could. She spotted the opened post on the kitchen table and her gaze drifted over the contents of the letter sitting at the top of the pile. When she saw who it was from, she couldn't stop herself from reading on, the contents of the letter stirring all sorts of emotions within her. She took a big breath before joining Wendy in the living room with the mugs of tea, whose face lit up at the sight.

'Ooh, what a sweetheart you are. I'm not sure what I'd do without you. Did Bertie behave himself on his walk?'

'He did, and we met a ten-month-old black Lab called Leo who gave him a right run around. They had such fun together, although I think Bertie was quite relieved when they left in the opposite direction. Anyway, how are you feeling now, Wendy?' Pia sat down on the end of the sofa nearest to Wendy's chair, her hands cupped around her mug of tea, while Bertie stretched out in the space in front of the fireplace.

'All right. If it wasn't for these useless legs of mine. Some days they just refuse to work.'

Pia had lived next door to Wendy all her life. She remembered her from when she was a little girl, a good friend to her parents, a happy and smiling face over the garden fence, and when she wasn't busy with her job as a teaching assistant at the village school or running the local Brownies group, then she was baking cakes or pottering about in her garden. Then she'd been a vibrant, energetic woman, always on the go, a well-known and much-loved member of the local community, always eager to help out anyone in need. These days, Wendy's spirit and compassion were still very much in evidence, but sadly her body was less willing, and Pia hated to see her friend so frustrated by her incapacity.

'Sorry, but I couldn't help noticing when I was out in the kitchen, the letter from Rushgrove Lodge?' Pia kept her tone light, knowing she needed to tread carefully as far as this particular subject was concerned.

'You can put that straight in the bin. I'm not interested,' said Wendy vehemently. 'That's Simon, you know, interfering from afar.'

'He's worried about you and only trying to help.'

'Well, he doesn't need to. I've managed all these years on my own; I'll get through this little hiccup as well.'

Pia reached out a hand and laid it on Wendy's arm, unable to quash the thought that this crisis was more than a minor hiccup. Wendy's arthritis had seriously impacted on her mobility in recent months and she was worryingly unsteady on her feet. She'd already had a couple of falls that had resulted in bruised ribs and a broken wrist.

'I've heard it's really lovely at Rushgrove Lodge. My best friend from school, Abbey, is the manager there.'

'I'm sure it is, but I won't be moving there. Someone else can have my spot.'

'All I'm saying is that it might be worth you going along for a viewing, just to see what it's like. You never know, you might decide you like it if you see it for yourself.'

'I won't,' said Wendy firmly. 'I'm not going anywhere without Bertie and no one can force me, so I would save your breath.'

Suitably chastised, Pia gave a kindly smile, knowing now wasn't the time to press the point. It really wasn't her place to do so anyway. She'd spoken to Wendy's son, Simon, several times on the phone, usually after the latest crisis, and he was just as concerned about Wendy as Pia was but there was only so much he could do from the other side of the world. He worked in the copper mines in Australia and only managed to get back to the UK every couple of years.

'Anyway, enough about me,' said Wendy, obviously eager to move the conversation on. 'What's the latest on the house?'

'It's all going through as planned; we have a completion date now, three weeks on Friday.' Pia kept her tone light, upbeat, although whether it was for Wendy's benefit or her own she wasn't entirely sure.

'I still can't believe Connor would do that to you, force you out of your own home. After everything you did for your mum and dad. All those years you spent caring for them, putting your own life on hold.'

'About time, then, that I got on with living my life,' said Pia brightly. 'Besides, it isn't like that. Mum and Dad left the house to both of us. Connor's getting married this year, so it's only natural that he and Ruby want to find a place of their own, somewhere to buy.'

'But they're making you homeless. Where will you go? Oh, I am going to miss you, Pia.'

'I shall miss you too, Wendy, but you won't be able to get rid of me that easily. I'll be calling round on a regular basis, that's for sure. And until I find a place of my own, I'm going to be staying with Connor and Ruby.'

Wendy let out a heartfelt sigh and Pia knew exactly how she felt. She was dreading moving out of the house that had been her home ever since she was a baby, with all the memories it held from her childhood and of her late parents. To her it was so much more than the unremarkable three-bedroom terraced house that it might appear to others. It was her home, her safe place and she could still feel the presence of her mum and dad within the fabric of the walls. She would miss it so much more than she was willing to admit to anyone, but it was time to move on. She'd stood still for far too long, as Wendy was keen to remind her often.

'Well, that's hardly ideal, is it?' the older woman said now and although Pia was inclined to agree with her, she just shrugged her shoulders nonchalantly.

If she stopped to think too long about all the changes she had in front of her then she might be too frozen with fear to do anything. She had to clear her parents' house of all the years of accumulated possessions, not an easy task when almost everything sparked an emotional reaction within her, find a new place to live and find a job that would pay the bills. Her inheritance from the sale of the house would tide her over for a short while, but she would need to work to fund her new lifestyle, but more than that she wanted to work.

Most pressingly, though, she was worried about Wendy. She glanced across at her friend now, looking frail and vulnerable in her armchair, and Pia felt a stab of fear, not knowing how often she would get to see Wendy in the future if she had to move away from the village. Places to rent in Norton End were few and far between. How would Wendy manage without someone checking in on her every day, making sure both she and Bertie were okay? Pia knew better than to mention her concerns to Wendy – she would only brush them aside, saying she was perfectly capable of looking after herself, thank you! Although these days Pia wasn't sure that was actually the case.

'It will all work out fine, for both of us,' said Pia. 'Just you wait and see. You know what we should do? Have a little leaving party It's such a big deal, me moving out from Meadow Cottages. I shall miss this place so much, but we ought to mark the occasion.' Pia knew there would be tears and sadness, but she had to keep reminding herself of the positives, all the happy memories she would carry in her heart. Excitingly, she could look to the future now too, even if that future was scarily uncertain at the moment. 'I'll put together an afternoon tea with some sandwiches, cream scones, cakes and some fizz. What do you think? Connor and Ruby will come along, I'm sure, and maybe we can invite some of the neighbours too?'

'Hmm, I'm not sure you moving away is cause for celebration, but if you want to, I suppose we could do.'

Pia spotted the reluctant curl of Wendy's lip, knowing her friend could never refuse the offer of some cake or a bit of a do either. Pia grinned. Despite her misgivings about the future, she was looking forward to a little party already.

2

Back at home, Pia shrugged off her coat and boots, and pulled up the ad she'd saved on her phone. She wished there was a telephone number on there, so she could call the company directly, but there was nothing apart from a generic email address, which she suspected would be inundated with applications. Without holding out much hope at all, she sent off her cover letter, along with her recently put-together CV.

The trouble was she knew that her CV was severely lacking in almost every area, even if it wasn't entirely her fault. Ten years ago she'd had great plans to leave home, to take up the place she'd been offered on a university course at the opposite end of the country, but the month before she was due to go, her dad fell ill and all her priorities changed in that instant. She'd planned to defer the start of her course for a year, but when the time came she didn't feel ready to leave her parents behind, not when her dad was still recovering from his stroke and her mum was recently diagnosed with cancer. There were those who told her not to put her life on hold, especially her mum and dad, but there was no way she could leave home knowing her parents were so vulnerable. Instead of gaining her independence, making new friends, studying hard and partying even harder, she'd eschewed all those pleasures to care for her family and she hadn't regretted it for a moment. She'd taken up short-term casual jobs when she could, bar work and shop work, but there wasn't anything that looked impressive on paper. So why was she even getting up her hopes for this particular job when she knew she had little chance of getting it?

She put the idea out of her head, returning to the task in hand. She sighed, looking at the mess around her. Already today she'd filled two black bags with rubbish and still it seemed as though she'd barely made a dent in the job. It was such a mammoth undertaking sorting through years of her parents' belongings and paperwork. She really needed to get cracking if she was going to be ready to move out in three weeks' time. Not knowing where she'd end up did nothing for her motivation or for her peace of mind. If it had been down to her then she would have happily stayed living at Meadow Cottages, but it simply wasn't an option. The house had already been sold to a lovely young couple who were expecting a baby. It was time for another family to make their own happy memories there.

It was a couple of hours later when she heard the familiar rumble of Connor's van pulling up outside the front of the house. She jumped up from where she'd been crouched on the floor and peered out the window to see his familiar figure sauntering down the front path.

'All right, sis?' he called, as he always did, as he let himself in through the back door. 'Are you having a cuppa?'

'Please!' she said, walking through to greet him, relieved of the distraction. As Connor pulled out mugs from the cupboard and popped teabags inside, she collected the milk from the fridge.

'So, how's it going in there?' Connor asked, glancing through to the living room at the chaos on the floor.

'I think "slowly" is the word. There's just so much stuff to go through; there's a load of your games and consoles up in the third bedroom. Do you want to have a look and see which bits you want to keep?'

'Honestly, Pia, anything of mine can go straight in the bin. I've already taken everything I want to hang on to. You need to be more ruthless and just chuck most of this stuff away. We can't keep it all and most of it's just rubbish.'

It hurt Pia to hear Connor sound so cavalier about all their parents' belongings. If it was down to him then she knew the job would be done by now. He'd have scooped everything up into bags and boxes and taken them to the tip. She couldn't do that; she had to go through each individual item, keeping anything that held sentimental value. She sighed, knowing that included most things. It was funny the memories that could be stirred by an old birthday card with her mum's thoughtful words penned inside, or the tattered box of Scrabble that they'd played so frequently when her mum was still able to do so. There were bits of old furniture too, a dark wood chest of drawers, and a set of oak chairs with a matching table, with no monetary value, but they'd been passed down from her grandparents so there was no way Pia could think about giving them away. At this rate she would need to organise a storage facility for all the bits she couldn't bear to part with.

'Don't worry,' she said, feigning a brightness she couldn't muster inside, 'it will all be done by the time the removal van turns up.'

'Do we even need one? We can probably get most of the stuff in my van. It's not worth paying out if we don't really need to.'

'It's all booked and paid for, and don't worry, it won't all be coming to your doorstep, if that's what you're concerned about.'

'Hey, you know we're happy to help in whatever way we can, until you find a place of your own, but I just don't think you'll be able to take all this stuff with you, wherever you end up going.' Connor looked around him, shaking his head.

Pia picked up a pile of the paperwork she'd already sorted through from the kitchen table and stuffed it into one of the many black bags littered around the floor, more for Connor's benefit than her own.

'So how are the wedding arrangements coming along?' Pia asked eager to change the subject.

'Yeah, we're pretty much there with everything. Only a couple of months to go now; I can hardly believe it. It's just a shame that Mum and Dad won't be there to be a part of it.'

'They would have been so excited – can you imagine? Never mind, we'll just have to make sure we celebrate as if they were there, and I'm sure they'll be with us in spirit.'

'Yep.' For a moment, Connor's gaze drifted out the window and he looked uncharacteristically pensive until he gathered himself. 'Ruby asked me to tell you: she's confirmed all the arrangements for the hen night. It's going to be on the Friday, the week after you move out from here. She thought it better to do it then so you'll have no excuses not to turn up.'

Pia gave a wry smile.

'Ruby knows me all too well, but don't worry, I'll be there,' she said, unable to hide her reluctance.

'It'll be fun, Pia. You need to get out more and enjoy yourself. This will be the ideal opportunity.'

Pia adored Ruby and thought she was the perfect match for her brother, Connor, but none of them would be surprised to know that a hen night in a cocktail bar in town that would quickly become very loud, raucous and messy was Pia's idea of hell. She'd already suggested that she didn't go, but Ruby had insisted that Pia was central to the celebrations, so she really didn't have much choice in the matter. It was only one night; how bad could it be? Knowing Ruby and her friends, probably very bad. Still, she couldn't worry about that now. She had plenty of other more pressing concerns: getting the house packed up, finding somewhere to live, and a job, making sure Wendy and Bertie were safe and well cared for. She was also reminded that she needed to find a wedding present for Connor and Ruby. That familiar sensation of panic took a grip in her chest.

'Talking about my social life, I was just saying to Wendy that we should have a little going away party, just some tea and cakes, and some fizz. I think she'd appreciate it. I know she's dreading me moving away. She won't admit it, but I think she's worried that I won't be here to pop in on her so often. Hopefully the new people will be friendly and keep an eye on her. Anyway, I thought late afternoon the Wednesday before moving day – she'd love you both to be there.'

'In that case, we will be, although you need to think about making some new friends too. Preferably some under the age of seventy-five?' Connor was grinning as he placed his empty mug in the sink. 'I'll take these black bags to the tip. Hopefully, there'll be a few more by tomorrow,' he said with a wink.

As he made his way to the back door, Pia's phone beeped in her pocket. She pulled it out to look at it, and gasped.

'Crikey, that was quick!'

'Anything exciting?' he asked, clocking her expression as she peered over her phone.

'Do you know,' she said with a big smile, 'I think it just might be.'

3

Pia couldn't believe that she'd had a response to her job application quite so quickly. Usually she would have to wait weeks for any sort of answer, if she heard back from her applications at all, and this particular invitation to interview had come through on the very same day, within the space of a few hours. It was strange, though, because she didn't have any further information about the company or where they were based, or even a contact name. She would have liked to do some background research on the company, but with only an email address to go on, her Google searches didn't lead her very far. What she did know was that the interview was the next day at 10 a.m. at the Treetops Cafe, which was odd in itself. Why not at the house? she wondered. Hopefully it would all become clear once she arrived for her interview.

It was a relief, then, when she turned up at the cafe the next day to find Lizzie Baker working behind the counter, a friendly and familiar face, who immediately came across to greet Pia.

'Hello, lovely, we don't often see you in here. Do you want to take a seat over by the window and I'll come over and take your order.'

'I'm actually supposed to be meeting someone, although I'm not sure how I'm supposed to recognise them,' she said, dropping her voice to a whisper as her gaze drifted around the cafe.

'For an interview?' said Lizzie. 'Ah, see the gentleman over there, with his back to us – that's him.' She squeezed Pia's arm in an encouraging show of support and Pia's stomach churned, as her nerves threatened to get the better of her. Part of her wanted to turn around and walk out again, but it was too late for that, so she pulled back her shoulders and marched over with a confidence that was entirely forced.

'Hello.' She smiled brightly. 'My name's Pia; I'm here for the interview.'

The man sitting at the table put down his phone and got up to greet her, and in that moment, Pia visibly startled, a myriad of thoughts and emotions bombarding her head as she wondered if she shouldn't just do what had popped into her mind a moment ago: turn and walk in the opposite direction. Instead, she blurted, 'Jackson! What are you doing here?'

'Hi, Pia. Why don't you take a seat?'

She pulled out the chair on the opposite side of the table and sat down, all the time staring at Jackson, as if she couldn't quite believe who she was seeing.

'It's great to see you. It's been a while. About seven or eight years, I'm guessing?'

'Ten,' she corrected him, still staring at him as she battled to get her breathing under control, not knowing if she was thrilled or outraged at his sudden reappearance in her life. One thing was for certain: she was shocked. Very shocked. 'I was eighteen,' she said, making it sound like an accusation. With a sudden urgency, she pushed herself up and out of her seat. 'I need to go; I'm supposed to be meeting someone here.'

Jackson looked up from beneath long black lashes, his dark eyes brimming with serious intent, and it was only the half-smile on his lips that softened his expression. She remembered that look from way back when, the way it'd made her feel.

'Sit down, Pia – it's me you're meeting.'

She slumped down in the seat just as Lizzie arrived at their table with an expectant look on her face.

'A cappuccino, please,' Pia said on autopilot, watching as Lizzie went off to see to her order, only wishing she could go off with her.

'I don't understand,' she said now to Jackson. She couldn't focus on what she was here for, not when her head was taunting her with memories of that last summer they'd had together. After finishing their A levels, they'd spent every moment of those long sunny days with each other: hanging out at Primrose Woods with their friends, riding through the lanes between the local villages on Jackson's motorbike and drinking cider at the back of the community hall. They'd made the most of that special time, knowing that it wouldn't last forever, that come the autumn she would be going off to college to study animal management and Jackson was heading up north to study financial mathematics at university. It wasn't supposed to be the end for them, rather a new beginning. Jackson had made Pia all sorts of promises: they would see each other at weekends, they would go travelling around Europe on the bike and they would reunite over the Christmas holidays. That was until Jackson had a change of plan, decided he'd had enough of education and that he was heading to the big city to make his fortune instead of going to uni. Not that he ever deigned to tell Pia any of this. He simply disappeared out of her life without so much as a word and she never saw him again. Until now.

'So, is this actually a proper interview, then? Or something else?'

'Yes, it's a proper interview,' he said, with a smile. 'Let me explain.' He rested his forearms on the table, his fingers interlocked together, as he leant across the table. She shifted her chair backwards, putting some distance between them.

He hadn't changed too much in the intervening years. His face was maybe a little thinner, the cut of his jaw and his cheekbones more prominent now. His hair was styled differently too. Back when he was a teenager, his jet-black hair was worn long and messily, falling over one eye, so that he continually had to rake a hand through it to clear it from his face. Now, it was cut short, further emphasising the strong lines of his jaw, making his eyes, dark as the night sky and just as romantic, even more striking. For a moment, she was transported back to her teenage self, remembering how she'd been mesmerised by those eyes, how she'd known even then that she would never forget them. And she hadn't, although perhaps she'd forgotten just how magnetic and intense they really were. She blinked her eyes closed for a moment to gather her thoughts and to compose herself, before returning her gaze on his features, waiting for him to explain.

'I've bought Primrose Hall. I moved in a couple of months before Christmas and I need someone to help me run the place. To act as my personal assistant, to help out with... well, basically everything.' Now she was reminded of that killer smile too, the one that offered a touch of sunshine to his dark, brooding features.

Their conversation was interrupted by Lizzie, who discreetly delivered Pia's cappuccino to the table, before returning to the serving counter.

'You live at Primrose Hall?' There was no way to hide her incredulity.

'Yep, I've always had a thing for the house ever since I was a kid. Me and my mates used to sneak in through the wire fencing and smoke cigarettes and drink cans of lager in the old porch. It was completely derelict back then – well, you'll probably remember; all the windows were boarded up and the grounds were completely overgrown. It was a wilderness, but I remember loving the place; it was completely magical to me as a kid. When I got the opportunity to buy the property, then I knew I just had to do it.'

'Wow!' It came out as a sigh. *The opportunity?* And a hefty bank balance too, she didn't doubt. She'd known that Primrose Hall had been restored to its former glory, had read an article about it in the local newspaper and seen the photos of the renovated seventeenth-century manor house looking resplendent against the backdrop of the surrounding verdant countryside, but she could never have imagined that Jackson Moody, her teenage crush, would be behind this transformation. 'That's amazing.'

It was very impressive, but then if anyone from school was going to leave the village under a cloud and come back years later to take up the role of lord of the manor, was it really such a surprise that it was Jackson?

'It's a job for an all-rounder, someone who doesn't mind getting their hands dirty, in all possible senses. That's why I've stipulated someone who can live on site so that they can deal with any issues if I'm not around for any reason. That wouldn't be a problem for you, would it, Pia?'

She shook her head, distracted by the reminder of the way her name sounded on Jackson's tongue.

'There'll be general office work to do, dealing with supplier accounts and any queries, organising my diary so that I know what I should be doing and when, and generally overseeing the running of the house and the staff, and the welfare of the animals.'

'Animals?'

'Yeah, we have a Shetland pony and a donkey, Little Star and Twinkle. Don't ask,' he said, seeing Pia's amused expression. 'I somehow acquired them just before Christmas. They needed a home, and I took them in – they were a great hit at the Christmas carols event we ran. Now I seem to be stuck with them. Weren't you going to study something to do with animals at uni?'

'Yeah.' So he hadn't entirely forgotten her hopes and dreams, then.

'I heard about your folks – I'm sorry.'

'Thanks.' She realised she probably wasn't giving the best account of herself, but she didn't care. She wasn't out to impress Jackson and she wasn't here to indulge in small talk either.

'I see the house is up for sale. Where are you going?'

'I'm not sure yet. If I don't find my own place in time, then I'll go and stay with Connor and his fiancée for a while.' She paused, examining the backs of her hands. 'You must have known it was me when I applied for the job. Why did you invite me along? Did you want me to come and see what a great success you've made of your life?' She couldn't hide her bitterness. She would finish her coffee and make her excuses and leave. This was all utterly pointless.

'No!' His brow furrowed. 'Of course not. Do you really think that badly of me?'

She shrugged. What did he expect her to think? There'd been no fond farewells between the pair of them. Jackson had been there one day and he'd disappeared the next.

'Yes,' Jackson went on now. 'I saw your name and thought it must be you – I mean, how many Pia Temples are there living in Norton End? – but that's when it occurred to me that you would be absolutely perfect for the job.'

'Really? And why would you think that?' She bristled at his presumption. 'You'll have seen from my CV that I don't have a great deal of experience, apart from retail and bar work. I think we're probably wasting each other's time here.' She went to stand up, but Jackson reached across the table, his eyes imploring her to stay.

'Come on, Pia, don't be like that. I promise you I'm not wasting your time. And let me be the judge of whether or not you would be right for this job. I'm keen to hire someone local, if possible. Primrose Hall is such a wonderful building, and so integral to its surroundings, that I want the building to benefit the whole community in some way. Our first event at Christmas was so successful that I intend to make it an annual do, and I've got plans to run open days throughout the year using the renovated stables as pop-up shops for local craftspeople. The person joining me will help organise and publicise these events.'

It sounded interesting and challenging and she couldn't help but be impressed by Jackson's enthusiasm, but then she remembered him as a young man full of fire and passion.

'Tell me a bit about what you're looking for in a job?'

She paused for a moment. She could hardly tell him that at this point in her life she would probably take anything offered to her. Anything with a salary attached. Something full-time. Over the years she'd done some casual shifts at the pub and in various shops, but she'd never held down a permanent position. She hadn't been able to, not when she was a full-time carer to her parents. At the ripe old age of twenty-eight, it was time that situation changed, one of the first steps in changing her life around.

'Something that would give me the opportunity to widen my skills, where I could be a real asset to the company. I might not have a huge wealth of experience, but I'm very willing to learn. I feel I've missed out on a career, and now I'd like to make up for that.'

'Well, the role at Primrose Hall is one that you could make your own, and it will certainly grow as we take on further projects. I'd be happy to invest in any training that you feel you might need.'

It was good of Jackson to pretend to be interested in her career aspirations, to make out that this was a proper interview, although she still wasn't entirely certain that he'd got her along for anything other than a trip down memory lane. It didn't matter; she'd got over Jackson a long time ago. She hadn't seen him in ten years and after today and her brief run-in with the past, she hoped she wouldn't need to see him for another ten years. That might be more difficult now he was living back in the village, but she had much more important matters to dwell on than Jackson Moody.

Now he nodded interestedly, still going through the motions, no doubt, as his finger ran down the screen of his tablet.

'And when would you be able to make a start?' he asked, which she suspected was his way of bringing the interview to a close.

'Well, I'm moving on 26th March so it would have to be after then.'

'The 29th seems as good a day as any.' He turned the tablet over, laying it on the table, and placed his phone on top before observing her with a warm smile. 'Thanks very much for coming along. It's been great to see you again, Pia. It's been far too long. I'll be in touch.'

'Yes, great, thank you!' She stood up hurriedly, suddenly desperate to get away. Inexplicably, she held out a hand to him and he looked at it, bemused, before taking it and accepting the gesture. She ignored the sensation of goosebumps travelling up her arm, feeling his hand in hers, and breathed a huge sigh of relief as she walked away. As far as interviews went, that was probably the most bizarre one she'd ever attended, but it didn't matter. She was just pleased that it was over. There would be other interviews, other jobs and they would all have the distinct advantage of not having Jackson Moody as her potential boss.

4

As she expected, Pia didn't hear from Jackson Moody in the following days, but that only came as a huge relief to her. Although she thought it very rude of him not to do her the courtesy of sending a rejection letter. The sooner she put that whole episode out of her head, the better. Even if erasing the reminders of Jackson from her mind might not be as easy as she first thought. Every time she closed her eyes, there he was, taunting her with those dark, intense eyes and that endearing half-smile. It was okay; she was bound to forget about him soon enough.

The following week, when Connor dropped in on his way home from work, as he usually did, to collect any rubbish bags for the tip or help to move any heavy pieces of furniture, he asked how the job-hunting was going.

Pia stopped what she was doing and put her hands on her hips, surveying the scene around her. She was making progress of sorts, but it was still a slow process.

'Slowly!' Everything in her life seemed to be moving at a snail's pace right now. She supposed it was only to be expected during this period of transition. 'There have been a couple of interviews, but they haven't really come to very much. Oh, the one I told you about, at the lovely bookshop in town, well, they offered me a position, but it's only for twelve hours a week and I really need to find something with full-time hours now. So I'm still looking. I didn't tell you about the interview I had at Treetops Cafe, did I?'

'I didn't know they were hiring.'

'It wasn't actually to work at the cafe. It was to work as a personal assistant in a private household. I saw the ad in the cafe window and thought I had nothing to lose by applying, but it was all very mysterious. I didn't know what to expect when I turned up for the interview, but you'll never guess who was waiting for me when I arrived.'

Connor raised an eyebrow in question, narrowing his eyes.

'Jackson Moody! Can you believe it – he's actually the new owner of Primrose Hall.'

Connor nodded as he sipped on the mug of tea Pia had prepared for him. It wasn't quite the reaction she had been expecting. She thought he might have been as surprised and shocked as she'd been, but he appeared distinctly underwhelmed by the news.

'Yeah, we ran into him and his girlfriend at the Christmas carols they held in the grounds of the hall. They've done a pretty good job at renovating the place.'

She felt the hackles rise on her back and couldn't help the sharpness of her tone. 'What? And you didn't think to tell me?'

Connor put down his mug and looked across at her, having the grace to appear sheepish. 'Well, I wasn't certain you'd want to hear that Jackson was back in the village. Then, well, the moment passed. Sorry, Pia.'

She shrugged. It was true. Why would she be interested? Their romance was a long time ago.

'Don't be. I've long since got over him. It was just one of those teenage things.' She busied herself with sorting through the accumulation of board games in the dark wood cabinet. She would keep the Scrabble, Monopoly and Cluedo, and the rest she would take to the charity shop. *His girlfriend, though?* Jackson hadn't mentioned anything about a girlfriend, although now she came to think of it, he had spoken in the plural. The inference was there if only she'd picked up on it.

'I'll go up and collect those bedside cabinets and that washing basket – they're all to go in the rubbish, right?'

'Yes please.' She sat back on her heels on the floor and reflected for a moment as she listened to the sounds of Connor's footsteps up and down the stairs. She couldn't help feeling deflated and dissatisfied, and she angrily blinked away the spontaneous tears gathering in her eyes. When she thought of everything Jackson had achieved in his life – a successful career in the city, a beautiful house in the country with staff and animals, and a happy personal life too by the sounds of things – she couldn't help comparing it to what she had accomplished since she'd left school. She was still living in her childhood home, although not for much longer. She didn't have a job, let alone a career, she didn't have a boyfriend, and she didn't have any animals, and by this stage in her life she'd planned on having a whole menagerie. What exactly did she have to show for herself after all these years?

She stood up and wriggled her shoulders, easing out the tension, drawing on her resolve. It was just a moment's self-pity; even she was allowed that. The stress of sorting out her parents' house was clearly getting to her. If anything, she would take Jackson's success as inspiration to move forward in her own life. Why was she allowing his reappearance in her life to make her feel so bad about herself?

'All done!' Connor reappeared, poking his head around the living-room door. 'I'd better get off. Ruby wants me home at a reasonable time as we're finalising the seating plan tonight. That will be fun,' he said, rolling his eyes. 'Oh, there's a letter here.' He handed over the envelope he was clutching in his hand. 'It was hiding underneath the doormat.'

'Thanks,' she said, suspecting it was even more bumf and could go straight in the black rubbish bag.

'Keep up the good work, sis, and I'll see you tomorrow.'

After Connor had left, she headed into the kitchen and flicked on the kettle. She'd had enough for today, and with another few bags on their way to the tip, she felt as though she was slowly getting there. She opened the back door, her gaze stretching down the length of the garden. Connor had come over at the weekend and given the grass its first mowing of the year, so it looked tidy at least, perfectly adequate for the couple moving in. But she was reminded of how beautiful it had been when her dad had spent his every spare moment out there, tending to his vegetable patch at the bottom of the garden, always so proud when he came in with his arms full of courgettes, potatoes and lettuces. He'd grown sweet peas up canes too, their fragrant scent and beautiful colours filling Mum's vases during the summer months.

She would miss this little oasis of calm, with all the memories of the happy family times they'd spent out there. Birthdays, anniversaries, all sorts of celebrations. She could hear the excited squeals and laughter now from when her dad would set up the sprinkler on the lawn and she and Connor would run through the spray on those long hot days, before turning the hose on each other, laughing until their stomachs hurt. *Happy days!* Her reminiscing was interrupted by Bertie's barking from next door. Something else she'd miss. Being able to peer over the fence to chat to Wendy and to laugh at Bertie's antics.

She wandered back indoors to make her mug of tea, pulled out a chocolate digestive and decided to head outside again to sit at the table, maybe the last opportunity she would get to enjoy the garden. Even though it was still only March, they were in the midst of an uncharacteristically warm spell and it was lovely to sit outside and feel the sun on her skin. The old and tatty garden furniture would soon be going to the tip so she would make the most of it while she could.

Her peace and quiet was interrupted by Bertie's persistent barking from next door. He could be a noisy boy at times, barking at the arrival of any visitors, or if he spotted any wildlife in the garden, but normally it was short-lived. Something was clearly troubling him today. Maybe he wanted to get outside while Wendy was taking an afternoon nap. Pia eased herself out of the chair and went across to the fence, standing on tiptoes to see if she could see him at the back door, but there was no sign of him, although she could still very much hear his protestations. With a sudden fear snaking down her spine, she dashed out of the side gate and ran around the other side of the fence, along the path that led to Wendy's back door. Thank goodness it was open.

'It's only me,' she called, as she usually did, and was greeted by an even more enthusiastic welcome than normal from Bertie, who ran up to her excitedly, dancing on his paws. 'What is it, Bertie?' she said, bending over to make a fuss of the dog. 'Wendy?'

Only there was no reply, just a muffled groan. Bertie paced up and down, leading Pia through the living room and into the hallway. The sight that met Pia there made her stomach fall.

'Oh good grief, Wendy, how long have you been like this?'

Wendy's crumpled body was lying at the bottom of the stairs and she was sporting a nasty gash on her forehead with blood running down her face, her leg sticking out at an awkward angle.

'Get me up, will you, love?' Wendy winced as she tried to lever herself up from the floor.

'No, don't try and move, Wendy. I'm going to have to call an ambulance. It looks as though you might have twisted that ankle.'

'I'll be fine once I'm back up in my chair. Don't fuss, Pia.'

Pia's heart broke to see Wendy so frightened and upset, but she knew she had no option but to call the ambulance. She'd been downplaying it when she said she thought it was a twisted ankle; from her viewpoint it looked very much broken and Pia couldn't help but wonder what this would mean for Wendy's much-valued independence.

After hurriedly phoning the emergency services, Pia grabbed a blanket and draped it over Wendy, bending down on her haunches to tend to her friend.

'It will be okay, I promise. Try not to worry,' she said, looking into Wendy's eyes as she stroked her brow. She tried to be reassuring and calm, but fear lodged in Pia's chest seeing the colour drain from Wendy's face as she groaned in pain.

Thankfully the ambulance arrived within ten minutes, the paramedics quickly taking charge and confirming what Pia had suspected. Wendy would have to go to hospital.

'Don't make me go, Pia. Please! I'll be fine here; you can keep an eye on me. Tell them, Pia.'

'I wish I could, Wendy, but you need an X-ray on that leg and a full check-over by the doctors.'

Wendy's eyes fluttered closed and she shook her head in obvious despair. A solitary tear ran down her cheek.

'Don't cry.' Pia tried to reassure her friend, knowing instinctively what was troubling her most of all. 'I'll look after Bertie, don't worry about that.'

'But how can you?' Wendy's eyes pinged open. 'You've got enough on your plate with the house move. What will happen to him? It would break my heart if he had to go to the kennels.'

'I promise you,' said Pia, squeezing hold of Wendy's hand and looking into her watery eyes. 'I will look after Bertie, of course I will. He'll stay with me for as long as it takes until you're better.'

'Do you mean that?'

Pia nodded and Wendy gave a relieved smile, dropping her head back on the rolled-up blanket provided by the paramedics. It was a promise Pia would keep. Somehow or other. She knew she wouldn't be able to take the dog to Ruby and Connor's place, though. Her search for a new place to live, somewhere that took dogs, had just become a whole lot more urgent.

5

After the ambulance left for the hospital, Pia quickly whizzed around Wendy's house, closing the windows, tidying and washing up and putting away the crockery. She didn't know when Wendy might be coming home, but she suspected it wouldn't be anytime soon, so she would need to pop in regularly to keep an eye on the place. She cleaned out Bertie's bowls and sorted out his food and treats, along with his bedding. He'd been on sleepovers before at Pia's so he would settle in quickly round at hers with any luck. She still had a couple of weeks before moving day. Surely a solution would have presented itself by then. Her mum always used to tell her, *Don't fret, things will work out fine in the end*, and she crossed her fingers in the air at Bertie, hoping that was true.

Later, Pia walked Bertie around the village, through the lanes, past the duck pond and the church before returning to Meadow Cottages, pausing for a moment to look at the sweet terrace of houses, the sight so familiar, so reassuring. Everything was changing, though. In a couple of weeks, Pia would be leaving for good and now she wondered if Wendy would ever return here. She'd spoken to the hospital, who'd confirmed that Wendy was comfortable but would need to go to theatre in the morning for an operation to fix her broken ankle. It looked likely to be a long recovery time.

'Come on, Bertie, let's get indoors,' she said, jostling herself out of her daydreaming.

Inside, Pia fed Bertie and he settled down on the sofa, making himself very much at home. She wasn't going to argue with him. He'd had a traumatic day and she was happy to see him content and curled up there. It was only when she came in with her cheese sandwich and mug of tea that she remembered the letter Connor had found underneath the doormat. She went in search of it and then settled down on the sofa next to Bertie, tucking her legs beneath her as she examined the envelope while she sipped on her tea.

It was a white, crisp envelope with her name written on it in black ink, underlined with an extravagant squiggle. Obviously hand-delivered. Intrigued, Pia opened it and pulled out the letter, scanning its contents. It took her a moment to make sense of it, to realise what the logo in the top right-hand corner of the A4 sheet of paper actually meant. *JM Enterprises. Primrose Hall.* Jackson Moody!

Dear Pia,

Thank you so much for meeting with me last week to discuss the vacancy of Personal Assistant at Primrose Hall.

I'm uncertain whether you received my email of 5th March with the details of the job offer, so am including again here just for confirmation:

I'm delighted to be able to offer you the position on a full-time live-in basis with a starting date of Monday 29th March as agreed. The attached contract gives details of your working hours, salary and additional benefits. If there is anything that needs any further clarification, then please do not hesitate to give me a call on the number above.

If you could confirm to me by return your acceptance of the terms in this letter, then I can make arrangements for your arrival here. You are welcome to drop by before your starting date to look around the estate, meet the team and to view your living quarters. If there is anything we can do to help during the moving-in process, then please do not hesitate to ask.

I'm very much looking forward to working with you and welcoming you to Primrose Hall.

With kind regards,
Jackson Moody

Shit! She scanned the contents again to make sure she hadn't imagined them. The email from last week, what was that all about? She hadn't seen it. Quickly, she pulled up her inbox on her laptop and scrolled through her emails, wondering how she'd missed it, but it wasn't there and it was only when she thought to check her junk box that she found the missing email, glowing at her accusingly. She'd been thinking Jackson was rude for not contacting her after they'd met at the Treetops Cafe when all the time he'd been waiting on a reply from her. She sighed, flinging an arm over Bertie's coat, smoothing down his fur. He looked up at her with big brown eyes and a gentle wag of his tail.

Not that it mattered. She would send a reply first thing in the morning, apologising for her delayed response. It wasn't as if she even wanted the job. She might be desperate, but she wasn't that desperate. Working for Jackson Moody would do nothing for her peace of mind; there were too many reminders from another time when she'd been young and carefree. She needed to start afresh, not be faced with the memories from her past every day.

Besides, since she'd completely ignored his letter, Jackson would probably have someone else lined up for the job now. Why did that thought make her feel quite so disappointed and regretful when she didn't even want the job? What a mess! Idly, she picked up the letter and read it for a third time. Her attention turned to the extra pages of the contract, where her eyes immediately picked out the salary details. She audibly gasped and looked at Bertie, as though he might be able to shed some light on the situation.

'How much? That can't be right, surely?' Bertie pricked his ears.

The salary was much more than she could ever have imagined, especially as all her accommodation expenses would be paid for too. Still, as her mum would say, if things seem too good to be true, then they probably are too good to be true. Her mum had been full of useful sayings like that. Pia wondered what she might tell her now, faced with this unexpected opportunity. It was a job, a good one, with a really decent salary, so wouldn't she be a fool to turn it down?

So she might have some unfinished business with Jackson, but clearly that was of no concern to him. She had to wonder if he even remembered that last summer. It had stayed in her mind only because it represented such a happy time before everything went pear-shaped and her life had transformed into one of caring and responsibility.

For Jackson, so much had clearly happened in the interim. He'd built a business, earned a fortune, restored a country pad and had secured a glamorous girlfriend, by all accounts. He'd probably not even thought of Pia until she'd turned up in his inbox looking for a job. Maybe Pia would need to put her pride to one side and accept the position as a stop-gap measure until something better came along. It would get over her two pressing problems at once: finding a place to live and getting a job that would bring in some decent money. If she did it for six months, she'd be able to save some money, by which point her small inheritance from the sale of the family home would have come through, and she would be in a much better position to decide what it was she really wanted to do and where she might want to live.

Honestly, it was the perfect solution despite her reservations about being in close proximity to Jackson again. She wasn't a teenager any more; she was a grown woman and she could put her feelings to one side to do a good job for Jackson and his 'team'. She only hoped that Jackson hadn't already offered the job to someone else.

'It will be fine, Bertie,' she told him, sounding confident as she ruffled the fur around his collar, until she suddenly remembered one huge, spotty dog in the ointment.

'Oh, Bertie!' she cried, nuzzling her head into his side. How could she possibly take up a new live-in position with a goofy dog in tow and without breaking her promise to Wendy? Her new resolve and positivity for the future tumbled, like confetti, to the floor around her.

6

Jackson stormed across the gravel driveway of Primrose Hall, climbed the steps to the camper van and wrenched open the door. He was greeted by a fug of smoking incense, which he wafted away with his hand.

'For Christ's sake, Ronnie! What is that godawful smell? And what have I told you about leaving the van around the front? It's a bloody eyesore. I haven't spent thousands of pounds doing this place up for you to turn it into a car park. Leave it around the back. There's plenty of space around there and you've got a great view of the grounds.'

'Ooh, someone's in a bad mood today. Scrub that. You've been in a bad mood for weeks now. If you're missing her that much, just ring her and tell her to come back again.'

Jackson shook his head. 'What are you talking about?' he asked, an edge of exasperation to his voice.

'Tara! You're rattling around in that house on your own now. Why don't you make it up with her and get her to come back. That place needs a woman's touch, and it might make you less grumpy.'

Jackson suppressed a sigh.

'It's never going to happen, Ronnie. It's over. Time to move on,' he said emphatically, closing down that particular line of conversation. 'Now are you going to move this thing or do you want me to do it for you?' He banged the side of the van.

'All right, all right. Keep your hair on. Would you like a nice cup of camomile tea first? I've just made myself one. It might do you good, darling. Calm you down a bit.'

Jackson took a deep breath and shook his head. His gaze travelled around the interior of the camper van, which was brimming with colourful fabrics and cushions. There was a small pull-out table covered with a gingham cloth, on top of which was an overflowing pile of books and magazines. By the sink was an assortment of mismatched crockery, and floaty kaftans hung from the grab handles on either side of the van. There wasn't a spare inch of space in view.

Jackson shuddered. All the clutter and chaos gave him the heebie-jeebies; he could barely stand to look at Ronnie's living quarters, so there was no way he would be stepping inside for a cup of disgusting herbal tea.

'I'm perfectly calm. Or at least I will be once this old jalopy is moved.'

Ronnie allowed Jackson's put-downs to roll off her skin. She was used to them by now and just shrugged them off with a smile, which only infuriated Jackson all the more.

'There's a perfectly good bedroom in the hall for you, you know that. Your own suite, in fact. Why you continue to insist on living out of this old caravan, I'll never know.'

'I don't want to live in that mausoleum. It's depressing.'

'Thanks a lot for that!'

'Oh, I know you've done it beautifully, and it's got all that state-of-the-art stuff going on, but it doesn't feel like home to me. This is my home, Jackson.' She held up her palms, proudly showing off the van, and all her belongings. 'It has been for years now. It's where I'm happiest. And I love the idea of being able to get up and go whenever the mood takes me.'

Jackson pulled his lips tight. Did he really expect anything different from Ronnie after all this time? He was used to her taking off without any notice, usually with a new man in tow. But surely she should be tiring of that lifestyle now. He knew he was.

'Well, if you do decide to do one of your disappearing acts, do you think you might let me know next time?'

'Oh, Jackson, don't be like that. Of course I'll let you know.' She waved a hand around vaguely. 'Not that I have any plans at the moment, but you never know,' she said, with her distinctive chuckle.

That was true. Life in Ronnie's world was often unpredictable, chaotic and impulsive, but Jackson was resigned to the fact that he was never going to change her now.

'Anyway, tell me.' She sat down on the bench seat covered in a colourful crocheted blanket and patted the space next to her, which Jackson entirely ignored. 'When are the new employees starting? It will be nice to see some new faces about the place.'

'The new groundsman, Mateo, is starting on Monday, and my exec assistant will hopefully start in a couple of weeks' time, although you've just reminded me. I haven't heard back from her accepting the offer so I will need to chase her up.'

Just at that moment, the sound of an engine rumbling along the driveway to Primrose Hall attracted both their attention. Ronnie pushed herself up from the bench to peer over Jackson's shoulder to see who the unexpected visitor might be, and Jackson turned, recognising the jeep as one of the Primrose Woods vehicles. Attached to the back of the jeep was a trailer and Jackson let out a heartfelt sigh.

'Not again,' he said, stepping down from the van as the jeep drew to a halt. A guy wearing the distinctive uniform of the Primrose Woods rangers jumped down from the cab, a smile on his face.

'Think this is one of yours,' he said, walking round to the trailer, where he unlatched the steel gate and grabbed hold of the small, cream-coloured Shetland pony that trotted down the ramp in a breezy manner.

'Cheers, Sam,' said Jackson, slapping the other guy's arm. 'Bloody pony. We should have called him Houdini, not Little Star. That must be the third time this month that he's escaped. That will be the first job when the new groundsman arrives next week. Sorting out the boundary fencing. Sorry again for the inconvenience.'

'Don't worry about it,' said Sam, unable to keep the smile from his face. 'It's not a problem. At least you're only next door; it's not far to bring the escape artist home.'

'You, mister,' said Jackson, addressing the pony with a serious expression, 'are on your last warning. Much more of this and you'll be looking for a new home. Do you understand me?'

Ronnie and Sam exchanged a glance and chuckled. Judging by the mischievous glint in Little Star's eye, Ronnie suspected the pony knew exactly what he was doing and had no inclination to change his behaviour anytime soon.

7

It was a good job Pia was an early riser because Bertie was raring to go just as soon as Pia turned over in bed the next morning to silence the alarm. Its insistent ringing stirred them both into action.

'All right, boy, let me throw some clothes on, and we'll head straight out.'

She gave a thought to Wendy, wondering how she was feeling this morning. Hopefully she'd had a comfortable night. She would phone the hospital at lunchtime to see if the operation had taken place and if she could visit her in the afternoon

Once she was dressed, Pia stepped outside and took a deep breath of the invigorating spring morning air. Fortunately, with Primrose Woods on her doorstep, Pia and Bertie could be walking the Woodpecker Trail within five minutes. Today, and for the foreseeable future, Pia would keep Bertie safely on his lead. She was used to letting him off and allowing him to gallop through the countryside, but occasionally he would head off into the undergrowth, catch the scent of a long-gone squirrel and take up the chase. Many a day she'd spent hours searching for Bertie, calling out his name, asking fellow dog-walkers if they had seen him, her panic increasing with every moment thinking that she might have lost him for good. Although he always turned up in the end, she didn't need that sort of stress in her life right now. She owed it to Wendy to keep Bertie as safe as she possibly could, and if that meant curtailing his independent streak for a short while, then she would have no hesitation in doing so.

Besides, Bertie was still having the time of his life as they strode out together at a pace, taking the route around the lake. He trotted along with his head held high, taking in the scenery, stopping occasionally if a scent caught his attention. Pia loved having a reason to walk in Primrose Woods and having a four-legged friend was the perfect excuse.

'Come on, Bertie, let's get you home and you can have some breakfast.' Pia laughed at Bertie's reaction, his ears pricking as though he knew exactly what she was saying, as they took the path that headed towards home. As Meadow Cottages came into view, Pia noticed someone standing in front of the house. She narrowed her eyes, trying to get a better idea of who it could be. It was someone wearing a wax jacket, that much she could decipher. They walked up the front pathway to her cottage and knocked on her door. Her curiosity roused, she walked a little faster. Maybe it was someone selling something, although it was a bit early in the day for that. Or perhaps it was a concerned neighbour who had heard about Wendy's accident and was calling to see how she was doing. It was only as Pia drew closer that she realised it was neither of those possibilities. Her heart lifted when she recognised the man, his tall and broad physique so achingly familiar, causing her heart to squeeze. She snatched a breath. Why exactly was Jackson Moody peering through the front window to her cottage?

She paused for the briefest moment, running her hands through her hair, attempting to tidy it. She looked down at her scruffy jeans and faithful old jacket, wishing she'd had the foresight to arrange a casually more elegant outfit, but who was she kidding. She'd never managed casually elegant in her life.

'Hey!' Jackson turned around, his face lighting up as he spotted Pia approaching. 'That's good timing. I was just driving past and thought I'd pop by. Do you have a moment?'

'Yeah, I guess. Do you want to come in for coffee?' The offer tripped off her lips before she had time to think about it. The house was a mess with boxes all over the floor, but Bertie was pulling on the leash, dancing around on his paws, and she didn't want to have any sort of conversation with Jackson with those kinds of distractions going on.

Besides, Jackson had already taken her up on her offer, nodding enthusiastically.

Pia led the way, going through the side gate, and let Bertie off his lead so that he went bounding down the garden. She unlocked the back door and gestured for Jackson to go inside.

'You look as though you're pretty busy here,' he said, immediately noticing the half-filled packing crates and the piles of items on every available surface.

Pia wandered into the kitchen, flicked the kettle on and pulled out two mugs from the cupboard.

'Tea or coffee?' she asked, turning to look at Jackson, who struck an undeniably handsome figure standing in the doorway, the faint scent of him, earthy and enticing, reaching her nostrils.

'White coffee, please. No sugar.'

She was pleased for something to do, to occupy her mind and settle her nerves. It was weird to have Jackson standing in her kitchen, knowing his gaze was appraising her. Once they'd been so close, but now there was an awkwardness wedged between them, or perhaps that was just in her imagination. Jackson looked more than comfortable now, resting his body against the worktop, his masculine physicality filling the room. She turned to face him, tucking her hair behind her ears, batting away her self-consciousness.

'Yes, it's taken a while because I've had to sort through all my parents' belongings, but I think I'm almost there. I've got the house clearance people coming next week to take away the larger bits of furniture, and the rest Connor will help me to move.'

'The real passing of an era, Pia.' The way his eyes hooked on to hers as he said her name felt far too intimate and she shrugged her cardigan off, throwing it over a kitchen chair. 'Look, I know you have a lot on your plate at the moment, but I wondered if you'd had a chance to look at the job offer I sent you?'

'Yes, I have, and I was going to call you this morning. I'm so sorry that I didn't contact you sooner, you must think me very rude, but your email went into my junk box and so I only saw your letter yesterday when you popped it through the letterbox.'

'No need to apologise. I thought there would be some kind of explanation. Anyway...' He looked hopeful now and expectant too, as he took the mug that Pia offered him. 'I hope you're going to join us?'

This was awkward. Pia took a sip of her coffee, even though it was far too hot on her lips. Her head was all over the place at the moment; she had so much to think about. The house move, Wendy, Bertie, finding a job and a place to live, which she would have to make a priority soon, and now Jackson Moody. She couldn't reconcile those things together in her mind, though.

'I'm grateful for the offer, Jackson, really I am. I was surprised, to be honest with you, and very flattered, but unfortunately there's been a change in my circumstances so I'm not going to be able to come and work with you, I'm afraid.'

She hoped she sounded as confident and decisive as she'd intended because she certainly didn't feel it inside.

'Oh...' Jackson looked crestfallen. 'Well, that is disappointing. Have you found another job, then?'

'Um... no.'

'But you've found somewhere new to live?'

'Not exactly,' she admitted.

'Okay, so...?' His brow creased and his lips twisted. 'If you don't mind me asking, what's happened to change your mind?'

She could offer any number of reasons why it would be a very bad idea for her to accept Jackson's job. She was unqualified for the position for a start. She had no formal training and no experience of being a PA. Most of all, though, she was ill-equipped to be thrown together with Jackson again. He might have completely forgotten about their ill-fated romance from that long-ago summer, but the memories had been taunting her ever since he'd made a reappearance. She wasn't about to tell him any of that, though.

'My next-door neighbour, Wendy, had a nasty fall yesterday and she's in hospital. We're very close; I've known her all my life. She's like a second mum to me.' An unexpected lump rose in her throat, and she swallowed hard and widened her eyes to ward off any show of emotion. 'I've promised to look after Bertie, her dog, for her but my suspicion is that it could be a long-term arrangement so I'm going to have to find somewhere to suit us both now.'

Pia could feel the panic rise within her as she said the words aloud. There was no way she could expect Connor and Ruby to take Bertie in. They lived in a very small flat without any outside space, which wouldn't suit the energetic dog. Besides, she'd never felt entirely happy about imposing on them anyway, not when they were just about to start their married life together. After she'd got rid of Jackson, she would make it her job today to find a rented house with a garden. How difficult could it be?

'I'm sorry to hear that,' said Jackson, looking genuinely concerned. 'But it wouldn't be a problem if you came to Primrose Hall. You'll have your own living quarters on the ground floor with your own private garden too. It's only small, but it's a safe, secure space for the dog and then of course you've got acres of land on the doorstep as soon as you step outside the back gate.'

'Really?' said Pia, not really believing it could be as good as Jackson was making out. Surely there must be a catch. Other than having to work for and live alongside Jackson, of course, which was one major catch all by itself.

'Really,' said Jackson, softening his response with a smile. 'Look, why don't you come and have a look round Primrose Hall. That's why I dropped by. I don't have anything in the diary this morning so I could show you around and it would give you a much better idea of what the position will involve. You can meet some of the team and see where you would be living. Bring Bertie with you if you like.'

In the matter of a few seconds, Pia managed to take in the mayhem around her, with the all-too-familiar reminders of her uncertain future. Jackson was offering her a job and a place to live, and a home for Bertie as well. It was the best and only offer she'd had. There could be no harm in checking it out, could there?

burst and reduced her eyes to scald off any show of emotion. The promise he broke, saw Borne had due, for her, but my suspicion is that it could be a long time as it people to have to have to find contentment so inferno to feel now.

8

'So this would be your living accommodation,' Jackson said, walking along a long corridor, which came off the main kitchen of the house. Pia followed, her head turning this way and that, trying to get her bearings, as Jackson opened up a door that led into a self-contained apartment. She took a deep breath, surprised by the scale and clean lines of the flat, which she found immediately welcoming. There was a compact galley kitchen and a dining area, a spacious double bedroom, all newly decorated, but it was the beautiful large living room that was the real show-stopper. It had high ceilings and full-length windows that overlooked a garden and then Primrose Woods beyond. There was a set of French doors that led out to the small garden, where they'd left Bertie when they'd first arrived, while Jackson had given Pia a guided tour of the house and the grounds. Pia peered out of the windows now, relieved to see Bertie mooching around quite happily.

'What do you think?'

'I think it's amazing.' There was no point in being coy. It was more than amazing; it was stunning. The house had such wonderful proportions and the parts she'd seen of it had been beautifully renovated in a way that retained and highlighted its original Georgian features, while giving it a contemporary yet warming atmosphere.

On their way around the house, Pia had been introduced to Frank, the maintenance man, Ivy, the housekeeper, and a lady called Ronnie who seemed to live in a camper van at the back of the house. Pia wasn't entirely sure who she was or what she did, but she seemed friendly enough. The one person she hadn't run into yet was Jackson's girlfriend, Tara. Pia had done a bit of online research on Jackson and his girlfriend, just to satisfy her curiosity, and had found photos of them both at the inaugural Christmas event at Primrose Hall. They made a gorgeous couple, her blonde supermodel looks complementing Jackson's dark and sometimes brooding persona.

From what she could gather, Tara had her own interior design business with a high profile on Instagram, her stagings of beautiful English country rooms with big squashy sofas, white walls and colourful contemporary art garnering thousands of likes and followers. She suspected Tara might be the creative genius behind the transformation of Primrose Hall.

'There's a double garage attached to the end of the stable block that is empty. You can use it for storage, if you need to.'

Pia nodded, trying to take it all in. She thought of the old bits of furniture at home that were headed for the house clearance company. None of them were of any monetary value, but she wasn't ready to let go of them yet. They held too many reminders of her parents. If she could safely store them here until she was in a better position to find her own place, then she wouldn't need to get rid of them.

'Is there anything else you need to know, anything else you'd like to ask?'

Jackson was observing her closely, one dark eyebrow quirked expectantly. He'd done a great sales job on the position at Primrose Hall, the living accommodation had sold itself and everyone she'd met so far had been friendly and welcoming. There was no reason why Tara wouldn't be exactly the same. Jackson had even won Bertie over, allowing him to gallop around the grounds and offering a few well-timed doggy treats.

'No, it's been really helpful. You have a beautiful home here, Jackson.'

'Thanks, does that mean you're able to start on 29th, as we discussed?'

Pia hoped she wasn't about to make the biggest mistake of her life, but with a broad grin, she looked directly at her new boss.

'Absolutely!'

* * *

'Honestly, Wendy, you would need to see it to believe it. The house is so beautiful and the office I'll be working in has views over Primrose Woods. It's very picturesque. Everyone I met there was really friendly. I'm a bit worried that I'll be out of my depth, but my new boss doesn't seem concerned.'

Pia shrugged, still unable to really believe that she'd found a great job and a place to live too.

'He's lucky to get you. You're very capable, Pia. It's just that you've never really had the opportunity to show it at work. This job will be the making of you, I bet.'

'I really hope so.' She felt a swirl of excitement mixed with dread every time she thought about her new job. Or more accurately, every time she thought of Jackson Moody.

Pia looked across at her friend, who was sitting up in bed with her leg elevated, looking so much better now, a few days after her operation. Even if she had been told she wouldn't be able to leave hospital until she'd been properly assessed and a care plan had been put in place, which might take several weeks. Pia leant across from her chair at the side of Wendy's bed and took her friend's hand, relieved that her recovery was well underway. She'd been buoyed too by Wendy's complimentary words and her apparent faith in her.

'You'll be pleased to hear that Bertie absolutely loved it at the hall. He'll be able to come to work with me at the office and, of course, there's plenty of outside space for him to run around in.'

'Are you sure this new boss of yours is happy having Bertie at the hall?'

'Absolutely. It was Jackson who suggested it in the first place. I wouldn't be going there if I couldn't take Bertie with me.'

'That's such a relief to hear, Pia. Thank you.' Wendy tapped Pia's hand fondly. 'I'm disappointed that I'm going to miss out on your leaving do; we were going to have an afternoon tea party before you left, weren't we? I was looking forward to that. You know, I wonder if I'll ever get back to Meadow

Cottages.' She glanced down at her leg encased in plaster. 'They're talking about some respite care for a few weeks, but then who knows what will happen. I can't see me ever managing those stairs at home again. Mind you, it wouldn't be the same anyway, not having you next door.'

'Stop it,' said Pia, fanning a hand in front of her face to ward off the tears. 'You know how I feel about moving away, but perhaps it's time for a change for both of us? It doesn't have to be a bad thing.' Pia wasn't sure who she was trying to convince, Wendy or herself. 'And listen, there's no way we're missing out on my leaving do. We can still have our afternoon tea; it might just be a bit delayed, that's all. Let's see how your recovery goes and then we can organise something just as soon as we know what your plans are.' Pia already had her own thoughts on that matter, but she would keep them to herself for the time being until she'd done a bit more research. 'That's another great thing about me moving to Primrose Hall: we'll still be very close to each other.'

Wendy looked marginally appeased. 'Honestly, love, I don't know what I'd do without you. You're like the daughter I never had.'

Pia smiled, as a swell of emotion bubbled up inside of her. The feeling was entirely mutual. Wendy was a constant in her life and she would do anything to make sure she was as settled and happy as she possibly could be, and if that meant pulling a few strings, then she was more than prepared to do it.

9

'So how are you feeling about the new job?'

Pia smiled and sat down at a window seat in the Treetops Cafe at Primrose Woods. Pia hadn't seen Abbey, her best friend from school, in ages but that was nothing unusual. They often went months without seeing each other, but then would immediately pick up where they'd left off when they did get together. Abbey was one of the first people Pia had texted when she found her new job and, knowing how busy she was likely to be over the coming months, she wanted to have a proper catch-up with Abbey over coffee while she still had the time.

'Excited. Nervous. Scared. All of those things and more. You must remember, Abbey, I've not really had what I'd call a proper job. Ever. I know I've done lots of casual jobs, but this is in a different league, and of course I'll be living in.' Pia widened her eyes, still unable to believe that she would actually be living at Primrose Hall in that gorgeous flat.

'Honestly, Pia, you'll be fine. What a great opportunity it is, though!' Abbey reached across the table and squeezed Pia's hand. She was so pleased for her friend. She deserved some good luck. She'd spent far too long worrying and caring for other people – it was about time she had the chance to follow her own dreams. 'We went to the Christmas carols at

Primrose Hall and we were blown away by the transformation. It's incredible what they've done to the house and to the stables.'

'Well, that will be one of my main responsibilities. Running the open days at the stables. They're hoping to make them regular events through the year. Craft fairs, food markets, art exhibitions, that sort of thing. I'm looking forward to getting started.'

'I bet you are. And what about your new boss? He's pretty gorgeous, isn't he?' There was a devilish twinkle in Abbey's eye. 'We got to meet him and his girlfriend, Tara, a couple of times over the Christmas holiday, first at the hall and then in the pub on New Year's Eve. He bought our table a couple of bottles of champagne.'

'Did he?' Why did that not surprise Pia. From what she knew of Jackson, she suspected he was fond of a big gesture. 'I've not met his girlfriend yet.'

'She's very glammy. Tall and blonde and really friendly. They seem like a great couple. I bet they'll be lovely to work for.'

Pia hoped so. She liked to think she could get on with most people so she would just get her head down and do her job. Her gaze drifted out of the window as she tried to push away the thoughts of what-might-have-beens.

'You know, Jackson and I had a bit of a thing that last summer after school.'

'What?' Abbey's brow creased. 'Hang on a minute. You already know him?'

'Yeah, he used to hang out with Connor back in the day, that's how I met him, and we got together for a few heady weeks after our A levels.' Pia sighed. It was another lifetime ago.

'Really? And you never told me?'

'Well, I think you'd gone off travelling that summer and by the time you'd got home, it was all over. Jackson was planning to go to university, I was planning to go to college, but he obviously changed his mind at the last moment and went to work in London instead. Shortly afterwards, Dad fell ill and so of course my plans changed too. I didn't see Jackson again – well, not until I turned up for the interview.'

'Wow, that's mad! Just think if you'd stayed together, you might be lady of the manor now.' Abbey had a big grin on her face, though she was joshing, of course, both of them realising what a mad idea that was. It hadn't stopped Pia from entertaining that exact same thought these last few days, mind you.

'Nah,' she said, waving it away as though it had been a minor, inconsequential love affair. 'It was only one of those teenage flings. I'm not sure Jackson remembers it in quite the same way as I do.' She gave a wry smile. 'Anyway, tell me, how's things with you and Sam?'

'Great.' Abbey beamed. 'We've actually set a date for the wedding now. It's going to be at the end of August, just a small intimate gathering with our family and close friends, about thirty of us in total. At the village hall. Of course, you'll be coming, Pia. The formal invitations are on their way.'

'I wouldn't miss it for the world. How exciting! I really can't wait.'

'Me neither. Let's hope it's a case of second time lucky, eh?' Abbey said, only half-jokingly.

'You bet,' said Pia, knowing exactly what her friend was referring to. Abbey's engagement to her ex-boyfriend had been called off just a matter of weeks before her wedding when Abbey discovered that he'd been cheating on her. *Good riddance* was Abbey's attitude, and Pia's too. She'd never liked Jason, and was only pleased that Abbey had moved on. She'd thought Abbey's new boyfriend, Sam, was lovely when she'd met him and so much nicer than Jason, by all accounts, kinder and more caring. 'Sam is definitely a keeper.'

'He really is,' said Abbey dreamily. 'I just feel so lucky to have found him. Anyway, I'll let you know the details for the big day when we've finalised them.'

'This is clearly going to be the year of the wedding, then, because we've got Connor and Ruby's wedding coming up soon too.'

'I know,' said Abbey excitedly. 'Romance is definitely in the air.'

Funny how Pia hadn't attended a wedding in years and now she had two coming up in the space of a few months. She'd heard of other people who'd been in her year at school getting married as well. She supposed they were at that age where they were settling down and having families, although Pia felt she was playing catch-up. She had a career to make for herself first, and hopefully she might dip her toes in the dating scene too, even if the very idea scared her senseless. Maybe some of the romance in the air that Abbey spoke of might rub off on her too.

After they'd drunk their coffees and eaten their toasted teacakes, Pia broached the subject she'd been wanting to talk to Abbey about.

'I don't know if you ever met my next-door neighbour, Wendy Peterson, but she's been friends of ours for years. She was very close to my mum.'

'The name rings a bell.'

'Yes, well, she's actually in hospital at the moment because she broke her ankle falling down the stairs. I found her, the poor thing. It was quite a nasty break and she's had to have a plate and some screws put in. Anyway, the reason you might recognise her name is that you recently offered her a place at Rushgrove Lodge.'

'Oh, of course! I have all her details in a folder on my desk at the moment.'

'Well, I hope I'm not talking out of turn, but I wanted to ask how long generally spaces are held open for potential new residents? Wendy was very reluctant to leave her home. It was her son in Australia who was pushing to move her into residential care, but I think this last accident has made her realise just how vulnerable she is on her own in that house. I can't see her going back to the cottage anytime soon. The hospital is talking about a lengthy period of rehabilitation. I'm just worried about where she's going to go and who's going to look after her.'

'We still have a room available for Wendy. I was reviewing her file only yesterday. Her son – Simon, isn't it? – he took the precaution of paying a deposit to reserve the room for a period of time so we could definitely still accommodate her. We do actually take patients from hospital for convalescence care. It's one of the areas we specialise in. Sometimes, depending on the individual's circumstances, we're able to get them back to being independent so they can look after themselves in their own home, sometimes they move on to another care facility and occasionally if we have the space available they stay with us as a permanent resident. Would you like me to make some enquiries with her son to make him aware that we're still in a position to take Wendy, if everyone thinks that's the right move for her? I have spoken to him on a couple of occasions before.'

'Would you, Abbey? I hope I'm not putting you in a difficult position.'

'Not at all. It's my job. And I'll tread very carefully. Leave it with me for a few days and I'll see what I can do.' Abbey gave a reassuring smile and Pia was filled with relief. She felt a responsibility for Wendy and wanted to do all that she could to ensure that she felt as happy and as confident as possible as she faced the changes ahead of her.

'Anyway, there's something you can do for me.' Abbey pulled out her phone and started scrolling. 'Dresses,' she said, with a wide smile. 'Who knew it would be so difficult? There's so much choice out there. I've found a couple of gowns that I like the look of, but I could do with a second opinion.' She placed the phone on the table between them so that they both could see. 'What do you think?'

Pia grinned, craning her head to look at the beautiful gowns, glad of the distraction from all the other pressing issues in her life. Mind you, offering advice on wedding dresses for her lovely friend's upcoming big day was important business in its own right. She was happy to throw herself wholeheartedly into the task. In the absence of any romance in her own life, she was more than happy to live vicariously through Abbey's wedding plans.

10

'Phew!' Pia let out a heartfelt sigh and collapsed onto the sofa in her new flat, throwing her arms wide. She was shattered and her limbs ached from lugging boxes around all day. Fortunately, she'd had the foresight to drape her patchwork blanket over the lovely cream two-seater, knowing that Bertie would naturally think it was his new bed and, of course, there he was curled up, his head on a cushion, oblivious to all the upheaval of the day.

Connor had turned up early that morning and loaded the van, doing a few trips the short distance to Primrose Hall. Jackson had given Pia the keys to the double garage, which was a huge space, fully fitted out with heat and light, to store those pieces of furniture and belongings that she wasn't ready to let go of yet. The move had gone remarkably smoothly and it was only when the last van load was packed up that she and Connor had taken a moment to sit on the old bench in the front garden to reflect on all the happy times spent at Meadow Cottages.

'Well, this is it,' Connor had said, wrapping an arm around Pia's shoulder. 'A final farewell to the cottage.'

'Yep,' she sighed, soaking up the view for one last time. 'I know in my heart that it's absolutely the right thing for everyone concerned, but I'm going to miss this place so much. At least we'll have our happy memories.'

'Of course we will. And you have to remember that Mum and Dad would have wanted you to move on and live your own life. They would have been so proud at what you've achieved already. You've really landed on your feet finding a job and a place to live at Primrose Hall!'

'I know. I still can't believe that it's my home now. I just hope it works out.'

'It will! And if it doesn't, for whatever reason, then you'll always have a room at ours. It might not be the size of the one you have at the hall and we can't offer views over woodland, but I just want you to know that you have an escape route if you need one. Not that you will, of course,' Connor quickly added. 'From what I've heard, Jackson Moody isn't such a dick as he was back in the day.'

'Thanks, Connor, I appreciate the offer.' Pia pondered on Connor's words for a moment, turning to glance at him. 'Was he? Were you close friends? I can remember you hanging out together for a while.'

'Yeah, but only as part of a group. I wouldn't say we were ever close. He was a bit of a wild child so I always gave him a wide berth. He used to be a bit mouthy and trouble seemed to follow him around. Had a few run-ins with the police, I remember.'

'Really?' She remembered Jackson differently, as being an exciting, adventurous and passionate young guy, although she supposed his rogue bad-boy reputation, which even she couldn't deny, had only added to his appeal at the time.

'Yeah. So you can imagine how I felt when I knew you two were seeing each other. I didn't dare tell Mum and Dad, and was just relieved when it was all finished.'

'It was only ever a teenage romance; it had ended before it had really begun.' She batted it away with a wave of her hand. It wasn't strictly true, though, not for her at least. She'd been besotted with Jackson back then, imagining they'd have a long and happy future together, and she'd thought about him all the time after they split, until her mind was taken up with more pressing concerns. 'So, you're not worried about me working for Jackson now, then?'

'No, not at all. He seems like a different man these days, settled in his work and personal life by the sounds of things. He clearly channelled all that youthful arrogance into making a success of his life. You have to admire what he's done. It's pretty amazing, really. And it's great that he's back in the village and looking out for his old mates.'

'Yeah,' she said brightly. Is that all she was to her old flame? Connor obviously believed so. She was still stuck in the past while Jackson had moved on, doing it in considerable style too.

Still, this was her home now, she mused, back in the moment. She looked all around her as she rested a hand on Bertie's back. It was all a bit surreal being here, knowing she would never be going home again. Thank goodness she had Bertie at her side, his sleeping presence providing all the moral support she needed right now.

'Oh, Bertie, it will all be fine, won't it?' She sighed, the act of saying the words aloud bringing all the emotions of the day to the surface. Tears rolled down her cheeks and small sobs escaped from her chest. She sniffed, wiping away her tears with the backs of her hands. Bertie lifted his head to look at her, curious, his nose sniffing in her direction as she hugged him tightly and he gave a gentle wag of his tail.

Suddenly being here in this beautiful flat, a loneliness engulfed her. At Meadow Cottages she'd been surrounded by everything familiar and reassuring; the views from every window, even the thread of the old carpet up the stairs stirred a reaction within her. All her belongings were in their rightful place, and of course she had her memories too. Here, although the flat was lovely and modern with everything she could possibly need, it felt strange and daunting. Had she made a big mistake in coming to live at the same place where she would be working? What if she could never settle here and she came to hate her new job and everyone who worked here?

She sighed, knowing that she wouldn't have that luxury. She would just have to get on with it now and make the best of the situation. Just then a knocking at her front door had both her and Bertie startling to attention. Pia jumped up from the sofa and wiped away a rogue tear before putting her face through some gymnastics so that she could regain some kind of normality to her features. She just hoped no one had heard her crying.

'Hi, Jackson,' she said brightly when she opened the door, seeing her new boss standing there.

'Hi, Pia. Welcome to Primrose Hall.' He held open his arms by way of greeting and although she knew it wasn't an invitation, she felt half inclined to throw herself into his embrace. She could really do with a hug right now. 'I just wanted to check that the move went okay and you have everything you need? If there's anything I can help with, just let me know and I'm sure we can sort it.'

'Thanks, yes, it's all good. I'm still surrounded by boxes, but I'm pleased to be here and looking forward to starting work on Monday.'

'Me too,' he said with a beguiling smile that reminded her of the young and wayward boy she'd known so well back in the day. She gave a small cough, covering her mouth with her hand, and pulled back her shoulders. She would need to stop reminiscing about the good old days if she was going to have any hope of making a new start here. 'Look, I wondered if you fancied dinner?'

He offered it casually and the mention of food made her realise just how hungry she was. She and Connor had grabbed a ham roll at lunchtime, but she hadn't eaten anything since and now she was ravenous, but dinner with her new bosses? That might be awkward, although it was probably something she couldn't sidestep at this moment. She dithered, hoping Jackson wasn't picking up on her hesitation.

'Well, when I say dinner,' he said, with a smile, 'I think I might be over-egging the offer. What I really mean is fish and chips from the local chippie.'

'That sounds great.' And much more relaxed than having something more formal. Pia was so intrigued to meet Tara at last. She'd seen photos of her online and heard a couple of people say how lovely she was so she suspected she didn't have anything to worry about on that front – it would just be good to get that first meeting out of the way.

'Good! Cod or haddock?'

'Cod please.'

'And chips, mushy peas and curry sauce?'

'All of the above please,' she said with a smile, her stomach rumbling at the thought.

'Great! I'll go and place the order. Usually it takes about half an hour, but wander along to the kitchen whenever you're ready.'

Just enough time for her to change out of her old clothes and freshen up. With a promise that she would join Jackson shortly, she jumped into the shower, experimenting with the buttons and marvelling at how powerful the flow was as she held up her face to the warm water coming from the rainfall head. The old shower at home had been temperamental, sometimes coming out in a dribble, then changing to freezing cold just when she had a head full of shampoo and sometimes clunking to a complete halt when she least expected it.

There were no such issues here. Everything was of the highest specification, and she gave a small squee of delight at her reflection in the mirror as she climbed out of the shower, revelling in the luxury around her. It was like being in a five-star hotel, not that she'd ever stayed in one of those. Perhaps living here wouldn't be such a hardship after all. Luckily, she quickly found some clean jeans and a blouse in the pile of clothes that needed hanging in the built-in wardrobes, which was her intended job for the weekend. Now, though, she only had one thing on her mind and that was her dinner date with Jackson and Tara. She could do this even if she didn't feel confident or relaxed or in control. She would just have to pretend.

'Won't be long, Bertie,' she said, throwing her arms around his neck and kissing him on his head. 'Wish me luck.' Moments later she wandered into the kitchen and she was taken aback again by just how beautiful the space was. There was an array of cream-coloured hand-painted cabinets, a matching dresser filled with blue and white crockery, and a gleaming Aga, all of which were set off by overhead oak beams and floor tiles in earthy, muted hues.

'Hey, great timing, I was just about to open this.' Jackson turned from where he was standing at the sleek marble island, a bottle of white wine in his hand. 'Do you fancy a glass?' he asked with that kilowatt smile that had first caught her attention and had not diminished any in the intervening years.

'Lovely, thanks.'

'Take a seat. Make yourself at home.'

She pulled out a chair at the long table and settled down, her gaze sweeping around the room, soaking up the atmosphere. It might take a little time for her to become used to these new surroundings. She was hardly accustomed to such luxury. For now, it was still a novelty as her eyes attempted to soak up every small detail of her new home. The whole house was stunning, like something from a glossy magazine. Even though it was growing dark outside, she could make out the beauty of the gardens through the double-sash windows and the sight of the woods in the distance. She must have exhaled a sigh as Jackson looked at her curiously.

'Everything okay?'

'Yes, I was just thinking, again, how amazing this place is. Could you ever have believed when you were a kid that you might one day end up living here?'

He joined her at the table, placing a welcome glass of wine in front of her. There was no sign of Tara and Pia gave a surreptitious glance in the direction of the doorway, wondering when she might be joining them.

'I guess not. Although Primrose Hall always held a special place in my heart. As a kid, climbing through the fence and hanging out in the grounds or, if the weather was bad, in the old stables, was exciting, but it also felt like an escape, a place of sanctuary, I suppose. And that's what it represents to me now.'

'That's really lovely, and I can see what you mean about it being a sanctuary. It's so quiet and peaceful here.' She took a sip of her wine, suddenly feeling weary after all the activity of the day. There were so many questions she wanted to ask Jackson, but she didn't want to overstep any boundaries.

She wondered about his family and if they still lived in the area. She remembered his dad hadn't been on the scene much and Jackson had lived between his aunt's house at one end of the village and his mum's place on the outskirts, although it only occurred to her now to wonder why. She'd felt so close to Jackson at one time, but really she knew so very little about him.

'Ah, that sounds like dinner.' Jackson jumped up from his seat and went to answer the knock on the front door. Moments later, he was back with a paper bag and a smile on his face. He faltered a moment as he unwrapped the fish suppers, looking at them and then back at Pia. 'Did you want a plate or are you happy...?'

She laughed at his awkwardness.

'No, it's fine. I'm more than happy to eat it from the paper. That's what I do at...' She stopped herself with a wry curl of her lip. This was her home now. 'Besides,' she said, recovering her composure, 'it tastes much better that way.'

'I think so too.'

So, it was dinner for two by the looks of things. Only two portions of cod and chips and no sign of Tara anywhere.

'Hey, I've just realised, you didn't bring Bertie along. Don't think you have to keep him confined to your room; he's very welcome to have the run of the house. I mean, he is house-trained, isn't he?' Jackson said with only the faintest trace of concern.

'Yes, definitely. He has very good house manners; it's just sometimes when we're out walking that he forgets how to behave.'

'Really, Pia, this is your home now, so don't feel you, and Bertie, have to make yourselves scarce. I'm actually off to London in the morning and won't be back until first thing Monday, so you'll have some time to get yourself sorted and find the lay of the house. Ivy and Frank should be around over the weekend so if you have any questions, you can always ask them or just text me. We'll get properly started on work on Monday morning.'

'Thanks.' It all made sense to her now. Jackson and Tara obviously had something on in London this weekend, which explained Tara's absence. Pia wasn't sure why she had built herself up into such a high level of anticipation at the prospect of meeting Jackson's girlfriend, but she supposed if they were living under the same roof then it was essential that they got on together. She wondered fleetingly if Jackson had mentioned to Tara that he'd once had a brief relationship with Pia.

Still, she was grateful that Jackson had gone out of his way to welcome her to Primrose Hall. The fish and chips had gone down a treat and she was really pleased that she would have a couple of days to acclimatise to her new living accommodation before starting the job on Monday, and finally meeting Tara too. If anything, she was more nervous about meeting

Jackson's girlfriend than she was about her new role. She was desperate to make a good impression. After all, Jackson knew her of old, but Tara and her would be starting afresh and she didn't want to get off on the wrong foot. Fingers crossed Tara would take to the other new member of the Primrose Hall family as well, an over-familiar and energetic spotty dog. She only hoped Bertie would be on his best behaviour when that moment came.

11

Waking up at Primrose Hall had been a surreal experience. As soon as her head had touched the pillow, Pia had fallen straight asleep and when her eyes slowly peeled open, she'd thought for a moment that she was still back at home in her own familiar bedroom. It only took a couple of seconds, as she acclimatised to the sunlight filtering through the blinds, for her to appreciate the reality of her new situation. It was a bitter-sweet moment. This wasn't her home, and her heart felt a pang of regret for everything she'd left behind. Still, there were worse places to end up, she told herself, trying to keep a positive frame of mind.

She reached out an arm to find Bertie curled up on the bed next to her, his warm, furry presence bringing a smile to her face.

'Come on, boy, let's get you outside.'

A little later as she stood on the threshold of the double doors out to the garden, she watched Bertie as he mooched around his new territory. He didn't seem to have any reservations about his new living arrangements and was happily exploring, his tail held high behind him. Perhaps she should take a leaf from Bertie's book, she thought to herself, and look upon every day as a new adventure. In every direction she looked she could see the trees of Primrose Woods towering above her and could hear the noises of the birds and the squirrels in the surrounding countryside.

There was a locked gate on the boundary of Jackson's land that opened up into the woods so she and Bertie really would be spoilt for choice on their daily walks, although the grounds of the hall were extensive enough in their own right so they didn't need to go further afield if they didn't want to.

Pia turned to survey her belongings dumped in the middle of the room. It would be her first job of the day. Sorting everything away. Fortunately, there was plenty of storage space in the apartment so it didn't take too long to put away her clothes and her personal items. There was a small kitchenette too, but Jackson had shown her some additional space in the main kitchen that she could use, a tall cupboard that had been emptied for her use. All her pots and pans, and her casserole dishes, would fit perfectly inside. She was just making a start on putting some items away when she heard a voice from behind her.

'Hello, lovely, how are you getting on?'

Pia turned to see Ronnie standing there, looking resplendent in a bright orange kaftan that reached the floor, her silver-blonde hair piled on top of her head, with tendrils escaping down the sides of her face. She had a beautiful face with kind, warm eyes accentuated by laughter lines.

'Great,' said Pia, uncurling her back to stand tall and running a hand through her hair. Bertie went across to say hello to Ronnie. 'I'm slowly getting myself sorted. I feel very lucky to be here. It's pretty amazing as workplaces go and this is a fresh start for me.'

'Well, it's nice to see a new face about the place, and if you ever need a listening ear or just an opportunity to have a rant about his lordship, then come and find me in the van. You'll always be welcome.'

'Thanks, Ronnie, that's good to know.' She faltered a moment before asking, 'So how do you know Jackson? Do you work for him as well?'

Ronnie threw back her head and laughed, her deep and warm timbre filling the kitchen with its amusement.

'Good grief no! We would probably end up murdering each other. No, I created the monster, I'm afraid.' At least she said it with a wide smile on her face. 'I'm Jackson's mother.'

* * *

During her first week at work, Pia learnt that Ronnie and Jackson didn't have the most conventional of mother–son relationships. He addressed her by her first name and seemed to be in a constant state of exasperation and impatience around his mum, while Ronnie wafted around the kitchen with a beatific smile on her face or retreated to her van if Jackson was in a particularly snippy mood. It puzzled Pia that Ronnie lived in an old beat-up van when Jackson had such a beautiful home where he could certainly house his mum, but then it wasn't up to Pia to muse on Jackson's personal relationships, even if she had spent a great deal of time since she'd arrived at Primrose Hall wondering when the elusive Tara might put in an appearance.

It was Friday afternoon and Pia was sitting with Jackson in the main office, which, like most other rooms at the house, had wonderful views over the grounds of Primrose Hall and the woods beyond. Bertie had made himself at home and had settled in front of the French doors, where he had a great view of any visiting wildlife and was ready to jump to attention should he be needed to scare away any bold squirrels on the lawn. For the first few days, Pia had shadowed Jackson and learnt about his consultancy company, his motivational speaking and his work for a charity he'd founded, for young, disadvantaged men. He seemed to have his fingers in many pies but his main focus was on getting some events up and running at the hall, mainly opening the renovated stables up to local craftspeople on the first Sunday of each month, and also organising some one-off events.

'So, we have one major date in the diary, which is the classic car show at the end of June. I have a couple of mates who are into their vintage motors, and they'll be coming along to exhibit, and they're also helping to spread the word. This is the spreadsheet of everything we have in place at the moment, but there's still a bit of work to do,' he said, pulling up the file on the computer. 'We need more participants, and we'll need to organise stewards and food vans, etc. Can I leave that with you to get started on next week?' He turned his head to glance at her and she nodded keenly. 'We'll have some motorbikes as well. They're a bit of a passion of mine, but right now we've only got my three bikes lined up, so we'll need some more entries there as well.'

'That's how I remember you,' she said, distracted for a moment, 'bombing about the local lanes on your bike.' Often without wearing a helmet, his dark hair whipping around his face. Sometimes she'd ridden pillion, hanging on around Jackson's waist for dear life, feeling exhilarated and alive. No wonder Connor had been so worried at the time.

Jackson gave a wry smile.

'Yeah, slightly different bikes now, big superbikes, although I like to think I'm a much better road user these days,' he said, as though he could read her mind. 'Well, I think you've got more than enough on your plate at the moment, but any questions then just ask or drop me a text if I'm not around.'

Later that day, on her way back to her flat after tidying up her desk and leaving copious notes for herself for Monday morning, Pia ran into Ivy and Frank in the kitchen, who were getting ready to leave for home.

'So, your first week at the hall is behind you,' Ivy said, with an interested smile on her face. 'How are you settling in?'

'Great,' Pia said genuinely. 'It's gone so quickly and there's still so much to learn, but I'm enjoying the challenge.' Bertie, who had been sniffing around the floor, spotted an opportunity and sat down obediently in front of Ivy, knowing that she was a good bet when it came to treats. Ivy duly obliged, finding a small titbit of ham in the fridge for the dog. Pia shook her head indulgently. 'Bertie's settled in very well too,' she said, laughing. 'Thanks both of you, for making me, or rather us, so welcome.'

Pia hadn't chatted to Ivy or Frank in any depth this week, there hadn't been the time, but whenever she'd bumped into them around the house, they'd always greeted her with a kindly expression and some friendly words, which had gone a long way to making her feel as though she belonged here.

'How long have you been working at the hall?' Pia asked them, as she helped herself to a glass of water from the tap.

'We both joined soon after Jackson moved in last year, so we've been with him from the beginning. He's a pretty good boss, so long as you keep on the right side of him,' said Frank, chuckling. 'You'll get used to his funny ways.' He glanced at his watch. 'I must go. I'm taking Penny out for dinner tonight and I shall be in trouble if I don't get back on time. Have a good weekend, you two.'

When Frank had left, Pia turned to Ivy. 'Funny ways?'

'Take no notice of Frank. Jackson can be intense at times, some might say moody, and retreat into himself if there's something on his mind, but underneath that tough exterior, he's a real softie.'

Pia caught the smile on Ivy's lips, the warm affection in her words. Pia had already seen that side to Jackson's personality.

'I knew Jackson, briefly, when we were kids – well, teenagers actually.'

Ivy gave a nod of understanding. 'That doesn't surprise me. He likes to employ people he knows. I'm sure he'll look after you very well.'

'He already has,' said Pia, reminded of how grateful she was to him for providing her with a job and a home. 'Did you know Jackson, then, before coming to work here?'

'Yes, I was best friends with Marie. His aunt? He lived with her for a time when he was growing up. They were very close.'

'Oh yes, I knew that. Is she no longer...' Pia's words faded away and Ivy shook her head.

'She died a few years ago now. Cancer. I got to know Jackson during Marie's last months and he always kept in touch with me afterwards. When he moved into Primrose Hall, he asked if I wanted to join him as his housekeeper. And here I am!' she said with a big smile. 'It's perfect for me, because it's just down the road from where I live and the hours suit. And who wouldn't be happy working in a place like this?'

'Exactly!' Pia said brightly, hiding a wave of disappointment. She'd been harbouring an idea that Jackson might have still held feelings for her in the same way that she had for him, when nothing could be further from the truth. He was just looking out for his old mates.

'Well, you have a great weekend!' There was so much more Pia could have asked of Ivy. Her curiosity about Tara was threatening to get the better of her, but she didn't want to appear nosy and intrusive.

All in all, it had been a great week. She had a job, a wonderful place to live and a four-legged best friend to share this journey. Wasn't that enough?

12

'Pia, I'm so glad you made it!'

To be honest, Pia would have much preferred to stay at home tonight, curled up on the sofa with a bowl of pasta and Bertie at her side, but seeing Ruby's face light up to see her, she knew that she'd made absolutely the right decision in coming along. This wasn't any old night out in a cocktail bar – it was Ruby's hen night and Pia knew how much she'd been looking forward to it.

'Come on, I've got you a seat next to me. Put this on,' Ruby said, laughing, handing Pia a badge that said *Bride Squad* and a sash proclaiming *Ruby's Hens*. As soon as she sat down, Pia was served a champagne cocktail and she savoured the taste on her tongue, enjoying the moment after the intense week at work she'd had. Pia already knew some of Ruby's friends and was introduced to the others.

'Pia's started a brand new job this week working at the Primrose Hall estate. She's PA to the new owner there. He's a bit of a high-flyer, isn't he?'

'I suppose he is,' Pia said, with a smile, as an image of Jackson's face popped into her mind. She knew he was a go-getting successful entrepreneur, but in her eyes he was still the same carefree teenager she'd once known.

'I went to the Christmas carols event at the hall last year and saw him with his girlfriend. There was a write-up in the local paper about them,' said Jenny, one of Ruby's bridesmaids. 'She's gorgeous; I think she's a model or something, isn't she? Mind you, he's not bad looking either.' She laughed.

'I haven't met Tara yet. I think interior design is her main focus, but she does a bit of modelling too. She's got a huge following on Instagram.' Pia should know. She'd probably spent more time than necessary checking Tara's social media accounts and she could confirm she was gorgeous, creative and talented. What a power couple she and Jackson made. Still, she wasn't here to sing the praises of her new bosses. She was here to enjoy herself and while she was reluctant about that initially, the effect of the champagne cocktail and the ambience and laughter all around them made her much more inclined to do so. 'So, remind me, how many weeks is it to the wedding now?'

'Pia!' Ruby chastised her. 'Are you not counting down the days like I am? It's six weeks tomorrow, can you believe it? I can't wait.'

'Neither can I. And it's good to have something positive to focus on and look forward to.'

'Yeah, it's been a tough time all around. It's such a shame that your mum won't be there to see us getting married. I know how sad Connor is about that. I'm just pleased that she knew about our engagement.'

'She loved you, Ruby, and she always said how perfect you and Connor were together. I said to Connor that Mum and Dad will definitely be there in spirit, dancing around the village hall like they used to in the good old days.'

'Yes, and talking of dancing, come on, let's get this party started.'

Ruby pulled Pia to her feet and gathered up all the other hens, beckoning them onto the dance floor. The DJ played a string of cheesy pop hits, which were just right for the occasion and had everyone bopping and singing along to the music. They weren't the only party in tonight; there were a couple of birthday celebrations and a group of well-behaved stags too over the other side of the bar. Pia couldn't remember the last time she'd been out partying, and she was surprised at how much she was enjoying herself. The champagne cocktails were going down a treat, and she felt light-headed and free for the first time in ages.

Back on the dance floor, twirling around on the spot, her arms held wide, Pia felt as if she didn't have a care in the world, until suddenly, in her enthusiasm, she lost her footing and stumbled straight into the arms of a guy who was doing his own particular wild brand of dancing.

'Hey, be careful,' he said, scooping her up beneath her arms to save her from toppling over.

'Oh, sorry,' she said, grabbing hold of the man's steady forearms. 'I'm not used to wearing heels,' she said, staring down at them accusingly before looking back up again into a pair of blue entrancing eyes, almost sending her wobbly again. She was sure her unsteadiness had nothing to do with the three champagne cocktails she'd already enjoyed.

'Me neither.'

She hesitated a moment, processing his words, before her gaze dropped to the floor. When she looked back again, he was laughing.

'I made you check, didn't I? Hey—' He pointed to the badge on her top. 'Are you the blushing bride?'

'No, that's Ruby.' She gestured towards her soon-to-be sister-in-law, who was in the middle of a circle of her friends doing the Macarena, arms flailing everywhere. 'She's marrying my brother in a few weeks' time.'

'Ah great, must be the season for weddings, then. My friend Steve is getting married too.' He nodded towards a guy who was attempting the same dance routine in a similarly enthusiastic manner. 'I'm Daniel, by the way.'

'Oh, I'm Pia; thanks for saving me from making a complete and utter fool of myself. I would definitely have ended up on the floor if you hadn't caught me.'

'My pleasure. To be honest with you, I'm never quite sure what to do in these places, apart from shuffling awkwardly on the spot, so it was nice to have some kind of distraction. A very lovely distraction, I might add.'

A smile played on his lips and Pia felt herself blush. Was Daniel flirting with her? It had been such a long time, how would she even know, although she appreciated the way his attention made her feel.

'I think I should probably go and sit down before I do myself or someone else even more damage. I could definitely do with a drink, though.'

'Do you mind if I join you?' Daniel asked, looking around at his group of friends, who were having a wild and boisterous time on the dance floor.

'No, not at all,' she said, noticing her own table was vacant as all the hens were still up dancing. She glanced at her watch, wondering how Bertie was doing being left on his own, and she couldn't help thinking about Jackson too. What did he do on a Friday night? Perhaps Tara would be home for the weekend? Pia wouldn't stay out too late as she didn't want to leave Bertie on his own in a new environment for too long. One more drink and then she would think about making a move.

Daniel was good company. He told her about his job as a firefighter, his six-year-old daughter, Chloe, from a previous relationship, who he was clearly besotted by, and how he liked to keep fit by cycling in his free time. Most of all she liked the way he showed a genuine interest in her, listening intently as she spoke about her family, the new job and Bertie, and she found herself opening up to him. It was easy when his sparkling blue eyes appraised her so thoughtfully and appreciatively.

They were getting on fabulously, oblivious to what was going on around them, until they were interrupted a little while later by Ruby, who came rushing over.

'Come on you two, stop being boring. Join in the party. The taxis will be here soon – back to mine for a nightcap?'

Pia would have to sidestep that invitation, already she'd stayed out longer than she'd planned, but one last dance wouldn't hurt. This time she kicked off her heels, knowing she would do less damage that way, and held Ruby's hands as they twirled around the floor together, spinning until they made themselves dizzy and laughing all the way. Every time she looked up and around, her gaze fell on Daniel, who was watching and smiling at her. Ruby pulled her close, whispering in her ear, 'Someone's got an admirer, I think!'

'We were just chatting, that's all. His name's Daniel. He seems like a nice guy.' She couldn't stop the wide grin from spreading across her face.

'Go for it, Pia,' said Ruby gleefully.

Later, as they collected their coats from the cloakroom, Ruby said, 'Are you sure I can't persuade you to come back to ours for a few more drinks? The night's still young.'

'No, it's been great, thanks.' Pia had enjoyed it much more than she'd expected to, but it felt very late to her. She was normally fast asleep by this hour. 'I've had a brilliant time, but I need to get back for Bertie.'

'Okay. Will you be all right getting home?'

'Yes, Daniel and I are going to share a taxi; he's on an early shift tomorrow so we'll get the taxi to drop me off first and then it will take him on to his.'

Ruby widened her eyes and wiggled her eyebrows. 'Well, just make sure you text me when you get back home to let me know you've arrived safely.'

It was funny, but Pia had a gut instinct about Daniel from the moment she'd first met him. Maybe it was because he had quite literally come to her rescue, but she sensed he was a decent, straightforward guy, with lovely eyes and a warm smile. She was more than comfortable to share a ride home with him, and if she'd thought it might be awkward, the two of them away from the heady atmosphere of the bar, then she needn't have worried. The chatter and laughter continued the entire journey home as though the pair of them had known each other for years and not just a matter of hours.

Although she'd told him about where she lived, it didn't stop Daniel from swooning as the taxi made the slow approach up the driveway to Primrose Hall.

'Wow, it isn't much, but it's home,' he quipped, craning his head to see the historic building out of the taxi window.

Pia did the same thing from the other rear passenger seat, marvelling at how beautiful the house looked lit up against the dark sky. It was the first time she'd seen it at night and it appeared just as majestic, perhaps even more so beneath the moon and stars. Despite its grandeur, it still managed to be inviting and welcoming. When the taxi drew to a halt, Daniel quickly dashed round to Pia's side of the car and took her hand as she climbed out of the car.

'It's been great meeting you, Pia. I'll drop you a text so that we can get together for a drink or maybe dinner next week, whatever you'd prefer?'

'That would be lovely.' She smiled. She hadn't thought twice about giving Daniel her number when he'd asked. She was already looking forward to the next time she would see him. He held up a hand to her face, his blue eyes latching on to hers. 'I really want to kiss you, Pia. Do you mind?'

'No.' She laughed. 'I don't mind at all.'

She closed her eyes, the touch of his lips on her mouth igniting all kinds of sensations in her body, feelings she hadn't experienced in ages. The scent of his masculinity, his aftershave, was a revelation and so very seductive too. She liked the way her body nestled into his arms, how she felt safe and protected being wrapped in his embrace, aware of the firmness of his body up against hers. It would be so easy to be swept away on a wave of desire, but she wasn't ready for that just yet. Reluctantly, she wriggled out of his hold.

'See you soon, Pia!' Daniel called, as she went running around the side of the house to the entrance nearest to her flat. When she got to the door she turned and waved and grinned to see Daniel still standing there, beside the taxi, waving back at her. As she fumbled with the key in the lock, she noticed a warm light glowing from inside Ronnie's caravan on the back driveway. She was up late, Pia mused. What might she be doing – reading, watching telly, crocheting, or maybe she fell asleep with a light on? Whatever it was, knowing Ronnie was there, a few steps away, gave Pia an internal hug of reassurance.

This was her new life, her new job, her new home, with a new family of sorts and all kinds of possibilities were opening up for her. With one final last wave to Daniel, she hurried inside. She was adapting to her new life much better than she could ever have expected.

13

Inside, Pia kicked off her heels and rubbed at her feet where the straps of her sandals had dug into them. She threw down her bag and collapsed on the sofa, the events of the evening running through her head. What a great night! Ruby'd had the best time, which was the main thing, and having met the other bridesmaids and friends, Pia knew that the wedding would be a wonderful celebration. Up until now, Pia had been so preoccupied with moving house and starting her new job that she'd barely given a second thought to the upcoming wedding. Now she was filled with excitement.

'Oh god!' She sat up straight. In a blinding moment of panic, Pia realised what she'd forgotten. How could she? 'Bertie?'

There was no way she could have overlooked a Dalmatian dog in her small apartment, but it didn't stop her from calling out his name. And looking behind the sofa, in the kitchen and even in the bathroom. Where was he? A feeling of dread rose in her chest, and she ran to the double doors that opened onto the garden and checked the handle to see if she'd left it open by mistake. It was locked as she knew it would be, but that didn't stop the pounding in her chest. She pressed her head to the window and gazed out into the dark night sky, wondering if she might have shut Bertie out before she left, without realising, even though she knew she wouldn't have done anything quite so stupid. Quickly she unlocked the doors and stepped outside, the cold of the night wrapping around her as her mind tried to make sense of what possibly could have happened.

'Bertie!' she called. There must be a logical explanation. If he had got outside somehow then he couldn't have escaped the small garden because Jackson had assured her that it was a totally secure space. But then perhaps he hadn't reckoned on Bertie's athleticism. Could he really have cleared the fence? She wouldn't put it past him. The thought of Bertie lost and alone in the dark of Primrose Woods brought tears to her eyes. What on earth would she tell Wendy? The very idea made her nauseous. Quickly she darted back indoors, pulled on her trainers and grabbed her hoodie. There was nothing else for it. She would have to go and search for him. Perhaps Ronnie might have seen him?

Dashing out of the door, she took the corridor that led into the main house and went into the kitchen in search of a torch. She pulled open drawers and cupboards, scrabbling around inside, but couldn't find what she was looking for. Desperation crept up on her, making her skin tingle. Not wanting to waste any more time, she would just have to make do with the feeble light on her mobile phone. It was better than nothing. As she hurried out of the kitchen, she heard a noise, the sound of voices, or maybe a television. The main drawing room was in complete darkness, but these sounds were coming from the snug. She hadn't been in there herself, but had taken a sneaky peek earlier from the top of the three steps that led down to the cosy room. It had two big squashy sofas, low tables and a huge TV screen that almost took over one wall. Ivy, the housekeeper, had told her that it was Jackson's chill-out room. She would hate to disturb him, especially if Tara was with him, but she had no choice. This was an emergency.

She knocked on the door tentatively, and immediately she felt a wave of relief hearing Jackson's voice.

'Hey, come in,' he called.

'I'm sorry to interrupt,' she said, almost falling through the door. She sounded breathless to her own ears. 'I've just got back after a night out and Bertie's gone... Oh!' Pia caught her breath as she reached the bottom of the steps and found Jackson reclining on the sofa, looking extremely comfortable, and he wasn't alone! A mix of relief, confusion and embarrassment swept through her body.

'What are you doing? I was worried sick. How did...?'

Her mind was trying to compute what was happening here and she was beginning to regret that last champagne cocktail. She might have expected to find Jackson snuggled up on the sofa with Tara, even if it wouldn't have made the best introduction to his girlfriend but, instead, the sight that greeted Pia was almost as surprising. Bertie was splayed out on the sofa, legs akimbo, while Jackson gently tickled his tummy. All she got for her concern was a gentle wag of Bertie's tail and a raised eyebrow from Jackson. Why did Pia have the distinct impression she was interrupting something here? On the main coffee table was a half-finished bottle of red wine, a glass, some books and Jackson's computer tablet.

'I'm so sorry, Jackson. What I don't understand is how Bertie got out in the first place.'

'Ah, that was me. I let him out. I used the master key. I hope you don't mind. I won't make a habit of it, I promise, but Bertie was barking continually and he sounded distressed. I was worried about him, thought he must have done himself some damage. Turns out he just wanted a bit of company, didn't you, mate?'

Jackson spoke casually as though it was no major inconvenience, but Pia was embarrassed. She knew only too well the racket Bertie could make when he started barking; she'd lived next door to him for long enough. She also knew that as soon as he got some attention he piped down.

'I really can't apologise enough. I'll make sure it doesn't happen again.'

'It wasn't a problem. Honestly. To be fair, Bertie's been pretty good company tonight, haven't you, boy? How about you? Did you have a good evening?'

'Yes, it was fun thanks. It was my sister-in-law-to-be's hen night. We went for cocktails.'

'Sounds great.' Jackson nodded, pressing his lips together. Was he really as relaxed as he was making out? She detected a hint of annoyance, but perhaps she was being overly sensitive. She couldn't help thinking how inconvenient it might have been had he been entertaining friends or spending some intimate time alone with Tara. And on that point, where exactly was Tara? Pia had expected to finally meet her this weekend, but there was no sign of her still. Perhaps she was away on holiday. 'Would you like a glass of wine?' he asked now, interrupting her thoughts, gesturing to the bottle on the table.

'No, I should probably get Bertie back.' She'd impacted on Jackson's time tonight much more than she would have wanted to. She would have to seriously rethink what to do with Bertie when she needed to leave him behind again.

Now, they both looked down at the dog, who looked as though he didn't want to go anywhere, perfectly happy as he was, sprawled out beside Jackson.

'Go on,' he said, with a persuasive smile. 'Help me finish this bottle off. There's a glass over there on the side.'

'Sure.' She could hardly refuse at this point after he'd doggy-sat for her all evening. She glared at Bertie, who was oblivious to her annoyance, before wandering across and picking up an empty glass, topping up Jackson's glass from the bottle and then filling her own. With the pair of them sprawled out on the corner sofa, she took a seat on the smaller one, the room suddenly appearing much more intimate from this angle.

'So how have you found your first week at Primrose Hall? Not just the job but living here too. Are you settling in okay? No worries or concerns?'

'No, it's been great, thank you. There's still a lot to learn about your various companies and the systems, but everyone's made me very welcome. I'm really excited too about getting the events up and running. We're going to be busy.'

'We are. I must admit it's a relief to have you here, knowing that we can move forward on some of these projects. I knew you were the right person for the job,' he said with a crooked smile.

'Thanks, Jackson. Did you really, though?' she ventured. 'I'm sure there must have been other better qualified applicants. I really don't have any experience of working in an office so I was surprised that you even offered me the job.'

Was it the alcohol making her so candid?

'Absolutely. I knew it wasn't so much about experience and skills, but more about finding someone who had the right attitude, a willingness to learn and the enthusiasm to take the role forward. That's you.'

The way he looked at her, his dark brown eyes appraising her, lingering on her features, sent a wave of desire through her veins.

'Well, thanks for putting your faith in me. I appreciate that.'

It was becoming hot in the cosy snug. She wriggled out of her hoodie and placed it over the arm of the sofa. If she wasn't with Jackson, then she would quite happily kick off her trainers and lie back on the sofa. It was that comfortable and she was that tired.

'I know this was a big move for you, Pia. Not only starting the job, but moving house too, so this is bound to be a period of adjustment. If I can help with anything, then just let me know. I want you to think of this as your home now and feel as though you can invite your friends or family round. Your boyfriend too, obviously?'

The unspoken question hung in the air, and she glanced across at Jackson, who had dropped his gaze to where his fingers had slipped beneath Bertie's collar, ruffling his fur.

'Oh, I don't have a boyfriend,' she admitted, 'but thanks anyway. That's good to know.'

She noticed the barely imperceptible quirk of Jackson's eyebrow before he reached for his tablet from the coffee table and closed the cover.

'I'm looking forward to meeting Tara, by the way. Will she be coming by this weekend?'

'Tara?' He turned his head to look at her, as though he might have misheard her question. This time there was no mistaking the rise of his eyebrow, the twist of his lips.

Oh god! Heat prickled at her cheeks. Had she got her name wrong? Why did Pia have the distinct impression that she'd said something out of turn? Trouble was, it was out there now. She could hardly pretend she hadn't mentioned her or just gloss over the subject, moving the conversation on to something less awkward.

'Yes... your girlfriend?' As if he might have needed reminding of that fact. 'I thought I might get to see her.' Pia's forehead crinkled involuntarily as she forced a smile. 'I thought she lived here.'

'No, she did, but we split. A couple of months ago.'

'Ah, I see. I'm sorry.'

'No need,' said Jackson, holding up a hand to stop her, obviously not wanting her to make a bad situation worse. 'Well, it's been great, Bertie,' he said as he untangled his limbs from the dog's and pushed himself up on the sofa, casually running a hand through his hair. Such a familiar mannerism, one that immediately transported her to another place and time. If she closed her eyes, she'd be able to conjure up the scent of him, the taste of him, but those sorts of reminders would only mess with her head. She reached for her hoodie, edging forward on the sofa, mirroring Jackson's movement. Meeting Daniel tonight had brought so many emotions to the surface, desires and longings she hadn't experienced in a long time. Finding out from Jackson that Tara was no longer on the scene was a revelation too and shifted something deep down inside of her. Could she dare to dream that she hadn't imagined the charged air between them, that there might still be an emotional connection between her and Jackson? She stood up, chiding herself. Dreams, that's all they were and the sooner she headed for her bed, and got them out of her head, the better.

14

A few weeks later and Pia thought that Bertie had adjusted well to his new environment. He loved getting outside, exploring the grounds of Primrose Hall, and there was an awful lot for him to discover, his tail held up high behind him as he trotted along, nose to the ground. She always thought he looked so comical, lolloping across the lawns, but she was pleased that he seemed so happy, and she was able to send Wendy lots of photos and videos to reassure her that he was doing fine. After their usual early morning walk, Bertie would settle down wherever Pia happened to be working, under her desk, or against the Aga, if she was in the kitchen.

'That animal! He is a menace!'

Pia had been making a coffee in the kitchen when Mateo came storming in and threw his gardening gloves onto the worktop by the back door.

'Oh, Mateo! What's Bertie done now?'

'No, it's not the dog, it's that pony. He has trampled over all the plants I've put in. They are all ruined.'

'Oh dear! Not again?'

Jackson's Shetland pony, Little Star, might have looked cute with his cream coat and long mane, but he was a little menace, forever escaping, chewing up the plants and leading Twinkle, the steady grey donkey, astray.

At least Little Star couldn't escape into the vast landscape of Primrose Woods any more now that Mateo had secured the fencing, but he was very much making his presence felt in other ways.

'I try to make a good impression. This is new job for me. I work hard and then this happens. What will Mr Moody say?'

'I'm sure he'll understand. I can appreciate how frustrating it must be, but it's not your fault. That naughty pony. How does he keep escaping from his paddock?'

'He squeeze under, he jump over. He undo gate with his nose. He is a super pony. He should be in circus. Mr Moody, he wants a low fence because it looks nice, but he doesn't think about those crazy animals.'

Pia fought hard to suppress the smile that was threatening to take over her entire face, because she suspected Mateo wasn't finding Little Star's antics amusing in the slightest. Pia had grown very fond of Little Star in these last few weeks, admiring his independent streak and wilful personality, and as for Twinkle, although he might sometimes be led astray by his pony friend, he was such a gorgeous and gentle donkey who was always pleased to see her, and often greeted her with a friendly bray. If she was having a low moment then Pia would take herself off, wander down to the paddock and have a chat with Little Star and Twinkle. She could tell, though, that Mateo didn't share her enthusiasm for the animals.

'I'll speak to Jackson about it and see if there's a way of making their space a bit more secure while still ensuring it looks good. Or maybe Frank would be able to help. He's very handy. Let me make you a cup of tea, Mateo. It sounds as though you could probably do with one.'

'Thank you, Pia.'

The gardener slumped down on a chair, looking thoroughly defeated, and Pia put an arm around his shoulder, giving him a gentle squeeze. The grounds of Primrose Hall ran into acres and Mateo had a huge job and responsibility on his hands, keeping them in tip-top condition. Her heart went out to him, having to contend with such a big task, a demanding boss in Jackson and a difficult pony who was hell-bent on causing as much damage as he possibly could.

'Apart from Little Star, how are you settling into Primrose Hall?' she asked him when they were both seated at the table. Mateo had started his new job a week before Pia arrived.

'It is good for me. Primrose Hall is beautiful. And Mr Moody a good boss. I like it. My home, so much better than my last place.'

Mateo lived on site too, in a converted apartment over the stone-faced triple garage. It gave Pia a sense of security and belonging to know that there were other people around, aside from Jackson.

'I like to live here forever,' he said, with a dreamy look as his gaze ventured out of the window.

'I know exactly how you feel,' Pia said, laughing.

Part of her still felt as though she was on holiday, that this was a lovely break away from the normal routine that had been so familiar to her for years. That she would soon return to Meadow Cottages and her life as she knew it and her time at Primrose Hall would be just a happy interlude. She continually had to remind herself that this was her new reality and there could be no going back, and while she was happy about that, after all the worry of being homeless and finding a job, it was still bittersweet that she had left that other part of her life behind for good now.

'Hello, you two!' Ronnie swept into the kitchen, her delicate floral fragrance reaching the table just before she did. 'Can I come and join you or is this important work talk?'

'No, please.' Mateo gestured to the empty seat beside him.

'Lovely, I'll just grab a coffee from the machine.' Moments later she was back. 'I can't tell you how super it is to have some new faces about the place. Jackson seems so much happier these last few weeks, which is always a good thing. I put it down to you two being here; it takes off some of his load.' She chuckled and her laughter rang out around the kitchen. 'It means he's not grumbling at me all the time.'

She took a sip from her mug, her face twisting at the heat on her lips.

'Don't get me wrong. I know he works hard, but he's a terrible perfectionist. I sometimes wonder how I came to be his mother. We're so different in many respects.'

'Did you ever think when he was a young boy that he would go on to achieve so much at such an early age?'

Ronnie's eyes widened, as she pondered Pia's question for a moment.

'He was always very wilful, single-minded and determined, so really it should come as no surprise. He was very smart, too clever for his own good, but of course he never settled to his academic work. He was much more interested in finding trouble, which meant he was often suspended from school. Then he didn't turn up for a lot of his exams. How he ever got a place at university, I still don't know. Not that it did him any good. He decided at the last moment not to go and shot off to London to make his fortune. We didn't see him for a few years.'

'I remember him leaving.' It was engraved on her heart. 'We hung out together for a while during that summer.'

'Did you?' Ronnie turned her attention on Pia, as though seeing her in a new light. 'I didn't realise. He never said.'

Why did that not surprise Pia? That summer had taken on special importance and meaning to Pia and was etched upon her memory. She was beginning to think that Jackson had scrubbed their brief romantic interlude entirely from his mind.

'No, I wouldn't have expected him to. It's a long time ago now, and Jackson obviously had much more important issues on his mind, building his empire.' She said it brightly, making light of its importance to her.

'Well, Jackson would say he's like me in one respect. He can walk away when things get difficult and start all over again without looking back. And he wouldn't mean that as a compliment.' Ronnie dropped her gaze to her hands clasped on the table. She shrugged. 'He resents me for the fact that I was often away in the van when he was a kid. He lived with my sister, Marie, in my absence, which I thought was a much more stable environment for him. The two of them adored each other, but of course, he saw it as me abandoning him.' She sighed, her thoughts clearly drifting to another place and time. 'We're all human, aren't we? We make mistakes. I know I made enough to fill a book, but at least we're back together now. Not exactly living under the same roof, I'm not sure we could manage that, I would definitely drive Jackson to distraction, but we're living under the same cloud space.' She held up her palms to the sky 'It seems to work for us.'

Pia felt a little uncomfortable that Ronnie was talking so candidly about Jackson. What would he think if he knew? From what she'd gathered about Jackson, he was private, keeping his emotions firmly beneath that assured exterior, but then again Ronnie was his mother, and she was outgoing and gregarious, seemingly a law unto herself.

'Anyway, Mateo, how are you?' Ronnie turned her gaze on Mateo, a smile on her lips, her hazel eyes shining brightly, and Pia noticed Mateo puff up under her attention. Pia looked at her watch.

'I'm going to have to leave you two to it. I'm meeting Jackson over at the stables. I'll see you guys later.'

Leaving Ronnie and Mateo chatting, and Ronnie's laughter ringing out behind her, Pia beckoned Bertie to her side and they slipped out the kitchen door and took the short walk across to the stable block. She spotted Jackson before he noticed her, taking in his black jeans, the tatty T-shirt that proclaimed some rock anthem, and a sleeve of tattoos sweeping over a masculine arm. The temptation to reach out and grab his arm, to look closer and run her hand along his tattoos, seeking out the pattern and design, was all too real. She dug her hands into the pockets of her hoodie.

'Hi, Bertie, how you doing?' Jackson's face lit up to see them, but Pia suspected that the warm welcome was mainly for the dog's benefit. Bertie danced on his paws around Jackson's legs as he leant down to make a big fuss of the dog. There was definitely a mutual appreciation society going on between the pair of them, and Pia wasn't entirely sure she approved. She had it in her mind that she and Bertie had the tightest bond, the pair of them against the world together, but Bertie seemingly had other ideas and was quite happy to go off with whoever was willing to make a fuss of him, especially Jackson.

'Okay, so I just wanted to run through the set-up for Sunday. It should all be pretty straightforward.' Jackson opened up the doors to the stables and led her inside.

The first of the craft Sundays was being held this weekend with all of the units booked out to different small businesses including a candle seller, a producer of home-made soaps and bath bombs, a small company that sold beautiful crafted wooden toys along with several other local artisans. A vintage van selling hot and cold drinks and a selection of filled paninis had been arranged to provide refreshments. The plan was to start out on a low scale to see how popular the open days were with a view to expanding and making them more regular events.

'Frank and I have kitted out each of the units with a single table and chair, as a starting point, but there's additional furniture in the main storage unit if it's requested. I'll be around, of course, but just so you know in case you're asked. We're going to use the hard ground at the back of the stables for parking, but that will all be marked up. It should be a good day if it all goes to plan.'

'I'm sure it will do. I really can't wait!' She paused a moment. 'Did you hear we had a bit of a problem with Little Star this morning?' They walked out of the stables and Jackson closed the doors.

'What's the little bastard done now?' he said, with a weary tone.

'He escaped the paddock, taking Twinkle with him, and then they proceeded to trample over the newly planted flowers. Poor Mateo wasn't impressed. I think we probably need to make sure the paddock is secure for the weekend so that they can't do any more damage between them. We don't want them to get out and terrorise the visitors.'

Pia said it lightly with a smile on her face, but she suspected Jackson hadn't picked up on her tone.

'You're right. I've been thinking for a while now that I should probably let them go. I only took them in because I thought they'd be a good draw at the Christmas carols, and they were, but to be honest with you, ever since then, that bloody pony has been nothing but trouble. Can you see if we can pass them on to a sanctuary or something?' He shrugged, as though getting rid of a pony and a donkey might be an easy task to add to her job list.

It seemed natural for them to walk over in the direction of the paddock where Little Star and Twinkle were grazing happily, oblivious to the havoc they'd caused.

'Jackson, I was joking. You can't just get rid of them because they don't suit your needs now. They're animals and this is their home. Look at them; they seem so content.'

They stopped at the paddock and Jackson rested his forearms on top of the fence, shaking his head ruefully. Little Star sauntered over and nudged his head in Jackson's direction.

'Well, I'm glad they're happy, but surely they'd be just as happy some-where elsewhere, stomping on someone else's flowers, disappearing onto someone else's land? It's embarrassing, Pia, to have the rangers from Prim-rose Woods continually having to bring Little Star home. They're more trouble than they're worth, these two. Make some enquiries and see what you can come up.'

'No. I won't.' Pia glared at him. 'I can't believe you would ask me to do such a thing.' She stood with her hands on her hips, annoyance bristling off her skin. 'If we send them away, who knows where they might end up and we don't know what sort of future we would be consigning them to. Besides, I thought you said you'd asked a little girl to name the animals at the Christmas event. What on earth will you tell her if she turns up here one day asking to see them?'

'Right. Fine,' he said tightly, exhaling a breath through pursed lips. 'So, what you're saying is that I'm stuck with this pair of reprobates?' He eyed the animals warily. 'I'll have a word with Mateo and Frank and get this paddock sorted. Maybe a nine feet tall chicken-wire fence will do the trick. What do you reckon?'

Pia caught the half-smile on his lips, but she couldn't return it. It wasn't a laughing matter.

'Hey, come on, Pia, don't look at me like that. I'm not a complete monster.'

She raised her eyebrows at him, her anger only just beginning to abate.

'I'm not,' he protested. 'I would have made sure they went to a decent home. I wasn't about to abandon them by the roadside. But you're right, of course you are, these guys are part of the Primrose Hall family now. I would probably miss them if they were to leave.' He pulled a doubtful expression, and this time Pia couldn't help responding to his crooked half-smile. It was difficult not to when he was chastising her with sparkling brown eyes.

'Look.' He glanced at his watch. 'There's a couple of calls I need to make so I'll catch up with you later in the office.'

Pia watched as Jackson strode away in the direction of the house.

'Honestly, Bertie, what is that man like?' She sighed, taking his head in her hands and stroking his ears down. He wagged his tail at the welcome show of affection. She clicked her tongue to beckon over Twinkle and Little Star and they duly came sauntering over. Relief washed over her. Although she was in no position whatsoever to make any grand gestures, she knew that she couldn't have stayed working for Jackson if he'd really gone through with his threat to re-home the animals. Animals weren't commodities. You couldn't just get rid of them when they no longer served your requirements. Although... what was that Ronnie had been saying earlier about Jackson's ability to turn his back on situations when they no longer served him well? Thinking about it, wasn't that exactly what he'd done to her that summer when he'd captured her heart and then cruelly walked away, without so much as a backwards glance?

15

On Sunday, Pia was up early to do a last-minute check of the stables, even though she'd checked them the night before, and she knew Jackson had done the same too. It was hardly surprising they both wanted everything to be as perfect as they could make it. Already she'd walked Bertie around the lake in Primrose Woods and now he was curled up on a blanket in front of the Aga in the main kitchen, where he would be happy to sleep for a couple of hours. Later, she would collect him and they would have a mooch around the grounds together when the main event was in full swing.

They couldn't have picked a better day for the opening of the craft fair at the stables. Primrose Hall looked beautiful, as it always did in any weather, but it looked especially magnificent that morning with the sun filtering through the woods, picking out the cream tones of the Georgian stonework. Swathes of sunny yellow daffodils greeted visitors along the length of the driveway to the hall.

Over at the stables, Pia made a point of introducing herself to each of the stallholders in turn, making sure they had everything they needed and having a sneaky preview of the gorgeous items they were selling. Already, she'd eyed a pretty wooden wreath engraved with the words 'home sweet home' hung with a red gingham ribbon, which would look good in her small kitchen. And she'd spotted some illustrated birthday cards with cute drawings of squirrels and foxes and deer so she would definitely buy a pack of those later to keep for emergencies.

Soon after opening, the first of the visitors pulled up in the car park and Frank was on hand to give directions and answer any questions. There was a steady flow of customers all morning and after exploring the stables, most people chose to linger outside, enjoying the scenery, buying refreshments at the vintage coffee van and sitting out on the wooden benches soaking up the ambience.

Seeing the array of delicious lunches coming from the van, Pia took the opportunity, after the rush had died down, to buy a panini with tuna mayonnaise for herself and she sat outside to enjoy a quiet moment, relishing the sun on her face.

'That looks good.' Jackson came over and laid a hand on her shoulder. It was the lightest of touches, but it was enough for her body to react to his closeness. As she looked up at him, her eyes snagged on his, sending a frisson of electricity along her spine. 'I'll be over to join you in a moment,' he added. 'I just want to go and speak to Frank, but I'll be back!'

The wide grin across his face was testament to his good mood today. She smiled as she watched him stride off. Why wouldn't he be in good spirits when the sun was shining and it looked as if their inaugural craft Sunday had been a great success? What she did know was that, in a relatively short space of time, Pia had become able to easily detect Jackson's mood. He wasn't one for shouting or great displays of anger. Instead, he would withdraw into himself, the tension held in his shoulders almost palpable. His brown eyes, usually so warm and friendly, would take on a hard, cool edge and that wide smile that held the potential to completely light up his face would be nowhere to be seen. Today, though, he was all smiles and sunshine.

'Hey, Pia.'

Her musings about Jackson were interrupted by the appearance of a dark shadow at the end of the bench. She looked up and was taken aback by her reaction at seeing Daniel standing there. She was genuinely pleased to see him again.

'Hello!' She felt a pang of guilt, realising she hadn't replied to his recent message. They'd been texting for a few weeks now, the conversation between them just as easy and flowing as it had been when they'd met in the cocktail bar. He'd been on night shifts, but as soon as he swapped to days he'd invited her out to dinner. It wasn't that she'd been ignoring him, although she supposed it might seem that way; it was just she'd been preoccupied with work. She'd been intending to reply but it had slipped her mind. 'It's good to see you. Have you had a look around?'

'Yes, it's great. We also seem to have bought rather a lot,' he said, with a wry smile, holding up a couple of brown paper bags and gesturing towards an older woman and a young girl standing behind him, who were also holding carrier bags. 'Can I introduce you to my mum and my daughter, Chloe.' Two faces beamed at her, the family similarity evident across the generations.

'Hi, it's great to meet you both.'

'Do you really live in that house?' Chloe piped up, her awe evident from her tone. The girl had long blonde hair with a centre parting and freckles on the bridge of her nose.

'I really do,' said Pia, with a smile.

'Cool, you must be very rich.' Chloe shook her head in disbelief.

'Ah, well, I only live here, and I work here too. I don't actually own the house and I'm certainly not rich, but I realise how lucky I am to call this my home.' She looked around her, seeing Primrose Hall through Chloe's young eyes. The grand house, the beautiful gardens and the stunning views of the surrounding countryside. Despite her initial reservations about working for Jackson, Pia had settled into life at Primrose Hall much better than she'd ever thought she would. Was this just the honeymoon period, though? she wondered fleetingly. 'Have you said hello to our animals, Twinkle, the donkey, and Little Star, the Shetland pony? They're over in the paddock.'

'No. Can we go and look, Dad?'

'Sure, why don't you and Nan wander over and I'll catch you up in a mo. I'll just have a quick chat with Pia.' A silence fell between them as they watched Daniel's mum and his daughter saunter across to where the animals were grazing. 'So, how have you been?'

'Good!' Left alone together there was a moment of awkwardness as they reacquainted themselves with each other's faces, as though meeting again for the first time. 'Although it's been very busy here,' she felt it necessary to add.

'I thought you might be, but hey, good job you've done here,' he said, nodding sagely, holding up his hands and looking all around him.

She laughed, reminded of how easy it was to talk to Daniel.

'I'd like to take credit for the beauty of Primrose Hall and the success of the open day, but I have to admit I have only played a very minor role.'

'Oh, I don't know. From my point of view it just wouldn't have been the same without you being here.' His eyes locked on hers and the intensity was broken only by the smile spread over his lips. She glanced away, seeing Jackson walking from the car park and across to the stables. His distinctive tall and broad frame strode out with confidence and purpose. *As if he owned the place*, she thought, with a wry smile. 'Right, well...'

'So, how's life with you, then?' she asked, turning her attention back to Daniel, realising it had drifted for a moment and thinking he might be ready to make a move. She didn't want him to leave just yet; she wanted to talk to him some more.

'Yep, great. I enjoy my Sundays with the women in my life.' He glanced across at his mum and daughter, who were petting Little Star and looked to be having a full-on conversation with the animals. 'We'll go home for a roast dinner shortly.' He pulled a face in mock despair. 'Really,' he said, shaking his head. 'My life is as exciting as that.'

'It sounds wonderful to me.' She laughed, a pang of nostalgia filling her chest. When her parents were alive, Sunday lunch was a highlight of their week. Her mum would always cook a roast and the table would be laid properly with a white starched cloth and the best plates and cutlery. Along with the succulent joint taking centre stage, there would be dishes overflowing with vegetables – no one made a cauliflower cheese quite like her mum – and the aroma of rich, delicious gravy would fill the air. There would be non-stop chatter across the table, and she and Connor would probably end up squabbling, but there was always plenty of laughter too. What wouldn't she give for one last opportunity to share another Sunday roast with her family. 'You definitely need to make the most of those times.'

Daniel cleared his throat. 'Look I don't know if you got my text... about dinner?'

'I did! And I was going to answer, but...' Her words trailed away, and she felt her cheeks tinge with embarrassment.

'Hey, it doesn't matter. It's not a problem. Maybe not dinner, then, but if you ever fancy going out for a drink or a walk or...' He shrugged. '...I don't know... anything, just drop me a text and we can get something sorted.'

'Yes!' She'd sounded far too keen, but then what was the point in pretending? 'I'd love to. I was going to reply, I promise.'

'I believe you,' he said, with a quirk of his eyebrow, and Pia suspected that neither of them could really be certain that she would have done so. She had so many other things on her mind right now – her new job, the upcoming wedding, Wendy, and looking after Bertie – that if she'd left it another day or two before replying to Daniel, then there was the possi-bility she might never have got round to doing it. And what a shame that would have been. All of those responsibilities were hugely important to her, but devoting time to her own personal needs had to be a priority as well now.

'So, dinner then?' he asked tentatively.

'That would be lovely,' she said. A bit of romance in her life was prob-ably just what she needed right now. It might stop her obsessing over Jackson too. With a date fixed for the following Friday, Daniel glanced over his shoulder, and said, with an air of reluctance, 'I should probably make a move, but it's been great seeing you again. I'll look forward to Friday. Pick you up at 7 p.m.'

'Great,' she said with a wide smile, waving with her fingers as he went to join his family. Chloe looked across at the same time and gave a big genuine wave too. What a lovely family Daniel had.

'Friend of yours?' Jackson suddenly appeared, slipping into the seat opposite her on the bench. He dropped his panini wrapped in a paper bag on the table and lifted his sunglasses to rest on his head, his gaze settling upon her face.

'Yes, Daniel. He is a friend,' she said, at a loss for anything else to say.

'Uh-huh,' said Jackson, looking at her intently. She wondered if he was waiting for her to expand, to tell him more about the extent of her relationship with Daniel, but she really didn't know that for herself at the moment. He was a friend and they were going on a date, and who knew where it might lead after that. It wasn't something she would feel happy discussing with Jackson anyway. Eventually, filling the silence, Jackson said, 'Well, today went pretty well judging by the visitors I've spoken to. Of course, this amazing weather has helped no end.'

'I know. It couldn't have been more perfect. Everyone says how beautiful this place is. And they were impressed by the different stalls too. I think they've all done quite well with sales.'

'So, same time next month?'

'Yes, it's on the office calendar. I've already had people asking if they can rebook their spot for the next time.'

'We'll see how it goes, but as we get further into summer we might increase the frequency of the open days to every fortnight or week, depending on what other events we have on the calendar. Thanks for all your help today, Pia.' He was looking at her again, his gaze lingering on her face, his scrutiny making her toes curl. He rested his forearms on the bench, leaning forward towards her, his hands clasped together.

'My pleasure,' she said lightly, and it really was. The time had flown by and she'd enjoyed being on hand to chat to the stallholders, and the visitors too. Now, though, she had other distractions at the forefront of her mind. Instead of meeting the intensity of Jackson's dark eyes, she looked down at his strong, tanned arms, which were within touching distance, if only she were to reach out with her hands. It was hardly surprising he was so bronzed. Any opportunity to escape the office and Jackson would be outside in the grounds of Primrose Hall, working with Frank or Mateo.

Sharing this moment of togetherness with Jackson in the early afternoon sunshine felt surprisingly intimate. They'd managed to pull off a successful day and that sense of accomplishment, the working towards a common goal, along with the rest of team, was bonding and energising. Now, his proximity was tantalising and off-putting in equal measure, so it was only natural that her thoughts drifted to that time when their relationship was so much more than just boss and employee. Then she might so easily have reached out for his hand, interlocking her fingers through his, sealing their emotional connection with a physical touch, and however tempting that idea might be now, she knew they wouldn't be revisiting that scenario.

Jackson was focused on his business and the future. It was only her who was very much stuck in the past.

16

Pia drew up in the car park of Rushgrove Lodge for the Elderly and went round to the back to let Bertie out. He leapt down, his excitement evident at finding a new location to explore.

'Now, no high jinks today, Bertie. You need to be on your best behaviour. Do you understand me?'

Bertie cocked his head from side to side as though he understood her every word completely, although the brightness of his eyes made no promises to actually heed her words.

Inside, Abbey Carter came out into the main reception and greeted her friend warmly.

'Hi, Pia, it's great to see you. And you too, Bertie. Now, I've set you up in the guest lounge with a table by the window, but we can open up the doors to the garden if you'd prefer to sit outside or if Bertie wants a mooch. Let me take you through and you can get yourselves settled.'

Wendy had been at the lodge for a couple of weeks now and was undergoing an intensive rehabilitation course from the visiting doctors and physiotherapists. Pia had visited her a couple of times and noticed that Wendy's mood had improved from when she was first in hospital. She had a lovely room with a window overlooking the garden and with her bits and pieces around her, some framed photographs of her husband and son, and one of Bertie too, it was much more homely and cosy than it had been in hospital.

Wendy was now able to get up on her feet and shuffle a few steps with the help of a mobility aid, although she had a little way to go before fully gaining her strength and independence.

Now, in the guest lounge, Pia placed the gold and silver helium balloons she'd brought along by the table, and Abbey brought in the tray of tea with some cups and saucers. The three-tiered cake stand was filled with sandwiches, cream scones and a selection of small cakes.

'Surprise!'

When Wendy was brought into the room on the arm of a carer, her face lit up, spotting Pia first and then Bertie. Bertie gave a small, joyful bark of recognition.

'Oh my goodness, what is all this?'

'Well, I said we'd get round to having our tea party so we thought today was as good a day as any.'

'Oh, Bertie!' With Wendy safely ensconced in her chair, Pia slipped Bertie's lead off and he danced around Wendy's chair as she leant over to pet him. 'I wish I'd known; I would have got some treats in for you.'

Pia delved into her pocket and pulled out a small packet, handing it to her friend.

'I know I can always rely on you, Pia!' Wendy was delighted, clapping her hands at Bertie as he performed his full repertoire of tricks – a sit, a down, a high five and a turn around – and he was rewarded with a treat each time.

When Connor and Ruby arrived, everyone tucked into the treats on the table.

'Honestly, Pia, I really didn't expect this. You are a good girl, looking out for me and knowing Bertie is with you, and happy and well cared for, it's such a huge weight off my mind.'

Bertie was sitting bolt upright, his head resting on the arm of Wendy's chair, adopting his best *I'm so adorable* expression in the hope of receiving more treats from his mum.

'Nice place, this,' said Connor, looking all around him as he bit into a dainty ham and mustard sandwich.

'Well, let me tell you, apart from the fact that it's full of snowy tops, I really can't complain.' It made Pia happy to hear Wendy laugh so naturally again, as if she didn't have a care in the world. 'You know that I was dead against coming here, but they've looked after me so well, and there is always so much going on that you can choose to get involved in or not. The food's not bad either.' She leant forward and surveyed the cake stand full of delights and plumped for a cherry slice.

'Anyway, tell me all your news,' Wendy asked, sitting back in her chair, revelling in the attention, her face beaming as she looked from Ruby to Connor.

'We're good. It's only three weeks to our wedding now, can you believe it? It's come round so quickly. We're so looking forward to it. I was at the village hall today, measuring up for the banners and balloons, and confirming the table layout,' said Ruby.

'So, there's no backing out now,' said Connor with a wry smile, adding just in the nick of time, 'not that I'd ever want to, of course.'

'I do love a wedding. Make sure to have plenty of photographs taken. I've got some space on the windowsill in my room for another photo frame.' Wendy turned to Pia. 'Abbey showed me the local paper yesterday with the piece in it about Primrose Hall. It had a picture of the owner. He's a bit of a dish, isn't he?'

Pia laughed. She'd thought the same thing seeing the article about the success of the open day. There were some lovely photos of the house and Jackson, looking every inch like a rock star turned country gent, as he rested his elbows against the fencing of the paddock, one leg casually crossed in front of the other. There was even a photo of him with the little girl, Rosie, who had given names to Little Star and Twinkle. Her mum, Katy, had taken one of the units in the stables selling greetings cards and a range of stationery items, and at the end of the day, she and Rosie and the rest of their family had gone across to visit the animals, and Jackson had taken the opportunity of a photo. He'd been impressed when Pia had put together a press release for the local newspaper.

'He's a really nice guy and a great boss,' said Pia, while not admitting that she wholeheartedly agreed with Wendy's assessment of Jackson.

'Well, you do know if you want to bring Jackson along to the wedding as your plus one, then you're more than welcome to,' said Connor, with his familiar crooked smile.

'Stop it! He's a great guy, but our relationship is purely professional.' Although she would only admit to herself that she'd entertained a few improper thoughts about him.

Bertie was beginning to get restless, so they opened the doors to the garden and Connor and Ruby took him outside for a wander.

'Oh, that's what I meant to tell you, Pia. I've had some news from Simon. You'll never believe it, but he's coming home.'

'For a holiday? That's lovely news!' Wendy hadn't seen her son in a couple of years, and although she always made light of him living on the opposite side of the world, Pia knew how keenly she felt his absence.

'No, he's coming back to live here.' She clapped her hands excitedly. 'I had no idea. He's retiring, apparently.' She shook her head as though it was a ridiculous notion. 'Can you believe it, at his age too? I think he's made a bit of money out there – he's worked very hard – but now he wants a change of pace. I know he's talked for years about running a fishery so I wouldn't be surprised if he ends up doing something like that. He's already got a house in Wishwell that he's been renting out so it will be lovely to have him back again.'

Pia smiled. So, it wasn't just the impromptu afternoon tea that had put a big smile on Wendy's face. The news that Simon was coming home had obviously lifted her spirits hugely. While Pia looked on Wendy as her family and would do anything for her, she was relieved that Simon would be on hand to care for his mum too.

A little while later, the others returned from the garden and Bertie settled down on the floor in between Wendy and Pia.

'Do you know your daddy's coming home all the way from Australia, Bertie? Won't that be lovely?' Wendy turned to Pia. 'I wonder if Bertie will remember him. He was only about a year old when Simon left. It was a bit of a shock when Simon asked me to look after Bertie while he was away. He was a big dog, even then, and I wasn't sure if I'd be able to manage him, but I could hardly say no, could I? He was pretty much still a puppy and so energetic, but we quickly got used to each other. Mind you, I was a lot more mobile in those days. We used to go for long hikes over at Primrose Woods.'

'I remember,' Pia said fondly. It really didn't seem that long ago and she knew exactly how Wendy must have felt, taking on the responsibility of Bertie and forming a bond with the good-natured dog, who was full of personality, as she'd done the very same thing recently. A swell of sadness filled her chest, thinking what it might mean for Bertie with Simon coming home. Would he want his dog back after all this time? *Of course he would. Who wouldn't?* Pia had always known that caring for Bertie was only a temporary arrangement, but she could never have imagined just how besotted and reliant she would become on that goofy, spotty dog. He'd been at her side every step of the way in this new stage in her life and he'd proved to be the best comfort blanket a girl could wish for. She didn't relish the idea of saying goodbye to the dog that had come to mean so much to her.

17

Pia had that Friday afternoon feeling and was looking forward to the weekend. It had been a busy and productive week at Primrose Hall, where, together with Jackson, she'd fixed dates for the craft Sundays for the rest of the year, organised some motivational speaking events and they'd even confirmed the date for the Christmas carols evening, even though it was still over seven months away. From what she'd heard, last year's inaugural event had been a huge success and Jackson wanted to make this year's even bigger and better than before.

She'd also tackled Jackson's huge pile of paperwork that had built up on one side of his desk. He'd joked that he might disappear beneath the mountain one day so Pia had set out to create a system for his invoices and VAT returns, scanning and filing them away. She set up folders on his computer for the different lines of his business and filled the barely used cabinet with those papers that needed keeping.

Getting to the end of her working week, she had a real sense of accomplishment. Although she'd had little previous office experience, she had quickly adapted to her new environment and was able to find her way around the computer system with the help of the manual, an internet search engine and a little intuition. She didn't wait to be asked. If there was something that needed doing then she would get straight on to it and Jackson was impressed by her can-do attitude.

Just at that moment he came bounding into the office and jumped into his chair, swivelling around on the spot with a big grin.

'Hey, you can't still be working, Pia.' He glanced at his watch. 'Turn that computer off. It can all wait until Monday now.'

'I was just about to,' she said with a smile. She leant forward to switch off her screen. Beneath her desk she stretched out her legs and twirled her ankles. Sometimes, and usually without any warning, she felt a wave of self-consciousness in Jackson's presence, her whole body reacting to his proximity. It was one of those moments now. She was never quite sure what triggered the response in her; maybe it was the subtle aroma of his aftershave wafting in her direction, or perhaps it was the way his dark eyes snagged on hers, lingering there for a moment, or the curve of his smile as he looked across at her. She wriggled in her chair, easing out the tension in her back, and twirled her feet some more.

'Are you rushing off?' he asked.

'No.' She shook her head. Was there something else that needed doing? She didn't mind. It was still early. She only needed to walk Bertie a little later and then get herself ready for her date tonight. Daniel was collecting her at 7 p.m. and she was looking forward to it. The first date she'd had in too many years to remember.

'Fancy a drink on the terrace? It's such a lovely afternoon out there.'

'Sounds great,' she agreed, and as she stood up, Bertie leapt up from where he'd been stretched out in one corner of the office – he seemed to have acquired a bed, or a blanket at least, in several rooms at Primrose Hall already – and he danced at her side as they headed outdoors. A few moments later, Jackson appeared, clutching a couple of bottles and glass flutes, and placed them on the table.

'What do you fancy, Prosecco or elderflower pressé?'

'Prosecco would be perfect,' she said with a smile.

'Good choice.' Jackson flashed her one of those sideways glances as he eased off the cork from the bottle and then poured the glasses. They sat down in the teak garden chairs, side by side, and surveyed the view in front of them. It was breathtaking. Jackson turned and raised his glass to hers and their eyes met over the top of their flutes, causing her heart to skip a beat. If she didn't know otherwise, it would be easy to imagine that she was on holiday in a beautiful resort with the man she loved at her side.

'It must make you very proud knowing that you've restored the house to its original beauty, the gardens are looking so wonderful now too.'

'Yeah, although I can't take credit for the grounds. We had a team in to do the major landscaping work, but it's great that Mateo is here now to do the maintenance and upkeep of the gardens. I can already see the difference he's made, and if we can ensure that Little Star does no more of his escaping tricks or tap-dancing on the flowers, then I think we're going to be fine.'

Pia laughed. She loved Twinkle and Little Star. It was part of her job description to care for the animals, but it didn't feel like an onerous responsibility. First thing in the morning she would throw on some old clothes and, along with Bertie, head over to the paddock to check that everything was well. There was a large barn to the side of their grazing field where they could shelter if they wanted to, and Pia would quickly get to work mucking out their home and ensuring they had the water they needed. If anything, she relished that alone time, out in the fresh air with only the animals for company, giving her a chance to get her thoughts and plans in order for the day ahead.

She looked upon it as her daily therapy session, an escape and a change of scene from the office.

'Do you remember what it was like when we used to come here as kids?' Jackson asked.

Kids? She remembered thinking how grown up she was back then, suddenly having a bit of freedom and independence, with hopes and dreams awakening in her mind, as well as in her body. Thinking about it, though, Jackson was right, they were just kids, finding their way, breaking hearts in their wake. Or at least having her heart broken.

'I do – the grass was so high, and I can remember the feel of it scratching against my bare legs. There were wildflowers everywhere; hollyhocks and poppies, and so many other flowers that I still don't know the names of. If I close my eyes I can still bring that picture into my mind.'

'Me too. That's why I wanted to keep part of the gardens as a meadow as a reminder of those days.'

'It's so beautiful.' She sighed again.

Like the inside of Primrose Hall, everything in the grounds had been created with love and a fine attention to detail. As well as the table and chairs they were sitting on now, there was a more formal dining set on the main patio surrounded by huge stone urns filled with blooming flowers in yellow and cream. To one side, out of sight, there was a built-in barbecue and pizza oven, and a little further down on the brow of the hill was a hot tub that offered glorious views of the valley below.

'How often have you used the hot tub?' she asked, regretting the question before it had even escaped her mouth.

'Ah, confession time. That wasn't my idea. It's really not my kind of thing; it's a bit tacky, don't you think?'

He picked up the wine bottle from the cooler and topped up their glasses.

She shook her head, not agreeing at all. It must have been Tara's idea, then. Perhaps she'd had visions of sharing romantic moments with Jackson under a moonlit sky. To Pia, the hot tub was such a luxury, especially in such an advantageous position. She could just imagine sitting in it, basking in the bubbling water with a glass of wine in her hand, watching as the sun came down, alongside the man she loved. Was Jackson really that much of a snob?

'I guess I'm stuck with it now, though. It's not been used yet. I had Frank check it out this week and it's all ready to go, so please, if you'd like to take the inaugural dip, then go right ahead. It needs christening.'

There was a smile on his lips as his gaze latched on to hers, and she felt her stomach tumble. Obviously, it was the wine affecting her equilibrium. The funny sensations inside her body had nothing to do with the man sitting beside her or the thoughts racing around her head.

'Oh, I haven't got a swimming costume.' It was the second thing she regretted saying in the space of a few minutes, but then she was beginning to make a habit of thinking and saying the wrong thing in Jackson's company, although he didn't seem to notice her embarrassment.

A little later, Jackson held up the empty Prosecco bottle to her.

'Another one?'

A whole bottle of wine? How had that happened? She'd only ever intended to have a glass, but sitting with Jackson, feeling the cool breeze on her skin and chatting away easily like the old friends they were had been far too enjoyable. She could quite happily have sat there all night, sipping on wine, talking, enjoying the ambience, but of course she had other plans.

'No, thank you. I should give Bertie a walk. He's been such a good boy all day.'

'Let me come with you.' Jackson stood up and collected the bottle and glasses from the table. 'Won't be a sec,' he said, heading back to the kitchen.

It wasn't an invitation, more like an instruction. Not that she minded. There was nothing she'd rather do right now than take a walk with Jackson, but she couldn't be too long.

She stood up and glanced at her watch. She would walk Bertie and then dash back to the flat to shower and change. If she had the choice she probably wouldn't go out at all now. After sitting outside and savouring the wine, she felt nicely mellow and relaxed and would be more than happy to stay in with a mug of tea, and cheese on toast. Or maybe a Chinese takeaway would hit the spot better. She put all such thoughts out of her mind. She didn't want to let Daniel down. It was her own fault for drinking too much wine. Tonight, she would stick to the soft drinks and at least she'd be able to have a lie-in tomorrow.

'Are we ready, then?' Jackson asked, when he reappeared. Bertie pricked his ears and went running ahead and Pia and Jackson exchanged a conspiratorial smile, as if they were young parents looking at a cherished child.

They walked down from the terrace and onto the lawns, taking their time before reaching the perimeter fence that abutted Primrose Woods. In every direction you looked there were either tall redwood trees, beautifully tended lawns or rolling fields in the distance with the magnificence of Primrose Hall standing proud behind them. She spotted Ronnie's van to one side of the house, the doors open, and saw Ronnie sitting in an easy chair outside, a multi-stripe blanket falling onto her lap from her crochet hook.

'Your mum seems happy in her own little world over there,' Pia ventured.

'She should do. She does exactly what she wants whenever she wants. Always has done.' Pia heard his wry chuckle but detected an edge of bitterness to his voice. 'You've probably worked out that Ronnie is a free spirit. She doesn't really do responsibility or conventional living.'

'You get on, though?' It wasn't really her place to ask and she hoped she hadn't overstepped a boundary, but it seemed an entirely natural follow-on from their conversation.

Jackson shrugged as though he'd never even considered the question before.

'She's my mother. I don't really have a lot of choice.' Jackson strode ahead and Pia realised it was the end of that particular conversation. 'What I'm going to do,' Jackson said, talking over his shoulder as he walked ahead, 'is to ask Frank and Mateo about the practicalities of putting a path along the entire perimeter fence. It's such a great walk, but while parts of it are passable at the moment, some other bits like here...' he pushed back branches with his hands and stepped over a sprawling rabbit hole that Bertie was currently investigating with his snout '...are not so accessible. Something suited to the environment, obviously, but something that would make it easier to navigate a route around the entire plot.'

'That sounds like a brilliant idea to me.'

It was one of the many things she admired about Jackson: his passion, alongside his vision. To anyone else, it might seem that Primrose Hall was a completed project, but Jackson wasn't the type to rest on his laurels. He was always looking forward, working towards his next goal. His energy and enthusiasm were infectious, and Pia felt grateful and lucky to be playing a small part in this stage of Jackson's grand plans.

The house came back into view and Pia's legs protested as they climbed the hill, but she suspected that was more down to the effects of the alcohol than the exertion of walking, although at least her head was a little clearer now. She paused for a moment, stretching out her spine and soaking in her surroundings. Every spot around Primrose Hall gave a different view of the landscape with something new to discover every time.

'Come on, Bertie!' Pia called.

What was that dog doing now? He'd got distracted, his attention taken by something in the depths of the shrubbery, only the back half of his distinctive spotty body and his tail visible from the greenery. It was a comical sight, but then a wave of alarm swept around Pia's body. She hoped that Bertie wasn't doing irreparable damage to any of Jackson's prized plants. Mateo would never forgive her! Pia called out Bertie's name again but to no avail. She was rewarded only by the increased wagging of his tail as he delved deeper into the bush. Thinking she would have to go over there and physically yank Bertie out of the bushes, Jackson stepped in and, using his index finger and his little finger in his mouth, whistled with such authority that immediately Bertie did a reverse manoeuvre and turned, his head cocked to one side to see what the fuss was about.

Pia laughed. 'Well, that was pretty impressive.'

'Come on, boy,' called Jackson, and immediately Bertie responded and came bounding over at such a speed that for a moment Pia thought he might not actually stop. Until she realised with alarming clarity that he really wasn't going to come to a halt. It all seemed to happen in slow motion, but even so Pia was in no position to do anything about it.

'Bertie, no!' she called half-heartedly, but it was far too late for that. With Bertie failing to engage his brake system, he clipped into her legs and took her straight off her feet with such force that she landed with an ungracious thump on the floor.

'Christ! Are you all right?' She looked up into Jackson's concerned face while Bertie looked on, bemused, too and proceeded to adorn her face with several wet kisses as though that might actually help the situation.

'Eugh, Bertie, get off,' she said, waving him away, while taking the hand that Jackson offered and clambering to her feet. She brushed herself down and flexed her limbs, making sure they were all still in working order. A pain radiated across her right hip where she'd landed, but she hoped and suspected that it would only be bruised and no serious damage had been done.

'Let me take a look at you.' Jackson held the tops of Pia's arms, his gaze running across her face and down her body. 'Do you think you've broken any bones?'

'No, I don't think so. I'm sure I'm probably fine; it was just a shock, that's all. The top of my leg hurts but I think it's just from where I landed.'

Jackson was still holding on to her arms with no sign of letting go and when his gaze settled on her face, she had to wonder if Bertie had had the right idea after all. Looking into Jackson's dark and caring eyes, she could easily believe that some of his over-enthusiastic and attentive kisses might make everything better.

18

Hanging on to Jackson's arm, she'd hobbled back up the hill, across the terrace and into the main kitchen at Primrose Hall. Jackson pulled out a seat for her and fetched her a glass of cool water while Bertie slunk off to his bed against the Aga, looking up occasionally with a mournful expression. Pia couldn't help but smile as Bertie had looked remorseful ever since Jackson had yelled at him when the dog had clearly thought that Pia falling over was a game and he'd been intent on not only showering her with kisses, but jumping over her crumpled body on the floor too.

'Oh Bertie, don't look so sad. It wasn't your fault,' Pia said, and Bertie responded with the tiniest wag of his tail.

'It was entirely Bertie's fault,' said Jackson gruffly, 'and if you do it again, you'll be going to the dogs' home. Do you understand me?' That too was greeted with a wag of Bertie's tail.

'You don't really mean that, do you?' Pia teased and Jackson grumbled something beneath his breath.

'Look, let me order us in some dinner. What do you fancy? An Indian or a Chinese? You choose.'

'Oh...' Pia felt her face drop. 'There's nothing I'd like more,' she said truthfully, 'but I've just remembered I'm going out tonight with a friend.'

She looked at her watch. She would need to get a move on if she was going to be ready for when Daniel arrived.

'Fair enough.' Jackson shrugged. 'You're feeling well enough to go out, though?'

'Yes, really. I'll be fine. I'm just a bit sore and bruised that's all.'

'Okay, well, that means it's just me and you then, mate,' Jackson said to Bertie, and Pia wondered if his light tone masked disappointment. What was her excuse? She was going out on a date, her first in years, and had been looking forward to it, but now she really wished she wasn't going. She would rather stay at home – and yes, she realised she did consider Primrose Hall to be her home now – to be with Jackson.

'Don't worry about looking after Bertie. I'm sure he'll settle down in the flat once I've gone.'

'Nah, you'll want to come and hang out with me, won't you, Bertie? We can keep each other company.'

While she was pleased that Jackson would be looking after Bertie in her absence, she couldn't rid herself of the niggle that she would be the one missing out by leaving them behind. The idea of a takeaway with Jackson was very appealing, sitting together at the kitchen table chatting some more, or relaxing on the sofas in the snug, but she knew it would be unfair to let Daniel down at this late hour. Even if she was still filled with regret when he came to pick her up later from the hall and they made the short journey into town.

'Have you had a good day?' he asked, giving her a sidewards glance as he rested his hands on the steering wheel of the car. There was no doubting Daniel looked attractive tonight in a pair of light chinos and a blue chambray shirt, his dark blond hair cut short against his neck, accentuating the strong lines of his clean-shaven appearance.

'Yes.' She nodded and smiled. She really needed to be right back in the moment. It wasn't fair on Daniel for her mind to be drifting elsewhere. 'It's been a good week, although Bertie did send me flying on our walk this afternoon. Honestly, he just came running at me and before I knew it I was flat on my back.'

'Oh god! That doesn't sound good. Bertie is your...?' Daniel scratched his chin, his face a picture of confusion and, seeing his expression, Pia laughed out loud.

'My dog – Bertie's the Dalmatian.'

'Oh yes, the dog, of course. I remember now. You told me about the dog. Well, that's a relief, I have to say. I did wonder for a moment what was going on up at that big house.' He chuckled, the sound of his laughter wrapping her in a warm embrace. 'You are okay, though?'

'Fine, although I think I might wake up tomorrow a bit bruised and battered.'

Arriving at the Italian restaurant, they were shown to a table at the back of the room and the aromas of garlic, tomatoes and warm bread wafting in the air reminded Pia how hungry she was. She hadn't eaten since lunch and the wine she'd shared with Jackson had definitely whetted her appetite, in all possible senses, so she was mightily relieved when the waiter arrived with a basket of bread and a bowl of olives. She was quick to dive in and as she tucked into a slice of home-made bread with a thick smearing of butter on it, she actually swooned with delight, as the sensations in her mouth exploded. Although she'd vowed not to drink tonight, Daniel insisted she have a least one glass of wine. He was laying off the booze because he was driving, and Pia, vacillating, quickly made her mind up when the waiter mentioned something about a Bellini. She thought it would be churlish to refuse.

As was always the case when she was with Daniel, the conversation flowed easily and they joshed each other in a way that anyone observing them from afar might believe that the pair of them had known each other for years.

'I told Chloe I was seeing you tonight and she was terribly excited.'

'Aw, she seems like a great kid.'

'She really is. No thanks to her psycho mother.'

'Oh...' His comment made Pia flinch and she wasn't sure how to react. 'Really?'

'Really.' He laughed bitterly. 'Best thing I ever did was walking out on that marriage. Thankfully Chloe takes after me.'

Daniel's words didn't sit right with Pia, but she wasn't going to press him on his failed marriage, especially when it seemed like a sore topic of conversation.

'Yeah, Chloe still thinks you're a rich celebrity for some reason. I've tried to convince her otherwise.'

'Ha ha, nothing could be further from the truth, I'm afraid. I really hope she doesn't end up too disappointed when she discovers I'm just a penniless country girl.' Pia took a sip of her Bellini, enjoying the fruity flavour, trying to ignore a nagging feeling of doubt about Daniel. She went on. 'Although I suppose I am rich in many ways if that doesn't sound too cringey. I'm really lucky to have found the job at Primrose Hall and to live in such a beautiful spot. My boss is great, really lovely, and the other people who work there have been so welcoming too. I've really landed on my feet. And isn't that worth so much more than mere money?'

Daniel pushed his lips together and nodded. 'Great that you get on so well with your new boss. He has a girlfriend, right? Did I read something about that online?'

'Yeah.' Pia nodded noncommittally, unsure why she wasn't been totally honest with Daniel, but she felt protective of Jackson and didn't want to be discussing his personal life. Instead, she took the conversation in another direction. 'Do you know, you'll probably think me mad, but I wouldn't be surprised if my mum was up there somewhere, pulling a few strings, making all this happen for me.'

'That doesn't sound mad at all,' said Daniel generously, with a smile. 'Maybe she's brought you and me together. You never know!' His eyebrows lifted and his eyes grew wide.

'Exactly. Who knows?' she said casually, her gaze drifting off around the restaurant. It wasn't what she'd been thinking at all. Her arrival at Primrose Hall and reconnecting with Jackson had felt pre-destined, but perhaps fate had something else in store for her entirely, something she couldn't even imagine yet.

Their starters of tiger prawns in a chilli and garlic dressing arrived.

'This smells amazing,' Pia sighed.

They ate and chatted, without any lulls in the conversation, and Pia didn't feel in the least bit self-conscious eating in front of Daniel as she'd thought she might. The main courses of sea bass for Pia and meatballs for Daniel were equally delicious and when they got to dessert, after both saying how full they were and how they couldn't possibly eat another thing, they plumped for a tiramisu and two spoons. Daniel was the first to dip in, scooping up a heaped teaspoon of the fluffy coffee-flavoured cream, but instead of trying it for himself he leant across the table with the spoon of deliciousness and hovered it over her lips. She smiled, opening her mouth, their eyes locking as the cream melted on her tastebuds.

'Is your brother's wedding next weekend?' Daniel asked a little later when they'd finally finished eating.

'Two weeks,' said Pia. 'I can't wait. And your friend's wedding must be coming up soon as well?'

'Yep, that's four weeks tomorrow. I wanted to talk to you about that, actually.'

Pia dropped her head to one side.

'I wondered if you'd like to come along with me as my plus one? All my mates from the fire station will be going and pretty much all of them have girlfriends so I think I'm probably going to feel like a spare part if I'm just sitting there by myself. I know you'll be able to help me out on the dancing front too when the time comes.' Daniel's gaze roamed her face before he quickly added, 'Not that it's the reason I'm inviting you, of course. I'd like you to come with me. It should be good fun, especially with you at my side. Obviously no pressure. Only if you wanted to, of course.'

Pia smiled, charmed by Daniel's self-effacing proposition.

'I'll tell you what,' she said, the thought suddenly occurring to her before she'd really had a chance to think it through. 'Why don't you come along to Connor and Ruby's wedding as my plus one? We can look upon it a trial run.' She giggled. 'But yes, thank you, I'd love to come along to Steve's wedding with you as well.'

'Really?' he said, his relief and surprise evident across his features. 'That's a great idea. And thank you. I'll look forward to it. I love a good shindig.'

Pia knew that her brother would be thrilled that she'd found a plus one to take to the wedding. He'd been going on long enough about her finding a man, including some ill-fated attempts at fixing her up with one of his friends, but despite his best intentions, she didn't need his help or anyone else's help when it came to her love life. She was perfectly capable of sorting that out for herself, even if she had completely neglected that area of her life in recent years. Who knew if anything would come from her fledgling relationship with Daniel, but she was excited and intrigued to find out where it might lead them.

After dinner they walked along the riverbank and when Daniel slipped his hand into Pia's, it felt like the most natural thing in the world. She loved the idea of being part of a couple, of sharing her life with someone who was kind and decent and funny. And wasn't Daniel all of those things? she thought to herself, as she snuck a glance at his handsome profile.

Later, when they'd returned to Primrose Hall, Daniel turned the ignition off in the car, and shifted his body in his seat to face her.

'Thanks so much for coming tonight. I've had such a great time. I hope you have too?'

'It's been great, Daniel, thank you.' It was the best date she'd had in years, even if it happened to be the only date she'd had in years. 'And thanks for treating me to dinner. That was really kind of you.'

It was no lie, she had enjoyed Daniel's company. He made her feel attractive and funny, and she loved the feeling of safety and security she experienced when he wrapped a strong and muscular arm around her shoulder. The sensation of his kisses was something of a novelty too. His mouth landed on hers, sending a flutter of butterflies around her body as a heat rushed to her skin.

She pulled away, looking into his ink-blue eyes, a myriad of thoughts fighting for attention inside her head.

'I'm sorry I can't invite you in for coffee. It's not something I feel comfortable with. I mean, as the new girl at Primrose Hall.'

'Don't worry, I didn't expect you to. Come on,' he said with a smile. 'Let me walk you to your door.'

Beneath the lights of Primrose Hall, Daniel took Pia in his arms and kissed her again, this time with more passion and urgency. It was lovely. Really lovely, or so she thought, as she tried to abandon herself to the moment. Only she couldn't. Her body tensed and soon she found herself wriggling away from Daniel's advances. The trouble was, as soon as she closed her eyes, it was someone else she imagined holding her, kissing her, filling her head with hopes and dreams, as he'd done once before. *Bloody Jackson Moody!* She pinged her eyes wide open. Why did he continue to invade her thoughts the entire time, taunting her with his presence without even realising he was doing it?

19

Wednesday afternoon and Pia was at her desk working on some social media graphics for Primrose Hall. Unusually, Jackson was in the office too. He was leaning over her shoulder, offering his advice on the images she was creating and she was doing her utmost to ignore the way his familiar scent and his masculine proximity made her feel.

More often than not, Jackson chose not to linger in the office too long. He would drift in and out, perch on the edge of his desk, chatting through with Pia any issues that might have come up, before dashing off again. She'd quickly come to learn that Jackson wasn't the sort of person to stay still for very long.

At least once a week Jackson would need to go into London to attend meetings or have lunch with one of his many associates, but if he was at home then he would most likely be found out in the gardens, in his old jeans and T-shirts, working alongside Frank and Mateo.

His laptop pinged and his fingers tapped on the keyboard.

'Ah, we have a visitor. We're not expecting anyone, are we? Or any deliveries?' He turned his laptop round so that Pia could see the screen. It was obviously some kind of CCTV system with several windows showing different viewpoints from every side of the house. She noticed the car approaching in the central screen, but didn't recognise it and imagined it to be one of their local suppliers. It wasn't that unusual to have unexpected visitors. What was puzzling her more was that there was CCTV in place at all. Although why she should be surprised about that discovery, she really didn't know. A property of this size with outbuildings housing expensive cars and motorbikes would definitely need a security system of some kind. It was the fact that Jackson had instant access to the outside camera system on his laptop that was troubling her. She cringed inwardly, feeling her cheeks colour, hoping he might not have seen her late-night smooches with Daniel.

'Let me go and see who it is.'

Jackson went off and Pia was left staring at his laptop, marvelling at how clear the images on the screen were. Clear enough that you would be able to see two people canoodling on them. *Oh god!* Now, though, Pia leant closer to the laptop to get a better look. As soon as the person emerged out of their car, she knew exactly who it was and it sent a shot of fear through her body.

'Pia, you have a visitor,' called Jackson, coming back into the office with a young raven-haired woman following behind.

'Ruby, what are you doing here?' Pia got up from her desk and went across to greet her, holding on to her upper arms and looking for answers in her troubled expression.

'I'm so sorry to just turn up like this, but I didn't know what else to do. Do you know where Connor is? I've tried calling him, but he's not picking up his phone.'

'I don't, but then he doesn't always answer when he's at work.' She looked at Ruby's face, which looked as if it was about to crumple. 'What on earth's the matter?'

'I've just heard from the caretaker at the village hall. They've had a survey done on the building because they were hoping to retile the roof after the summer, but apparently they've discovered asbestos in the ceiling so they've had to close the building down for the next couple of weeks while further investigations are carried out. They've said, categorically, we won't be able to go ahead with the wedding reception.'

That's when Ruby broke down in tears, the anguish and emotion she'd obviously only just been holding on to during the journey over in the car escaping in noisy sobs.

'That's awful, and such a shock, but try not to worry; I'm sure there'll be a way around it,' said Pia, sounding much more confident than she felt.

'Pia, we're getting married in ten days' time in peak wedding season! Where on earth will we find another venue at this late date? Somewhere that we can afford? It's a complete disaster! We'll probably have to end up cancelling.'

'Let me go and make a cup of tea, or else a cold drink. What would you like... um...?'

'Ruby,' Pia said for Jackson's benefit. 'My soon-to-be sister-in-law,' she said with as much positivity as she could muster.

'Well, that's hardly likely to happen now, is it?' Ruby sighed. 'But thank you. I'd love a tea if you're making one. And sorry for barging in like this.'

Ruby grimaced as Jackson went off in the direction of the kitchen.

'I'm so sorry, Pia. I didn't know what to do or where else to go when I heard the news. And then when I couldn't get hold of Connor, I jumped into the car and it just made its way here. I haven't told anyone else. I don't want my family panicking.' She fell silent for a moment, tilting her head in the direction of Jackson's departure. 'Phew, he's hot, isn't he?' she said, fanning her face with her hand at the same time.

Pia smiled and shook her head indulgently. At least Ruby wasn't too distraught that she couldn't appreciate a good-looking man when she saw one. And at that moment Pia was very grateful to Jackson, who returned a few minutes later with two mugs of tea and a plate of biscuits. *What a sweetheart!* He discreetly backed out of the office, leaving Pia and Ruby to their conversation.

'What will we do, Pia?' Ruby looked at Pia imploringly.

'Speak to Connor tonight and see what he has to say. Then maybe ring round some of the other village halls in the area to see if they have any availability. Or what about some of the local pubs or hotels? I could help you ring round if you like.'

'We couldn't afford to even if we wanted to. We were doing this on a budget as it is, so we're not going to have the money to pay out on another venue. It's not as though my mum or dad have big enough places to have it at either of their houses. I really don't know what we'll do. I'll be devastated if we have to cancel. It would be like a bad omen for the start of our marriage.'

At that moment, Jackson wandered in with Bertie at his side, who had got into the habit of following Jackson around everywhere.

'How many people did you have coming to the wedding?' Jackson asked.

'It was about sixty in total.'

'And who was doing your catering?'

Pia glanced across at Jackson, wondering why he was asking such direct questions. Ruby wouldn't want to be reminded of a wedding arrangement that she might be cancelling as soon as tomorrow.

'We're having a buffet. My mum and my aunts were going to be doing it between them. Just something simple: cold meats, quiches, cheeses and salads, that kind of thing.'

'And what about the service?' Jackson was perched on the edge of his desk, scrolling through his phone, seemingly showing a half-hearted interest in Ruby and Connor's predicament. Pia wished he would stop with the third-degree questioning. She wasn't sure it was helping. 'Where were you having that?'

'At the village church. That's not the problem. It's the reception that's the difficulty. What am I supposed to do with sixty hungry people intent on having a good time?'

Pia and Jackson exchanged a glance and Pia shrugged her shoulders, trying to think.

'There must be a way. Perhaps Connor knows someone at work that might be able to help?' Pia was really clutching at straws now.

'I don't think so. It's going to be awful if I have to ring around everyone to tell them it's cancelled. Who knows when the village hall will be back in action? We might have to postpone the wedding until next year,' she said sadly, her bottom lip wobbling dangerously. 'Oh—' She let out a strangulated yelp. 'I've just realised we're going to lose all our deposits: for the cake, the photographer, the flowers and the disco. I'm sure there are others too. Connor will be furious.'

Ruby started crying again and Pia reached for the box of tissues on her desk and handed them over, putting an arm around her shoulder.

'I'm sorry this has happened to you, Ruby. It's so disappointing, but let's try and find another venue. There must be something out there. Speak to Connor and then perhaps we can brainstorm and put together a list of possible venues.'

Ruby looked doubtful.

'And then at least we can say we did everything we could to make your wedding go ahead,' Pia added. There was a pause in the conversation while both Ruby and Pia drifted off into their own thoughts. As for Jackson, something had obviously distracted him because he was busy on his phone, wandering in and out of the office, talking intensely to someone. Pia felt a pang of guilt, realising he was probably just waiting for Ruby to leave so that they could get back to what they were doing. She hoped he would understand. This was a family emergency after all.

'I've just got to get the electrics checked out and the PA system installed, but I've been in touch with my supplier and they can do it this weekend.' Jackson was back and talking to Pia as though Ruby wasn't even in the room. How rude, thought Pia. She knew he had work to do, but he must be able to see just how devastated Ruby was.

She looked at him, nonplussed.

'Great,' said Pia, without enthusiasm, picking up a pencil and scribbling down on her pad: *electrics, PA system, weekend*. She needed to show willing, but surely this could wait until after Ruby had left. She looked at the words she'd just written, not having the faintest clue what Jackson was talking about.

'No, I mean the barn.' Jackson was insistent. 'It's pretty much finished; it just needs the audio installation fitted. They were due to do it next month, but I've just spoken to them on the phone and they've agreed to bring it forward to this weekend. I know the guy who runs the company.'

Jackson was looking at her expectantly as though waiting for some sort of response, but at that moment Pia was at a complete loss as to what exactly was the right answer. She just nodded and smiled, which she hoped might satisfy Jackson's interest.

Jackson laughed, looking from Ruby to Pia.

'No, you're not getting it, Pia. The barn. Don't you see? It's the perfect place for a wedding. Come on, come and have a look.'

Jackson turned and strode out of the office with Bertie following closely behind, and Pia and Ruby were left gawping at each other, mouths open in amazement before quickly dashing out after Jackson, their excitement building with every step.

20

Jackson walked at quite a speed and while it was easy for Bertie to keep up, Pia and Ruby took small galloping steps to catch him up as he waited at the entrance to the barn. He opened the doors and gestured to them to go inside. Pia and Ruby both gasped as one as they stepped over the threshold.

'Oh my goodness, this is amazing,' said Ruby, her head craning to look at the oak beams above.

The walls were newly painted, the dark cream colour separated by the light oak vertical beams around the barn. The effect was rustic, traditional and charming. Light filtered in through the fully glazed doors on one side of the barn.

'All the doors open up onto the gardens so it's a pretty flexible space.'

'This is the first time I've seen inside,' said Pia, seemingly as taken aback by the sight as Ruby. 'What were you intending to use this for?'

'Well, originally I thought it might be a good place to store some of the vintage cars that I hope to buy one day.' He smiled and Pia wasn't entirely sure if he was joking or not. It was far too swanky to be used as an upmarket garage. He walked around the spacious barn, appraising the room as if he was seeing it for the first time too. 'But really it was only ever intended as a place for parties and one-off events. It would also work for our Sunday open days if and when we decide we want to grow them. To be honest with you, I never wanted it to be a dedicated conference centre for corporate businesses. This is my home, so I want the facility to be used for those occasions that I think are worthwhile, preferably benefiting the local community. And I can't think of anything more fitting than your upcoming wedding reception, Ruby. You are more than welcome to use the barn. If you want to, of course.'

'Oh my god! Do you actually mean it, Jackson?' Ruby's face lit up with excitement before falling with disappointment just as quickly.

'But we could never afford somewhere like this.' Ruby's excitement was bubbling beneath the surface but Pia could tell that she was daring to imagine her wedding reception in the beautiful old barn. 'How much *would* it cost?' Ruby ventured.

'Nothing.' Jackson's response came quickly and decisively. 'You're welcome to use it for free.' He gave a genuine smile. 'Really, I wouldn't offer otherwise. Besides, me and Connor, we go back a way.'

Ruby looked at Pia, her eyes wide, anticipation emanating from her entire being. The tears that had been so in evidence today erupted again but now they were tears of happiness.

'There's a small kitchen area through that door, with a fridge and plenty of storage, and a couple of toilets too. So you should have every-thing you need – well, apart from tables and chairs...' Jackson grimaced at the realisation of the major flaw in his grand plan.

'I'm sure we could sort something out,' said Pia quickly. 'Borrow them from somewhere?'

'Yeah, there's a couple of contacts I have that might be able to help. I can give you their numbers if you like. It's up to you, Ruby. See what Connor thinks and then just let me or Pia know what you'd like to do.'

'Oh, I don't need to think about it,' said Ruby, wiping away her tears on the back of her hand. 'This will be absolutely perfect for our reception and, honestly, it's so much classier than the village hall.'

Jackson and Pia exchanged a glance and grinned, as Ruby ran to the centre of the barn, holding her arms out wide and spinning around on the spot, her happiness filling ever corner of the room.

'Thank you so much, Jackson. Really, I cannot thank you enough.

You've made me the happiest woman in the world.' She pursed her lips together, pressing a finger to the corner of her mouth. 'No, that can't be right, can it? Isn't it my future husband who's supposed to do that? Never mind, you come a very close second. Is it okay if I bring Connor round to take a look? He's going to be so impressed.'

'Yeah, sure. Just let us know when.'

Ruby ran across to Jackson and threw her arms around his neck, jumping up to wrap her legs around him too, which took Jackson somewhat by surprise. Trapped in Ruby's over-enthusiastic embrace, Jackson flashed a look of bemusement at Pia, as if she might be able to do something to help. Pia grinned as Jackson looked mightily relieved when he was finally able to extract himself from Ruby's hold.

'Right, I'm going to leave you both to it. I have a couple of calls to make. It's been nice meeting you, Ruby. Anything you need to know or ask, then Pia's probably your best bet.'

Pia watched him stride out of the barn. She'd barely uttered a word since they'd come inside. She hadn't trusted herself to. Or else she might have been in serious danger of breaking down in tears like Ruby. She was still trying to process what Jackson had just done. He'd been under no obligation to offer his quite frankly beautiful barn as a replacement wedding venue, but he'd done it, seemingly without any qualms whatsoever.

'I can't believe he just did that,' gushed Ruby, breaking into Pia's thoughts. 'Your boss is the most amazing guy ever.'

For a while now Pia had suspected he might be, and this afternoon's events had proven, if she'd actually needed any proof, that he was the very special human being she'd always known him to be.

21

A couple of days later, Pia rat-a-tat-tatted on the door of the caravan.

'Special delivery!' she called.

Moments later, Ronnie emerged, wearing a long flowing skirt, a flowery blouse, and with her ash-blonde hair, highlighted with natural silver streaks, piled high on her head.

'This parcel just came for you.'

'Oh thank you, darling, that will be my herbal teas.' She took the box from Pia. 'Why don't you come inside and have a cuppa. Mateo and I were just having one.'

Pia poked her head round the door to see Mateo sitting on the side bench with a mug in his hands.

'I will be back to work soon. This is my break,' he said, looking alarmed.

Pia laughed. 'Don't worry, I'm not checking up on you, really! And thanks, Ronnie, I'll have a cup of peppermint tea if there's one going.'

Pia settled herself on the steps to the caravan in view of both Ronnie and Mateo, and Bertie lay down on the ground beside her. She could see why Ronnie loved it here so much. It was surprisingly spacious inside the van, for two people at least, with every convenience that you might require. Ronnie had certainly made it homely with her collection of colourful cushions, exotic fabrics draped around the seats and units, and her set of mismatched, vibrant crockery. She probably had one of the best views of the surrounding landscape too, as she overlooked the valley and Primrose Woods to one side. And should Ronnie ever get fed up with the view, for any reason, then she could simply tootle off in her van to find another spot.

'Did you hear that my brother, Connor, and his girlfriend are holding their wedding reception here, a week tomorrow?'

'I knew about the wedding. Mateo was telling me about it.'

'Yes, I am putting together pots and baskets for the outside of the barn. It will look beautiful.'

'I had no idea it was your brother, though,' added Ronnie. 'How lovely!'

'Yes, well, they had a bit of bad luck. They were due to hold their reception at the village hall, but it was closed down suddenly. They're having some safety checks carried out, apparently, but it was the worst possible timing for Connor and Ruby. With less than two weeks to go, they were left without a reception venue. It was so wonderful of Jackson to step in and offer the use of the barn.'

'Yes! Jackson to the rescue again!' Ronnie laughed. 'You know at one time they were talking about making a dedicated wedding venue here. Well, that was Tara's plan at least. Jackson's ex?' Pia nodded; she would never admit it, but she knew far more about her boss's ex-girlfriend than she really needed to know. 'I'm not sure Jackson was so keen on the idea, though,' Ronnie went on. 'I think she even got to the stage of applying for and being granted the licence to perform civil ceremonies here.'

'Oh, that's interesting. I mean, Connor and Ruby will just be having the reception here, but I can definitely see why Jackson and Tara might have wanted to explore that possibility. The barn is such a beautiful building and with the glorious backdrop of the grounds and gardens, any wedding photos would look amazing.'

'Yes, well, as I say, I think Tara was the driving force behind that idea. She had lots of plans for this place – well, that was before they split up. As you've probably already found out for yourself, it's Jackson's way or no way. I think she might have even had the idea that she and Jackson could get married here themselves.'

'Oh, really?' So their relationship had been a serious one, then. 'It's a shame they split up,' said Pia, at a loss for anything else to say. There were a dozen questions she could quite easily have asked but it certainly wasn't her place. Her curiosity about Jackson and Tara would have to remain unsated if she didn't want to show she had more than a professional interest in Jackson, although Ronnie seemed quite happy to volunteer the information.

'Yes, I'm not certain Jackson's the marrying type. Once he gets too involved with a woman, he always reaches a point where he gets cold feet. Afraid of commitment. A bit like his father, I suppose.' She let out a hollow laugh. 'And once someone has served their purpose to Jackson, he's very good at cutting them out of his life for good. It was a shame. I really liked Tara.'

Pia nodded, sipping on her tea. Perhaps Ronnie didn't know the full story of what had gone on between Jackson and Tara. It was unlikely that he would tell his mum every detail of his relationship history, but Ronnie's words hit a nerve with Pia. Wasn't that exactly what Jackson had done to her once upon a time? For some unknown reason, and she'd spent several years wondering why, he'd tired of her and walked away without looking back. And if he was capable of doing something like that once, then he would certainly be able to do it again.

22

Back at the main house, Pia walked through the kitchen and then into the office, stopping with a start in the doorway as her eyes alighted on a beautiful basket of flowers sitting on her desk.

'Oh my goodness!' she exclaimed, looking over her shoulders as though someone might jump out to surprise her. Not that there was anyone around. Curiously, and with a pretend air of nonchalance, she wandered over to her desk, wondering who they might be for – another delivery for Ronnie, perhaps – and tentatively reached into the middle of the arrangement and pulled out the card. Her name was written in ink at the top and a sear of excitement shot through her body.

To Pia
I'm so happy to have met you.
Counting down the days until the next time.
Love D xx

D? Daniel, of course! Who else? He seemed keen, probably a bit too keen, if Pia was being honest. It was a lovely gesture, though. She picked up the basket and turned it around in her hands, admiring it from all angles, trying to ignore the seed of disappointment in her stomach. The

flowers acted as a reminder that she'd had several texts from Daniel that
she hadn't replied to yet. Frankly, it was hard to keep up with them all.
When she was at work, she thought of little else apart from her job and
now the upcoming wedding was playing on her mind too. She'd only given
Daniel a cursory thought since their date night and was beginning to think
that having a plus one in tow might be far too demanding and time-
consuming. She read the card again, running a finger around its edges.

Quickly, she composed a text to Daniel. He probably thought she'd
fallen off the edge of the world. She couldn't make him wait any longer for
a response.

Hi Daniel,
Thank you for the lovely flowers.
They're beautiful, it was very sweet of you, and much appreciated.
Will look forward to catching up soon.
Pia xx

She snapped her phone shut and hoped that her short message might
keep Daniel happy until the next time they met, which would probably be
at Connor and Ruby's wedding now. She really hoped she'd done the right
thing in inviting him along. It had seemed like a good idea at the time,
taken by the moment and aided by glass or two of fizz; it had been a spontaneous and carefree thing to do, but now she was having second thoughts.
Still, it was too late to do anything about it. She could hardly uninvite him.
Her phone buzzed on the desk and she knew instinctively it would be from
Daniel again. It sent an uncomfortable shiver along her spine. She
wouldn't look at the message. He must understand that she had work to do
and couldn't spend the whole day texting. The basket of flowers would
look great in her flat; she knew she wouldn't want to keep them hanging
around the office as a constant reminder.

Picking up the basket, she headed for the door at the same time as
Jackson came walking down the corridor, almost bumping into her.

'Ah, I see you found the flowers. Very nice,' he said matter-of-factly.
'From your boyfriend or a secret admirer perhaps?'

His tone was jovial, a smile on his face, but still his question made her cringe inside. If he'd read the card in the bouquet, then Jackson would know exactly the nature of Pia's relationship with the sender of the flowers.

'Just a friend,' she said breezily. 'I'll just go and pop these in the flat and I'll be straight back.'

So it must have been Jackson who'd taken the flowers in. Annoyance crept over her shoulders. She really didn't want her personal life intruding on her working life, giving Jackson any reason to think she wasn't fully committed to her job. Quickly dumping the basket of flowers next to the sink, thinking she would water them later, she hurried back into the office.

Jackson was leaning back in his chair, his long legs crossed and extended onto his desk, staring aimlessly out of the window. In his hand he held a pencil, which he twirled round and round in his fingers, giving off a nervous energy that put Pia on edge too.

'Everything okay?' she asked with a tentative smile.

'Yep, all good.' The heavy silence that punctuated the air suggested to Pia that perhaps Jackson wasn't as good as he made out so she took the hint and focused her attention on her laptop, scrolling through her emails. Clearly, Jackson was in no mood for talking. His presence in the room and his dark mood were all-pervasive and she had to wonder for a moment if she'd done something to upset him. Now she was just being paranoid. It wasn't all about her. Thankfully, at that moment Bertie decided to get up from his stretched-out position by the French doors where he'd been catching the rays of sunshine filtering through the glass and went across to Jackson, nudging his hand with his nose.

'Hello, boy,' Jackson said with a smile, and Pia was sure she detected the resulting exhalation of relief from Jackson as he stroked Bertie's head.

'It's a beautiful day out there, isn't it?' Pia said, unable to stop herself from filling the silence. 'If the weather's anything like this on the day of the wedding, then Ruby and Connor will have the most amazing day.'

'Yeah. Do you have everything in place? Is there anything else you need from me?'

'No, we've managed to organise tables and chairs, thanks to those contact numbers you gave us, and some extra crockery and cutlery. We're all so grateful for everything you've done. You've gone above and beyond.'

'It's not a problem. Besides, you're part of the Primrose Hall family now.' His gaze hooked on hers, and she glanced away, feeling a heat fire her cheeks. She liked the way he said that, his words making her feel a small part of something much bigger. As though she really belonged here.

'Your mum, I mean Ronnie, was saying something about you once considering using the barn for weddings?'

He sighed. 'Yep, but then I realised I didn't want the place overtaken each weekend with party guests. Drunk party guests at that. Then the hall loses its exclusivity, what makes this place special. I'm not averse to hosting wedding parties here, but it would definitely have to be on a case-by-case basis, on my terms.'

Pia smiled, remembering something Ronnie had said about everything needing to be done Jackson's way.

'Obviously if you came to me and said, "Jackson, I'd like to have my wedding here," then of course it would be an immediate yes. So, you know, do bear that in mind.'

He was challenging her with that stare again, the one that lingered a bit too long and made her toes curl, the half-smile on his lips doing nothing to make her feel any better.

She laughed, a bit too loudly.

'Oh, well, that's not going to happen. Well, not any time soon at least.' She laughed again. 'I haven't even got a boyfriend.'

Oh god! She cringed, wondering why she was so keen for Jackson to know she didn't have a boyfriend. He must have got the message by now. She'd told him enough times already.

'Well, you never know. If things should change...' His words drifted off. 'I still want to do some further work over there. I'm thinking of creating a long walkway that comes off one end of the barn, covered by a pergola with vines growing over. It would make a versatile space that could be used for dining or as a reception area. With some fairy lights entwined, it would look pretty magical of a night.'

'That sounds amazing. I can just imagine it.' Pia had goosebumps over her arms thinking about it. 'Oh, by the way, I hate to tell you, but my family, and I think Connor and Ruby's friends too, are all drinkers. I hope they don't get too drunk at the wedding.'

'I'll be disappointed if they don't,' Jackson said with a smile. 'Please don't worry. I was only kidding when I said that. I'm looking forward to everyone having a great time.' He tapped his fingers on the desk, growing restless. 'I should go and try to find Mateo. You haven't seen him, have you?'

'I saw him a little while ago. He was taking his break round at your mu —I mean, Ronnie's.'

'Really?' Jackson sighed heavily. 'Those two seem to be spending an awful lot of time together. I really hope she's not trying to lead Mateo astray. He's a bloody good gardener. I don't want to lose him.'

'I'm sure that won't happen. I think they're just friends. They seem to get on very well.'

'You really don't know my mother, do you?' He shook his head wryly. 'She's a desperate romantic. And her sights are set firmly on Mateo now.'

'And is that such a bad thing?'

His eyes snagged on hers and this time she held his gaze, not wanting to look away.

'It is when it impacts on my life and, as far as Ronnie's concerned, it invariably does. She'll probably want to drag him off into the sunset any day now. And while I don't mind what she does – I'm used to her following her heart and disappearing off for months at a time – I really don't want her taking Mateo with her.'

Pia laughed loudly and self-consciously, unsure of how to react to Jackson's comments. She thought he might be joking but judging by his expression it was clear that he wasn't.

'Look, I'm going to get out of here for an hour or two. Clear my head. I'll be back later.'

'Sure.' She could feel the pent-up energy radiating from his body. All she wanted to do was wrap her arms around his body and hug him tight, help to soothe his troubled soul, but she suspected that wasn't in her job description. She didn't want him to leave, and almost called out after him when he turned and waltzed out the office, but stopped herself just in time.

If she and Jackson had met up again just as old friends, down at the pub, then she wouldn't have felt so reticent about asking him questions, probing him about his mum, and his ex, Tara, or the passion that drove him, and most importantly, the reason why he'd walked out of Pia's life without any explanation whatsoever when she was still a teenager. There was so much more she wanted to learn about him, but as his employee she felt those topics were very much out of bounds. Minutes later, when she heard the unmistakeable roar of a motorbike revving up outside, she ran to the window to see Jackson's black-clad figure sitting astride the monster machine, and her stomach tumbled as she watched him zoom down the driveway until he was firmly out of sight. 'Be safe,' she whispered to herself.

23

A couple of hours later and Pia had just stepped out of the shower after her day at work when there was a knock on the door to her flat. Quickly throwing on a dressing gown, she went across and opened it to find Ronnie standing there dressed in a bright orange kaftan with a towel tucked under her arm. She looked as though she was off to the beach.

'Are you off out somewhere tonight?' Ronnie asked.

'No. I was just getting changed. Why? What did you have in mind?'

'Do you fancy a dip in the hot tub? With a glass of rosé?' She whipped out a bottle of pink chilled wine from her bag. 'I've asked Frank to get it going for me. I don't think it's ever been used. It's such a lovely evening out there – what do you say? Shall we give it a whirl?'

'Oh Ronnie, I'd love to, but I don't have a swimsuit. I'm more than happy to come along, though, and perch on the edge. And drink lots of wine with you.'

'Perfect! I'll go and find some glasses and see you over there.'

When Pia made it over to the hot tub, Ronnie was already inside, luxuriating in the water, her arms outstretched on the lip behind her, looking like a glamorous film star.

'Oh my goodness! This is the life. Mateo doesn't know what he's missing.' She twirled an ankle around, her painted toenails visible just beneath the water. 'Said he was going to take a nap. Honestly! Anyway, why don't you pour the wine, darling?'

'Good idea.' Pia took the wine from the cooler and poured the two waiting glasses on the side. She had to admit, seeing the bubbles frothing in the tub, that it looked very inviting and she wished she could jump in and join Ronnie.

'So tell me, what's rattled Jackson's cage today?' Ronnie asked, sipping on her wine, as Pia settled down on the step beside her, her gaze transported to the golden horizon in front of her.

'Er...' Where Jackson was closed off and kept most things personal to himself, Ronnie was much more of an open book. Pia didn't feel comfortable chatting about her boss, especially to his mother. Besides, she would be the last person to know what was going on inside Jackson's head.

'I heard him go out on the bike earlier and normally when he does that, it's because he's wound up over something. He's always done it, even when he was a kid. At eight or nine he would run off, usually after I'd grounded him, and jump on his pushbike and head into the countryside. I would end up walking the roads of the village, calling out his name, asking people to keep an eye out, and he'd roll back home hours later. The locals got to know him, and they'd say, "Has he done a runner again?" It was embarrassing. Then when he got a moped things only got worse. It gave him even more freedom and I barely saw him. I tried to discipline him, but there was no getting through to Jackson. He would never listen to me. I used to dread the calls from the hospital or the police saying he'd been in an accident or else he'd been cautioned. He was a law unto himself. Just like he is today. Only now when he gets in a black mood, he heads off on a much bigger and scarier bike.'

'You still worry about him.'

'Of course I do. You never stop worrying about your children, even if they are a six-foot-two successful businessman who believes he doesn't need anyone's help. I have to be careful, though, or else I get told off for interfering.'

'Well, you know, you've clearly played a huge role in forming the man Jackson is today so I think you need to give yourself a big pat on the back for being part of his success.'

Ronnie laughed. 'I'm not sure Jackson would see it that way, but I think you're right, I should take a bit of credit. All the worry and grief he's put me through over the years, I deserve to bask in his golden glow at times. And I suppose it doesn't get much better than this, does it?' Ronnie twirled her outstretched arms in the water. 'Oh, Pia, you need to get in here. It's so lovely and relaxing. Why don't you just slip off your top and trousers and jump in? It wouldn't matter.'

'No, I couldn't,' said Pia, laughing, although it was sorely tempting. The last thing she wanted was to be found in her undies by her boss.

'Oh, there we go, talk of the devil,' said Ronnie.

The unmistakeable throaty roar of Jackson's bike heralded his arrival and Ronnie and Pia exchanged a look of understanding and relief at his safe return. About ten minutes later, after presumably putting the bike away, he joined them outside.

'I'm glad to see this is being put to some use at last.'

Pia glanced up at Jackson, his broad tall frame towering above them, his dark eyes shining with amusement. He seemed different to when they'd spoken in the office earlier. More relaxed somehow.

'Do you not fancy it, Pia?'

'I would, but I haven't got a swimming costume. I'm going to order one, though, and then I'll be in here all the time. Don't you worry.'

'There's one in the office if you want it.' He clearly noticed her puzzlement. 'A swimming costume. Brand new. I ordered some the other day when you mentioned you didn't have one.'

'Oh.' She felt her cheeks redden, a heat running around her body. That was weird. 'You ordered me a swimming costume?' How would he have known her size? The thought that he may have been surreptitiously eyeing her body to check out her size unsettled her.

'Not you specifically.' There was a wry smile on his lips as though he was reading her mind. 'Several. Swimming costumes and trunks in different sizes. Your comment the other day made me think it would probably be a good idea to get some in so that any visiting friends or guests can use the hot tub if they want to. They're in the tall cupboard in the office.'

'You really do think of everything, don't you?'

'I try to,' he said, with a nonchalant shrug.

'Go on, Pia,' said Ronnie enthusiastically. 'Go and find a cozzie and come and join me in here. It's absolutely lovely. And what about you, Jackson? Are you going to join us too?'

'No, I don't think so. Some other time. I'm going to put something on for dinner. Do you want to eat, Pia or do you have other plans for tonight?' His gaze drifted off into the distance and Pia had the distinct impression that he wasn't bothered with her response, one way or the other.

'No, I don't, but...' She hesitated, looking from Pia to Ronnie. 'I don't want to intrude.'

'You wouldn't be. How does mushroom risotto sound? It's one of my specialities.'

'I can vouch for that,' said Ronnie.

Pia nodded, her thoughts wandering. So not only was Jackson a successful entrepreneur with a beautiful house and lifestyle, and undeniably good-looking too with a strong and athletic body, he was also an accomplished chef by the sounds of things. Was it any wonder that she found herself becoming increasingly distracted by his charms?

'Do you want to have some dinner too?' he asked Ronnie.

'No, I've got a date with Mateo!' she said, taking a sip from her wine, pursing her lips together coquettishly.

'Please tell me you haven't,' said Jackson with a resigned sigh.

'Well, not a date exactly, but he's coming round to the caravan for some supper. I've got a vegetable hotpot in the slow cooker.'

'Ugh, poor guy,' said Jackson, with feeling. 'Tell him if he'd prefer risotto then he'd always be welcome here.'

'Oh, stop it, you! I'm sure Mateo will love it. He's a much less demanding man than you, Jackson.'

'Just please don't scare the poor guy away. It took me long enough to find him. I don't want him running for the hills.'

'Honestly, what on earth do you take me for? Mateo and I are just friends.'

'Hmm, you forget I know you of old, Ronnie. Okay, just two for dinner, then. Shall we say seven thirty-ish?' he said, turning to Pia.

'That sound great,' she said, excited by the thought of dinner with Jackson, even if she was a little apprehensive too. Being alone with her boss when they were working was one thing, there was always something to focus her mind on, but spending down time with Jackson set her mind off in another direction entirely. Still, she would look forward to being cooked for and until then she would have a couple of hours to enjoy the delights of the hot tub. Dashing off to find one of the swimsuits, Pia returned a few minutes later, hoping Jackson may have made his excuses with Ronnie and left. No such luck.

'All okay?' he asked, looking her determinedly in the eye as she stood in front of him in the turquoise all-in-one swimming suit, which somehow fitted perfectly.

'Great.' She beamed. 'I can't wait to get in.'

'Good, well, I'll leave you to it and I'll see you later for dinner,' he said, before turning and walking away.

'What do you think?' Ronnie asked, chuckling to herself, clearly amused by something as Pia tentatively stepped into the hot tub and gasped with delight as her feet touched the water.

'Oh, it's wonderful and so warm too.' Pia splashed the water over her body and sat down on a seat opposite Ronnie. Reclining, she took a sip of the delicious, crisp pink wine. 'It's every bit as good as you said it would be.'

'I think it's the perfect way to end the day, isn't it? I can see us being in here every evening with a glass of wine if the weather stays like this. Can you think of anything more civilised?'

Pia laughed. She really couldn't imagine anything better. Other perhaps than Jackson joining her in the hot tub too.

24

It was funny that when Pia had first accepted the job at Primrose Hall, she'd had it in her mind that it would only be a temporary assignment. Something to tide her over until her small inheritance came through and she could find her own place to live and a more suitable job, although what that might be, she really didn't know. What she did know was that she'd been woefully unqualified for the job at Primrose Hall and that she hadn't wanted to work for Jackson Moody for any length of time.

Only she hadn't reckoned on settling into her new home and job quite so happily. Everyone at the house had been hugely welcoming, Jackson especially, and although the job had been something of a steep learning curve, Jackson had given her the time and space to find her own way and carve out the role for herself. Whenever she had a spare moment she would get on the computer and run through the tutorials on the different software packages so that now she had a pretty good understanding of them all. She'd quickly reached a point where she felt that her input was actually helpful to the smooth running of Jackson's various business interests, and he was always quick to tell her how valuable he found her contribution.

It had helped having Bertie at her side. Everyone loved him and his presence in the house had brought a much-needed light-hearted vibe to

Primrose Hall. It was impossible to stay down for long when you had a goofy dog to laugh at, and she knew Jackson appreciated having him around. The only trouble was Pia wondered how much longer she would be looking after Bertie for. Simon, Wendy's son, was coming back over the weekend and Wendy had already told her how much Simon was looking forward to seeing his dog again.

Now she'd found this safe haven with Bertie and Jackson, and the other members of the team at Primrose Hall, she couldn't imagine a time when she would ever want to leave it behind. What troubled her most of all, though, was that those decisions regarding her future might not be entirely within her control. If Simon wanted his dog back then Pia would lose her best buddy and if Jackson was ever to decide he no longer needed her services, then she could find herself looking for a new job and some-where else to live too. She suppressed a sigh. Now wasn't the time to think about those sorts of concerns. She was determined to enjoy the moment for as long as that moment was destined to last.

'Something smells delicious,' said Pia, as the aromas of garlic, mush-rooms and wine met her nostrils. After her dip in the hot tub, she'd quickly changed into a sun dress and joined Jackson in the kitchen with a swirl of excitement lodged in her stomach. Bertie was already there, following Jackson around the kitchen in the hope of any treats going.

'What can I do to help?' she asked.

'You can grab a couple of pasta bowls from the cupboard and some knives and forks too. Then just sit and chat to me.' He turned and graced her with one of his megawatt smiles. 'How was the hot tub?'

'Oh my goodness, it was just wonderful. You really need to try it, Jack-son. With the views of the woods and the valley, and a glass of wine in hand, it was simply magical.'

'Talking of which. You were on the rosé, weren't you?'

She nodded, debating whether she would continue with the wine or opt for a soft drink, but before she could make up her mind, Jackson had presented her with a chilled glass of pink wine, which she was hardly about to refuse. Before coming to Primrose Hall, she'd rarely drunk alcohol – it had been something reserved for high days and holidays, which had been few and far between, sadly – so it was lovely to be able to enjoy a glass or two with either Jackson or Ronnie when the opportunity presented itself.

Music was playing in the background; she couldn't recognise the singer, but it was soulful and mellow, and her body relaxed into the chair as she watched Jackson move between the central island and the worktops confidently and effortlessly. She looked all around her, soaking up the atmosphere.

'So, did you come up with the plan for renovating the house or did you get designers and architects in? Everything's been done so perfectly.'

'Well, I'm glad you approve,' he said, raising an eyebrow at her. 'I had a very clear idea in my head how I wanted the house to look. Obviously, architects were involved in drawing up the plans, but it's pretty much as I first envisaged it to be.'

Pia nodded, impressed by Jackson's creativity and vision.

'Tara chose the colour scheme and sourced the drapes and cushions. She's an interior designer by trade so it made sense for her to do the soft furnishings. I had some input too, in the overall scheme, but she brought everything together. I'm pretty pleased with the results.'

'You should be. It's gorgeous.' So a team effort, then, Pia mused, waiting a few moments before asking, 'Were you together for very long?'

'Me and Tara?' He spooned risotto from the saucepan into bowls, his attention focused on the task in front of him. 'About three years, I think.'

'A long time, then. Ooh, thanks,' she said, as Jackson placed a bowl of creamy risotto in front of her. 'This looks amazing.' She swirled her fork through the rice, releasing its heat and the heady concoction of aromas that stirred her appetite. 'I'm sorry it didn't work out for the pair of you.'

He shrugged nonchalantly. 'These things happen. I never think there's any point in looking back and dwelling on what might have been. Do you?'

'I suppose not,' she said, softly, knowing she'd been guilty of doing exactly that. She wouldn't dare to mention the amount of times Jackson had popped into her thoughts over the years. She tried the risotto, which was just as tasty as it had promised to be.

'If things don't work out, for whatever reason, in your personal or business life, you just have to learn from it and move on and look to the future.'

'Yes, I guess you're right,' she said, wondering if it was really as easy as

Jackson made it out to be. To simply forget about the past. Was Tara of a similar frame of mind, or had she been left wondering what had gone wrong between her and Jackson and if she could have done anything differently to have saved their relationship? As Pia had once done. One thing was for sure, it confirmed to Pia that Jackson hadn't looked back or spent years regretting his brief fling with her. She wondered if he even remembered that it had actually happened or if he'd scrubbed it totally from his memory.

A little while later, after Pia had savoured every delicious mouthful of her dinner, she pushed her empty bowl forward.

'That was lovely. Thanks for cooking, Jackson.'

'My pleasure,' he said as he cleared the bowls from the table. 'It's one of the ways I like to relax. And it's even better when I have someone to cook for,' he said, fixing her with a look that released butterflies in her chest. 'Oh, hang on.' He was leaning across the granite worktops and peering out of the kitchen windows onto the driveway of Primrose Hall. 'I think we might have company, although who it could be at this time of night, I'm not sure.' He picked up his phone to look at the security footage. 'I don't recognise the car. Ah, looks like it might be a taxi.'

Pia felt a whirl of dread in her chest. She really hoped it wouldn't be Daniel turning up uninvited with another bouquet of flowers in his hands. She quickly checked her own phone. Anyone else that she knew would have texted to let her know they were coming, but she had no messages. A few minutes later, there was a tentative knocking on the door and Jackson went across to answer it.

'Yes, can I help?' he said brusquely.

'Jackson, hi! I really hope you don't mind me turning up like this?' A man stood at the outside entrance to the kitchen, suitcases on either side of him.

Pia's immediate response was one of relief when she realised it wasn't Daniel, but that was before she noticed Jackson's stricken expression.

'What...?' It took Jackson a moment, probably a few moments, before he realised who it was standing on his doorstep. 'Jesus Christ! You'd better come in.'

25

'What are you doing here?'

Jackson's shock at the arrival of his visitor was palpable, and suddenly Pia felt as though she was intruding on something personal. The man, in his late fifties or early sixties, was darkly tanned with sparkling eyes, and hair accentuated with silver flashes at the temples. He looked familiar, as though Pia had possibly met him somewhere before until she had a moment of dawning realisation.

'Oh, sorry,' said Jackson, filling the awkward silence that had permeated the room. 'Pia, meet my dad.'

'Hello there,' he said warmly, his voice low and gravelly, and Pia had to wonder why she'd had even a moment's doubt about the identity of this man, seeing the half-smile that lit up his face, so reminiscent of his son. He came across and held out a hand to Pia.

'Lovely to meet you...'

'Rex!' the older man said, filling in the blank.

'Well, I'm sure you two have got lots to catch up on so I will leave you to it. Thanks for...'

'No, don't go, not yet.' Jackson clasped her wrist in a vice-like hold, his eyes imploring her to stay.

'Okay, sure,' she said, brightly, her gaze drifting between father and son. 'Would you like a drink, Rex?' It wasn't really her place to offer, but someone needed to do something to fill the awkward stand-off. Rex's arrival had rendered Jackson speechless. 'If that's all right with you, Jackson?'

'Sure, the beers are in the fridge,' he said to Pia.

'Thanks.' Rex held up a hand to stop her. 'A coffee or a tea would be great, though. I've been sober for over three years now,' he told Jackson proudly.

'Really?' Jackson nodded, clearly impressed, although she could tell he wasn't about to say so. 'How long are you back for?'

'I'm back for good, son. It seemed the right time. I'm not getting any younger and I couldn't ignore the pull of home any longer. And where else was I going to go? I'm staying with an old mate and his wife in the village until I find a place of my own, but in the taxi on the way here I thought, *I know, I'll go and see Jackson*. You don't mind, do you?'

'No, not at all.'

Pia had never seen Jackson look quite so uncomfortable in his own home. She filled the kettle and pulled out three mugs from the glass-fronted cabinet, glad for something to do, although she still felt as though she was intruding by listening in on their conversation. Bertie was curious about their new visitor and sniffed around at his feet, until he received the attention he demanded from Rex, who rewarded him by enthusiastically ruffling his fur and telling him what a good boy he was.

With the tea made, she handed a mug to Rex and he settled down on the window seat indicated by Pia, his gaze travelling around the kitchen.

'You've got a lovely place here, Jackson. I've been following your career online and in the press, so I knew you'd done pretty well for yourself, but to see it for myself, well, let's just say, I'm very proud of you. And a lovely young lady here too. It's great that you've made such a great success of your life.'

'Oh no, we're not together in that way.' Pia was quick to correct him. 'I work here for Jackson, that's all.'

'Ah, well, I hope I haven't spoilt your evening by intruding.'

'No, not at all,' said Pia, waving a hand around, although she sensed she probably wasn't speaking for Jackson as well.

'Coo-ee, Jackson, are you there?'

Pia and Jackson exchanged a worried glance when they heard the approach of footsteps along the corridor.

'I wondered if you had another bottle of that lovely rosé in your fridge. I promise to replenish your stocks – it's just that Mateo and I are about to watch that film you were talking about and we could do with a little... Oh good grief!' Ronnie came to an abrupt halt at the entrance to the kitchen when her eyes alighted on the late-night visitor. She grabbed hold of the doorframe as her legs swayed beneath her.

'Rex Moody! Bloody hell! What stone did you crawl out from under?'

'Ah, darling Ronnie, it's lovely to see you again too.' Even Pia could tell his words were dripping with sarcasm. 'Although had I known you'd be here, I might have thought twice about dropping by.'

'Dropping by? Dropping by? It's been a lifetime, Rex. You can't just swan in here after all those years, as though you've never been away, and expect everyone to be pleased to see you.'

Rex raked a hand through his hair in a mannerism Pia had seen in Jackson on many an occasion. If she'd felt awkward earlier when Rex arrived, now she felt wholly uncomfortable with Ronnie in the room as well, feeling an air of antagonism radiating between Jackson's parents. She wanted to plan her escape, but how could she possibly when Jackson had specifically asked her to stay?

'I came here to see my son, not you, and until he asks me to leave then I shall stay right where I am whether you like it or not.'

'You're all right to stay, Dad.'

'Jackson! Why would you say that? Don't be taken in by him, please!' Ronnie came striding into the kitchen, unable to take her eyes from Rex, as if checking it was really him and not a figment of her imagination. 'I know exactly why you're here, Rex. You've got wind of Jackson's good fortune and thought you'd sweep in, pretending to be the loving long-lost father, thinking you'll be able to benefit from his newfound wealth. Well, it's not going to happen, do you hear me?'

'I'm glad to see your opinion of me hasn't changed at all in the inter-vening years, Ronnie.' Rex gave a resigned sigh. 'You aways held me in such high regard, didn't you? I could never do anything right in your eyes.

Anyway, I really don't care what you think of me, any more. I gave up worrying about that years ago. It's Jackson I'm here to see. You're right, I have been off the scene, for longer than I intended, but let's be honest here, you always made it as difficult as possible for me to see Jackson when he was a kid.'

'You're still blaming me after all this time. Jackson, can you believe what he's saying? He needs to go. It's not fair on me, your mother, remember. When you think what he put me through. All those years. If he stays around here, then I'll have no option but to leave.'

'Don't be ridiculous, Ronnie. You're over-reacting,' said Jackson tightly.

'Well, it wouldn't be the first time,' said Rex unhelpfully.

'For Christ's sake, will the pair of you stop it. Ronnie, take the bottle of wine and leave. You being here is not helping the situation at all. I'll speak to you in the morning.'

'Typical.' Ronnie, hands on hips, stamped her foot like a toddler in mid-tantrum. 'Why would I expect anything less? Really!' She sighed heavily, her exasperation clear to everyone in the room. She turned on her heel, suddenly remembering what she'd came in for and dashed across to the huge American-style fridge and yanked open the door, finding what she was looking for. 'I see how it is and where your true loyalties lie, Jackson. Where they always have.' She dashed out of the kitchen, but there was no mistaking her muffled sobs.

'I should go after her,' said Pia, glancing across at Jackson, who nodded his assent. She was relieved; she just wanted to get out of the heady atmosphere of the kitchen, although she hated seeing Jackson's mum so distressed.

'Hey, Ronnie, come back.' She ran after her, grabbing her arm and turning her round to face her. 'I'm sorry you're upset. I can understand what a shock it must be after all these years.'

'Honestly, Pia.' Ronnie put down the bottle of wine she'd been holding onto a nearby console table and leant against the wall for support. Her expressive hazel eyes were filled with tears and her skin flushed with emotion. 'What does he think he's doing here? Turning up out of the blue after all these years. Making me feel bad about myself. What does he want?' She exhaled heavily. 'What really riles me is Jackson's reaction. He's always sided with his father ever since he was a small boy. I might never have won any awards for best mother of the year but I tried my hardest for him. He's never forgiven me for leaving him at home with my sister, Marie, when I went off travelling.' She paused, clearly wrestling with her thoughts. 'I mean, I could hardly take him with me, even if I'd wanted to. He needed to go to school. I thought I was doing the best thing for him but looking back, I wonder what I was thinking. Perhaps I was guilty of being selfish.' She shrugged. 'We all do things we regret, don't we?'

Pia nodded her support.

'It wasn't that I totally abandoned him. I knew he was safe and well with Marie, but I suppose Jackson wouldn't have viewed it in the same way. What gets me, though, is that I did nothing different from his father. Rex disappeared from Jackson's life for years at a time, but when I did it, I was castigated as being a terrible mother.'

Pia stroked Ronnie's arm, making soothing sounds. 'Don't upset yourself, Ronnie. Emotions are running high tonight, but I'm sure in the cold light of day everything will seem better. I think Rex just wanted to see Jackson, and surely that can be no bad thing? You shouldn't beat yourself up over things that happened in the past. It's a long time ago and I'm sure both you and Rex have changed a lot since those days. Besides, I'd say Jackson has done pretty well for himself and as parents you two should be incredibly proud. Come here.'

Pia opened her arms wide and pulled Ronnie into her embrace, and Ronnie dropped her head on Pia's shoulder.

'I'm not sure Jackson is quite so forgiving as you make him out to be, but I just hope he'll see fit to forgive me one day.'

'Honestly, I'd be surprised if he hadn't already done so, if there was anything to forgive in the first place.'

Ronnie pulled back, looking at Pia's face, and ran a hand along her cheek, stroking her hair away from her face. 'Honestly, love, I'm so pleased that you've come to Primrose Hall. You really are a breath of fresh air and just what we need around here – a bit of girl power.'

26

Pia didn't return immediately to the kitchen, thinking Jackson and Rex might appreciate some alone time together, now the initial shock of finding his dad on his doorstep had worn off for Jackson. Instead, she wandered into the snug and perched on the edge of the sofa, dropping her head in her hands. What an evening! There was never a dull moment at Primrose Hall, that was for sure. She was considering taking herself off to bed, leaving Rex and Jackson to catch up, but before she could make up her mind about that, the door to the snug was flung open and Bertie came bounding down the steps to greet her, obviously delighted at having found her. He was closely followed by Jackson.

'Ah, that's where you got to. Your coffee had gone cold so I've made you a fresh one. Are you coming through?'

He held out a hand to her and she pushed herself up off the sofa end and went across to his side, looking up into his face.

'I thought you might want some time alone with your dad?'

'No, it's fine. Come and join us. Please,' he said, taking her hand in his, looking at her imploringly.

'Are you okay, Jackson? It must have been quite a shock.'

'Yeah.' He nodded, a wry smile on his face. 'It's all good, though. He's not really changed that much. He's older and greyer, but that voice and that smile, I'd know those anywhere.'

'You look so much like him.'

'Do you think?' He shrugged, her comment eliciting a small smile. 'Everyone says it, though.'

They were standing within a whisper of each other, and Pia was still holding on to the hand Jackson had offered. She recognised something in his expression, a vulnerability and a connection that she simply couldn't ignore.

'Do you need a hug?' she ventured.

He nodded and she wrapped her arms around his broad chest, holding him tight, relaxing into the warmth of his embrace, feeling an over-whelming sense of relief, as though Jackson was comforting her, rather than the other way around. Determinedly, she fixed her gaze on the side wall of the snug, not allowing herself to close her eyes, or to pull back to look into his face, knowing that emotions were running high and not trusting herself not to console him further, more intimately. It was just a reassuring hug between friends, that was all.

'We should go and join your dad,' she said eventually.

'Yep, you're right,' said Jackson, gathering himself, and releasing his hold on her, their eyes snagging for the briefest moment as they pulled apart. 'Come on then, Bertie. Let's go.'

Moments later, Rex stood up from the window seat as Jackson and Pia returned to the kitchen.

'Sorry about all of that with Ronnie, love. What must you think? I didn't come here to upset anyone, I promise. It just didn't occur to me that Ronnie would be here.'

'It's not a problem,' said Jackson. 'You know Ronnie of old. Sometimes I think she's mellowed and then other times, well...' He gave a wry laugh before turning to Pia. 'I've said to Dad that he must stay here tonight and then I can run him down to his friends in the morning.'

'Only if you're sure, Jackson,' Rex butted in. 'I don't want to cause any trouble.'

'Absolutely. Don't worry. Ronnie lives in her van at the back of the house so you shouldn't run into her in the middle of the night.'

'Does she really?' Rex threw back his head and laughed. 'She really hasn't changed at all, then. Good on her!'

* * *

The following morning, Pia woke early and as she lay in bed with the events of the previous evening running through her head, she strained her ears for any noises that might be coming from the kitchen. Satisfied that all was quiet, she quickly threw on some jeans and a sweatshirt and headed outside with Bertie.

It was her favourite time of day when the air was clear and crisp, the birds chirped noisily in the trees and the scents and hues of the countryside greeted her afresh. Walking through the gardens of Primrose Hall on their way to the paddock, there was always something new to notice, with the changing of the seasons and the blossoming of the shrubs and flowers that were always a feature of her walks. Today the glossy leaves of the rhododendrons were touched with dew.

After she'd seen to the animals, Pia and Bertie took the beaten path around the edge of the estate, Pia smiled as Bertie padded along in front of her, his snout twitching in the air and his tail curling up behind him. Squirrels darted in and out of the shrubbery and up the tall redwood trees, usually just before Bertie caught their scent and went on a wild but fruitless chase after them.

Pia felt her phone vibrate in her pocket and pulled it out to look. She sighed, seeing a couple more messages from Daniel. He'd texted her last night, asking after her, saying how excited he was to see her again, and she'd quickly forgotten about the texts in the midst of everything else going on. Now there were more messages and a sense of dread that she would need to reply. Perhaps it was far too soon to be thinking about having a boyfriend when she didn't have the emotional time or energy to give to someone else.

Back at the hall, she entered through the main kitchen door and was greeted by the aroma of coffee wafting in the air.

'Just in time,' said Jackson, turning to greet her, holding up a mug in her direction, the smile on his face causing an involuntarily fluttering in her chest. 'How was your walk?'

'Great – it always gets us off to the best start to the day, doesn't it, Bertie?'

The dog was mooching around, checking out his food bowl to see if it had been filled in his absence and Pia took the hint, bending down to pick it up before filling it with Bertie's kibble.

'Good morning!' Rex wandered in with a big smile on his face, looking relaxed in his short-sleeved shirt showing off tanned arms.

'Morning. Did you sleep well?' she asked him.

'Like a baby! It's good to be home.' His mouth twisted in a cheeky smile, his distinctive laughter ringing around the kitchen as he took a seat at the kitchen table. With impeccable timing, Ronnie arrived at the exact same time.

'What are you still doing here?' she said crossly, looking between Jackson and Rex. 'You told me you were dropping by. That suggests that if you had any decency then you would pop off just as quickly.'

'Good morning, sunshine!' said Rex cheerfully. His greeting grabbed Ronnie's attention, her face lighting up momentarily, before she remembered she was still cross with Rex, even if Pia was sure she noticed Ronnie blush too.

'You always used to call me that.' Rex's casual use of the endearment had clearly taken Ronnie by surprise.

'I know. You *were* my little ray of sunshine.'

'I was just going to make some breakfast, Ronnie.' Jackson pulled out a frying pan from the corner cupboard, put it on the hob with a drizzle of oil and went across to the fridge. 'I thought a full fry-up would suit this auspicious occasion. Us all being back under the same roof. What do you think?'

'Huh, well, clearly, I'm not as delighted as you lot,' she said haughtily, casting a glance in Rex's direction and shaking her head, 'but...' She caught the whiff of bacon as Jackson placed some slices in the pan. 'I can't remember the last time I had a cooked breakfast so why not?' she said with an air of forced nonchalance.

'Great, do you want to grab the juices from the fridge, Pia?'

'Sure.' With an uneasy truce called between Rex and Ronnie, who sat at opposite ends of the oak table, Pia felt happy to potter around the kitchen, helping Jackson. She poured the juices, gathered the plates and sauces and laid the table, chatting aimlessly about the weather and the beauty of Primrose Woods and hall. Thank goodness for Bertie. His happy presence, as he wagged his tail and trotted between Rex and Ronnie in search of attention, helped to lighten the atmosphere.

As Jackson loaded plates with bacon, sausages, mushrooms, hash browns, tomatoes, beans and eggs, Pia collected the toast and popped it in a basket, before placing it on the table. Mateo wandered into the kitchen with an apprehensive expression on his face as he looked between everyone gathered at the table.

'Good morning. I not stay. I collect keys.'

'Mateo, you're more than welcome. There's plenty of food. Come and join us.' Jackson introduced Mateo to his dad and Rex stood up to shake his hand.

'Ah, Mateo. I heard your name mentioned last night. Are you two together, then?' he asked casually, indicating between Ronnie and Mateo.

'I don't think that's any of your business.' Ronnie patted the seat next to her for Mateo to come and sit down, flashing him a wide, conspiratorial smile.

'No, no, no! I am just gardener here. We not together. I have wife. She no longer here. She died. Ronnie is my friend. She is lovely lady, but we not together.'

'We're still getting to know each other, aren't we, Mateo?' Ronnie held out a hand to him, which Mateo entirely ignored as he shifted on the spot, looking anxious. 'It's early days for us, isn't it? Such a sweet man,' she said with feeling and, Pia suspected, entirely for Rex's benefit.

'No, I not want to cause upset. I just gardener,' said Mateo. 'I leave you to your breakfast.'

Mateo picked up his keys, said his goodbyes and couldn't leave that kitchen fast enough.

'Nice fella,' said Rex, grinning at Ronnie, his eyes locking on to hers for a moment, before he tucked into his breakfast eagerly, still chuckling to himself.

27

The day of Ruby and Connor's wedding dawned with the promise of clear skies and warm sunshine. Pia climbed out of bed and peered out of the window, excitement filling every cell in her body for the day ahead. Bertie greeted her with a kiss on her face as he did every morning, and she wiped it away with the back of her arm, groaning in mock disgust, but loving the daily ritual all the same. She would give Bertie a long walk around Primrose Woods first thing to hopefully tire him out before handing him over into the care of Frank for the day, who had very kindly offered to doggy-sit.

On the way to the woods, Pia had stopped off at the barn and peered through the windows. She knew it was all ready for the celebrations because she had popped in yesterday afternoon to help Ruby and Connor put up swathes of gold ribbons across the rafters and arrange the tables and chairs that had been delivered that morning. White starched linen cloths draped the tables and with the gold-edged plates, cutlery and glassware in place, the barn was transformed into the most magical and charming wedding venue. Clusters of balloons surrounded the top table as well as at the double doors to the entrance of the barn.

Pia took the opportunity to take lots of photos of the inside and exterior of the barn, which she could always use for promotional purposes, if

Jackson should ever change his mind and decide he wanted to host more wedding parties, after all.

'It looks so beautiful,' Ruby had sighed. 'In my wildest dreams I could never have imagined it would look as amazing as this. I really cannot thank Jackson enough. He is going to come and join us for a glass of champagne tomorrow, isn't he?'

'He said he would, yes!' Although Pia would probably need to remind Jackson about that. His head was all over the place at the moment, ever since his dad had resurfaced in his life. It didn't help that Ronnie was still being temperamental too, wafting in and out of the house, moaning to anyone who would listen about Rex's reappearance.

Pia's awkwardness and embarrassment at finding herself in the midst of the drama playing out at Primrose Hall had been overwhelming. She'd tried to take a step backwards and not get involved in the family dynamics, but it was difficult when she worked for Jackson and Ronnie used Pia as a sounding board. Most of all, Pia's heart went out to Jackson. As owner of Primrose Hall, he was a confident and assertive businessman, in control of all his many ventures, but faced with the reminders of his fractured upbringing, Pia could detect Jackson's hurt and vulnerability bubbling just beneath the surface. The look in his eyes as his gaze had flittered between his dad and Ronnie that night in the kitchen had stirred a protective response deep within Pia and all she'd wanted to do was to take Jackson in her arms and reassure him that everything would work out fine.

Still, now wasn't the time to worry about Jackson's family dramas. Today was all about new beginnings and happy times, sharing in Connor and Ruby's special day. Pia had been full of excitement and apprehension, and she was sure she couldn't have felt more nervous if it had been her own wedding day. The service in the village church had been beautiful, so touching and intimate, and the swell of love that came from Connor and Ruby's friends and family in the congregation was palpable and sent goosebumps along Pia's shoulders and arms. It was a good job she'd thought to put a pack of tissues in her bag because tears gathered in her eyes and she needed to dab them dry. She couldn't help thinking of her mum and dad, imagining how proud they would be to see Connor looking so happy, marrying the woman he loved. Pia felt their absence keenly, as a deep hole in her chest, but she also felt certain she could sense their presence around her and imagined them both looking on fondly.

It was lovely to see so many familiar and friendly faces, and she was delighted that Wendy had made it along, with the help of her son, Simon, who did a good job at navigating the wheelchair down the church aisle. Pia was also surprisingly pleased that Daniel was at her side. He really did scrub up well and looked handsome in a deep blue three-piece suit that brought out the turquoise of his eyes. She appreciated the way he looked at her, as though she was the most beautiful woman in the room, the way he laid a gentle hand on her arm when he spoke to her and how his hand slipped into hers when they stood up to sing the hymns. She liked it, the feeling of being part of a couple, and she supposed it was only natural that her thoughts would drift to imagining her own wedding one day. She aspired to having the same sort of marriage that her parents had shared, one filled with laughter, and kindness, and support, and although they did occasionally have humdingers of rows, it usually all blew over quickly, neither of them holding grudges for long, and making up with kisses and laughter. Oh, how the memories were taunting her today!

When the guests had made the short journey in minibuses to Primrose Hall, then Pia had no time whatsoever to dwell on the past. She was too busy chatting with everyone and snapping pictures of the happy couple. They were so many beautiful spots for photo opportunities at Primrose Hall: in front of the rustic barn, which looked stunning adorned with the hanging baskets and trugs, prepared by Mateo over the last few days. Then they moved across to the paddock where they shot joyful photos with Little Star and Twinkle, who made everyone laugh with their antics as they barged their heads through the middle of Connor and Ruby, intent on being centre stage. Primrose Woods provided a wonderful backdrop for some romantic shots and of course some more formal pictures were taken at the front of the house beneath the stone portico.

'There you are! I thought you'd done a runner on me.' Daniel appeared at her side and placed a proprietorial arm around her waist.

'Oh, sorry,' she said brightly. 'I was just taking some photos for the family album. Have you had a drink yet?'

'Yep, but I could do with another. Come on, let's go and get one together.' He dragged her away, through the crowds of people milling around outside, until he found the table where glasses of fizz and elderflower pressé were laid out. Swiftly, standing by the table, he downed a glass of champagne and then picked up another.

'That's better. It's thirsty work, this wedding lark. Have I told you, you look absolutely beautiful today. Stunning, in fact.' He pulled her close again and kissed her on the lips, which ordinarily might be considered a nice gesture, but for some reason, she felt embarrassed by his full-on attentions when all she wanted to do was enjoy the celebrations with the rest of the guests. She wanted to chat and share stories about Connor and Ruby, enjoy the drink and the wonderful buffet that had been put together by Ruby's mum and her aunties.

'Oh look, there's Wendy and Simon – I need to go and say hello. Are you coming?'

Daniel peered at the bottom of his now empty glass.

'I'll just get a refill and then come and find you again,' he said with a resigned smile.

She supposed it was awkward for Daniel, not really knowing anyone. He was more than welcome to tag along with her, but he seemed to be happiest hovering near to the bar with a drink in his hand. She wanted to speak to as many people as she possibly could, catching up with old friends and relatives, determined to make the most of every moment.

'Pia, isn't this lovely?' Wendy held up her hands to Pia, who took them and squeezed them in return. 'I'm so pleased I was able to get here and be a part of this wonderful day. Thanks to you all for inviting me along, and, of course, to Simon as well.'

'Yes, hello! It's so lovely to see you!' Pia and Simon exchanged a hug. It had been several years since they'd last seen each other.

'And you too! It's great to see Connor finally settling down,' he said with a smile. 'They make a lovely couple. You know, I must thank you for looking out for Mum in my absence. I can't tell you what a relief it was knowing you were next door and popping in to see her each day. I felt helpless to do anything being so many thousands of miles away.'

'Honestly, it wasn't a problem at all.' Pia gave a self-conscious smile, unsure of what else to say. She hadn't looked out for Wendy out of a sense of duty; she did it because she was her friend and she cared for her.

'Oh, I've told you, Pia is an absolute sweetheart. Like the daughter I never had.' Wendy reached up and squeezed Pia's arm and Pia nodded her agreement, unable to say anything in response as tears filled her eyes again. 'Of course, I can't help thinking about your mum and dad today, and how much they would have loved all this.'

'I know, they would have been in their element, chatting to everyone. I'm sure I can hear their laughter now. I bet they're up there somewhere, looking down on us all,' said Pia wistfully.

'Pia, I wanted to thank you too for looking after that mad dog of mine, Bertie. How is he doing? I wondered if I might snatch a glance of him today?'

'Oh, he's absolutely fine.' Pia plastered on a wide smile, but Simon's question filled her with dread. 'Of course, he's won the hearts of everyone around here and made himself very much at home. We've got Primrose Woods on our doorstep so he gets plenty of long walks, which he loves. Frank, the maintenance guy here, is looking after him today, but after the food and all the formalities I'd be more than happy to take you down to the house so you can say hello.'

Simon's face lit up. 'Would you really? I was hoping that might be possible, if it's not too much trouble. I've missed that daft dog so much.'

'I bet! Look, I should probably go and mingle, but I'll definitely come and find you a bit later and we'll go and see Bertie.'

Pia wandered back towards the barn, where Connor and Ruby were greeting their guests before everyone went inside for the buffet. Pia quickly found Daniel and took his hand and they hung back to let the other guests go through first.

'Are you hungry?' Pia asked him.

'Starving! Looking forward to my lunch and getting to spend some time with you at last,' he said, lifting his face up and leaving a kiss on her cheek.

'Yes, me too,' she said. She'd been far too busy, and probably far too excited, to eat breakfast. Her whole being had been abuzz with anticipation from the moment she'd woken up this morning. Even her unsettling conversation with Simon couldn't put a dampener on the day. After all, she'd always known that looking after Bertie would only be a short-term arrangement, only she hadn't thought saying goodbye to him might come quite so soon. She couldn't worry about it now, though; she didn't want anything to spoil her enjoyment of the day. At least she knew Bertie would be going to a good home with someone who really loved and cared for him and wasn't that the most important thing?

The buffet was a welcome distraction and everyone commented on how wonderful the spread looked. As well as silver platters of sandwiches, and mini pastry bites, there was a whole poached salmon, a honey-glazed ham, a succulent beef joint, quiches and big bowls of colourful salads. Pia filled her plate, suddenly realising how hungry she was.

After everyone had tucked into the delicious desserts, which included a selection of lemon tarts, chocolate profiteroles with fresh raspberries and strawberries, plus several cheese platters with biscuits and grapes, the speeches began, which were all very informal and funny. A wonderful sense of goodwill radiated around the eaves of the barn and there was so much love and laughter in the room. When Connor stood up and paid tribute to his beautiful bride, it sent collective goosebumps around all the guests. When he mentioned his and Pia's dear parents, she could no longer contain the tears that had been brewing beneath the surface all day, and then when he expressed his gratitude and love for her, his sister Pia, the tears turned into full-on sobs.

Afterwards, as everyone gravitated outdoors, Pia met Connor in a heartfelt hug.

'I meant every word I said. These last few months have been difficult, but knowing that you're always there, Pia, makes all the difference. It means the world.'

'Oh, me too, you,' she said, before grimacing, realising she was making little sense. 'You know what I mean, Connor!'

She was so taken aback by Connor's sincere words. Normally he didn't go in for sentimentality or declarations of his feelings – he was more often to be found chiding her to be more proactive, giving her his advice on what she should be doing with her life – so to hear that he did truly love and appreciate her meant everything.

'I really do,' he said, as he held on to her forearms, appraising her fondly. 'It's been such a brilliant day, hasn't it? And being here at Primrose Hall has made it all the more memorable.'

'Yes!' Ruby, who had been standing back, allowing Connor and Pia to share their own special moment, stepped forward. 'We haven't seen Jackson yet. Is he going to pop down? I'd really like to thank him again personally.'

'I'm not sure what he's up to. I've got to go up to the house. Simon wants to see Bertie again so while I'm up there I'll have a word with Jackson and see if I can get him to come down.'

Pia left Connor and Ruby chatting to their guests. Everyone had spilt out from the barn and were standing in the sun, or sitting on the benches put out by Frank, enjoying the beautiful surroundings, a sense of bonhomie wafting in the air. It was a good time for Pia to slip off to the house. Daniel was quite content with a beer in his hand, admiring the view across the valley.

The interior of Primrose Hall offered a cool, calm and peaceful respite from all the activity and hubbub of the wedding party. Pia took a moment in the kitchen, poured herself a glass of water and took a sip, before wandering off in search of Bertie.

'Hey!' Just as she walked out of the kitchen and along the hallway, she came face to face with Jackson. His face lit up to see her and she suddenly felt self-conscious under the appraisal of his penetrating gaze. 'How's it all going over there?'

'Oh! Really great. Everything's been perfect. The ceremony, the food, the weather, and of course the barn. It looks so beautiful and so many people have commented on what an amazing space it is. We're just having a breather after the speeches before the evening shenanigans kick off. Everyone's just soaking up the lovely surroundings. Ruby wants to know when you might come over and celebrate with a glass of champagne?'

'Soon. I'll get changed and wander over in a while.' From Pia's viewpoint, Jackson looked pretty decent as he was. In ripped jeans and a white fitted T-shirt that clung to his biceps, showing off his tattoos to maximum effect, she wondered if he could look any better. She doubted it, although she could concede that it probably wasn't the perfect wedding reception attire. She was struck by a desire to reach out and wrap her arms around his chest, to run her hands along the contours of his arms, a longing that swept over her entire body. She took a mental snapshot, to consign the image of Jackson to her memory.

'Great,' she said brightly. 'I'm just off to find Frank. I told you about Wendy, my old next-door neighbour at Meadow Cottages? Well, her son is home from Australia and he wants to say hello to Bertie. He's Bertie's original owner.'

'Oh, home for good? Does that mean Bertie might be moving on soon, then?'

Pia grimaced, a pain stabbing in her stomach at Jackson's natural assumption.

'I don't know. It's possible.' She shrugged, not wanting to face that thought.

'You'd miss him,' Jackson said, noticing her fallen expression. 'But you know something else, I would too.'

'Yep.' Pia nodded, her gaze locking on his for a moment. She could really do with a hug right now, but she couldn't get into the habit of hugging her boss. It would be far too addictive. 'I should probably go and track the little heart-stealer down!'

Pia walked past Jackson, smiling up at him as they crossed. She suspected everyone at Primrose Hall would miss Bertie's sunny presence if he were to leave. She could only hope Bertie might take an instant and wholehearted dislike to Simon, bark and growl at him so that Simon might believe Bertie wasn't the sweet-natured dog he'd left behind. Even if that was probably the most uncharitable thought she'd had in a long while.

'Oh, Pia?' Jackson called out her name and she turned to face him, her skin tingling with anticipation from his proximity.

'Yes?'

'Well, I just wanted to say that... um, well...' He opened up his palms in front of him, his mouth moving involuntarily. 'You look really lovely today.'

28

As she went off to track Frank down, Jackson's words replayed over and over in Pia's head. His comment had made her pink with pride and happiness, but it hadn't been so much what he'd said as the way he'd said it. His gaze had roamed over her body, a smile hovered at his lips and that moment where'd he stumbled over his choice of words had been charged with an energy that sent goosebumps along her limbs. Obviously, she'd had far too much Prosecco to drink today.

A little later, she walked out of the house with Bertie at her side and headed back towards the barn, where Simon and Wendy were sitting out on the lawn in the sun. Simon, on spotting Bertie, called out his name and Bertie, loyal as ever, went sprinting over, ears pricked and tail wagging. Did Pia really expect anything different from Bertie? He was incredibly happy to see Simon, as though he actually remembered him from all those years ago, delighted to be reunited with his long-lost owner.

'Hello, boy! Look at you. He's got so big,' said Simon, getting down on his haunches and going in for a bit of good-natured rough and tumble with Bertie.

'Well, I suppose he was still very young when you left. He's a grown-up boy now, aren't you, Bertie? And most of the time he's very well behaved.

It's only when he's distracted by a squirrel or some other wildlife that he completely forgets his recall,' Pia said, laughing.

'Would you mind if I took him off for a walk, over at Primrose Woods, perhaps? It's such a lovely afternoon, and it will be great to have a bit of male bonding, won't it, Bertie?'

'Oh… I suppose, if you really wanted to.' Pia quickly tried to cover her dismay. 'He has had a long walk today…'

'If I remember Bertie of old, he's never going to say no to another walk.'

'That's true,' piped up Wendy. 'You can keep me company while Simon walks him.'

'Sure,' she said, her voice high. 'Perhaps keep him on the lead, though, because sometimes he runs off and then it's not always easy to get him back, and he's not keen on small, yappy dogs, so keep him away from those. The most random of things will spook him so, you know… you just need…'

'Pia, he'll be absolutely fine, I promise you. I'm a very responsible dog owner,' Simon said, laughing. 'We'll have great fun, won't we, Bertie?'

Feeling as though her young child had been snatched from her arms and taken away by the child catcher, Pia watched, with a sense of regret, as Bertie trot off happily on the lead, alongside Simon. She turned her attention to Wendy.

'Stop worrying, they'll be fine,' said Wendy, chuckling.

Pia placed her head on Wendy's arm, and looked up into her face, smiling. She was so relieved and happy that her old friend had actually made it to the wedding. Wendy was making good progress with her recovery even if there was still a long way to go in regaining her independence. It made Pia shiver to think how differently it could have turned out if Wendy had taken a heavier fall; it really didn't bear thinking about.

'How are you getting on at Rushgrove Lodge? Are you enjoying your stay there?'

'Honestly, I am. I never thought I'd say that, but it's funny how quickly you adjust. I miss the cottage, of course I do, but what's surprised me most of all is that being away from home has taken away a level of anxiety that I had, about looking after the place and keeping everything clean, and getting up and down the stairs. I don't have to worry about those things any more. I'm eating much better too now that someone else is cooking for me. I miss Bertie hugely, but I have to be realistic. I'd never be able to look after him in this condition. And of course you're no longer at the cottages, so in a way there doesn't seem a lot for me to go home for.'

Pia's heart twisted to hear the sad note to Wendy's voice.

'I've come to terms with the fact that I can't do what I did ten, or even five years ago. This accident has made me realise my limitations. I don't know what the future holds, if they might need my room at the lodge for someone more deserving, but I'll have to cross that bridge when I come to it. The lodge is lovely, and the people are so kind there. I don't want them sending me to some grotty old place, with a load of old, miserable fogeys. You do hear some stories.'

'They won't do that, Wendy,' Pia said with a smile, stroking her arm in an attempt to reassure her. It was only natural that Wendy should be worried about her future and Pia could understand her concern, wondering if she might need to be uprooted again. She hoped for Wendy's sake that wouldn't be the case. 'I'm sure Simon could talk to Abbey at the lodge so that you can make some longer-term plans together. It will all work out fine, I'm sure,' Pia said, squeezing Wendy's hand. She was keen to move the conversation on to a more light-hearted topic. 'Would you like another drink?'

'Perhaps I'll have some of that sparkling elderflower if there's any going.' She glanced at her watch. 'When Simon comes back, I think we'll probably get on our way. It's been such a lovely day, I'm so glad I could be a part of it, but all the excitement and fresh air has worn me out. I will definitely be ready for my bed by the time I get home.'

Pia went off to fetch the drinks, relieved that Wendy spoke about the lodge in such glowing terms. Her friend was going through a period of transition, having to come to terms with a new reality and making those mental adjustments, but Pia could tell Wendy was in a much better place both mentally and physically than she'd been at her old home. It couldn't be easy, but at least Simon was back to help support his mum as she faced this new stage in her life, which came as somewhat of a relief to Pia as well. She loved Wendy dearly, but it was good to be able to pass some of the responsibility of her welfare on to her son.

Back with the drinks, Pia sat down next to Wendy and they soaked up the sun together, having fun watching the other guests as they made good-natured comments about their fashion choices for the day. Pia deliberately avoided the subject of Bertie, not wanting to voice the inevitable consequence of Simon's return from abroad.

Later, when Simon and Bertie came back from their walk, they both looked as though they'd had the best time. Simon had a wide grin on his face, and Bertie was looking up at him adoringly.

'I don't know what you were worried about, Pia. Bertie was as good as gold. And his recall was fabulous. Every time he slipped out of sight, I just gave him a whistle and he was back at my side within moments.'

'He obviously knows who the boss is,' said Wendy, chuckling.

Pia smiled, suppressing a sigh. Of course Bertie did, the little so-and-so. Bertie might feel irreplaceable in her life, but she suspected she was highly replaceable to Bertie and he would go off happily with anyone who gave him the attention he demanded with long walks, food and plenty of cuddles.

'Thanks again, Pia, for letting me see Bertie again. It was a proper treat, wasn't it, boy? Once I'm properly settled, I'll be in touch, if that's okay?'

'Sure,' she said, as a feeling of nausea rose in her chest.

Once Wendy and Simon had said their goodbyes, Pia took a moment to herself on the bench. Bertie dropped his head onto her knee and looked up at her imploringly with those big brown eyes that always melted her heart, as though asking for her forgiveness. Honestly, what was it with the men in her life, toying with her heart and then casting it aside with casual abandon. *Bertie. Jackson*. Then another man popped into her head. *Daniel!* With a twinge of guilt, she realised she'd completely forgotten about him. What a terrible hostess she was!

'Come on, Bertie, we have to go!' The dog jumped to his feet, ears pricked, always excited for the next adventure.

29

After handing Bertie back over into the care of Frank, Pia hurried back in the direction of the barn, looking out for Daniel. He wasn't where she'd left him and she was just mooching around outside, her gaze scanning the huddles of people, when she felt a sudden pair of hands on her waist, which made her jump out of her sandals. Daniel's smiling face appeared over her shoulder, his hands gently squeezing her hips.

'There you are! I thought you'd abandoned me.'

'Daniel, I'm so sorry. I got distracted by Bertie. It's all his fault,' she said with a smile.

'I forgive you. This time,' he said, chastising her with a frown.

Frustration seeped through her body and she subtly extracted herself from his hold. Perhaps it hadn't been the best idea to invite Daniel along. It wasn't fair on him when her attention was distracted elsewhere and she was flitting all over the place, chatting to different people. She'd probably make a rotten girlfriend; she was far too wrapped up in her own world at the moment. Still, Daniel seemed happy enough with a beer in his hand, making the most of the hospitality.

'Right, now I've found you, I'm not going to let you go again.'

He pulled her towards him and kissed her on the lips, and she smiled as she pulled away.

'Come on, let's get a drink,' she said, eager to distract him. 'The dancing should be getting started any moment now.'

When the light grew dim, people started gathering indoors and settling at the tables that had been rearranged around the edge of the barn. Jam jars filled with tea lights cast a soft glow around the room. Pia and Daniel joined Connor and Ruby at a table and the newlyweds were up and down, speaking to their guests, before the band, a local group of youngsters, started up and Connor and Ruby took to the floor to a chorus of applause from everyone.

'They look so happy together,' sighed Pia, grateful that her brother had got the wedding day he deserved.

'Let's hope it lasts,' Daniel quipped with a side smile that Pia chose to ignore.

It wasn't long after the first dance that other people started spilling onto the floor. Daniel jumped up, took Pia's hand and dragged her onto her feet.

'Hey, I didn't think you liked dancing.'

'You've seen my moves before. You know what a great dancer I am. It would be a shame to deprive these people of such a great sight.'

She hoped he might be joking, but he gave a demonstration, throwing his arms and limbs around unselfconsciously. He was certainly enthusiastic and Pia suspected that all the booze he'd imbibed today had loosened his inhibitions. Still, wasn't that what weddings were about, getting tipsy and making merry?

The girl singer orchestrated the revellers in a group dance that had everyone sliding to the left, then sliding to the right, clapping their hands and twirling on the spot, resulting in great hilarity when inevitably people went the wrong way, twirled when they should have clapped and bumped into their neighbour with surprise, and lots of apologies.

'Oh, look,' Ruby exclaimed, falling into Connor's arms. 'Jackson's here.'

Pia turned to see her boss standing just inside the doors of the barn, her gaze snagging on his as it had done in the hallway of the house a few hours ago. From across the room Jackson looked incredibly handsome in a charcoal suit and an open-necked white shirt, the sight sending a rush of heat around Pia's body. For a few moments it was as though everyone else had faded away and it was just the two of them, Jackson and Pia, connected by an invisible thread across the room. That was until she came to her senses, suddenly feeling self-conscious. Daniel, oblivious to Pia's distracted state, wrapped an arm around her waist and pulled her into his embrace, making up his own moves to the group dance. She allowed herself to be led half-heartedly around the floor by Daniel, but she had one eye on Jackson the whole time, who was now sharing a drink with Ruby and Connor.

'I should go and say hello to my boss,' she told Daniel. 'Won't be a sec.'

Without listening to Daniel's sulky protest, she left him behind and wandered over to where Jackson was standing.

'Hi, you made it,' she said with a smile, trying to cover up her awkwardness.

'We were just telling Jackson what a fabulous day it's been and how this venue has far exceeded all our expectations,' Connor said.

'We'll be forever grateful to you, we really will. You know what we need? A photo of us all together.'

'I'll take it,' Pia volunteered.

'No, you'll need to be in the picture too,' said Ruby. 'I mean, without you and Jackson, we would not be standing here today. Auntie Sue!' She beckoned a lady sitting on a nearby table. 'Can you come and take some photos?'

Pia supposed that was true, but as she stood alongside Jackson, smiling into the camera, his hand slipped casually around her waist and she realised she would never be able to forget Jackson now even if she wanted to. Sneaking a glance at his handsome profile, she suspected she would never want to. She'd tried it once before, but still he'd managed to infiltrate her thoughts over those missing years. Now, he would have a place in the family album for years to come.

She was hyper-alert to the sensation of Jackson's hand on her back, which sent ripples around her entire body. It was the lightest of touches, but still it sent a thrill of anticipation and excitement beneath her skin that was so very different to the way Daniel's touch was beginning to make her feel. His exuberance and enthusiasm made him heavy-handed and she'd caught herself recoiling from his touch several times already today.

'Ooh, I love this song,' said Ruby as the band played the opening bars to a sixties classic. 'Will you come and dance with me, Jackson?'

Pia suppressed a smile, noticing Jackson's face fall for a moment before he gathered himself.

'Yes, of course.' He shrugged off his jacket, hanging it over the back of a chair, before rolling up the sleeves of his shirt, holding out a tattooed arm gallantly.

'Come on, sis,' said Connor. 'Let's show them how it's done.'

They bopped around the floor, Connor practising his jiving skills on Pia, in a way reminiscent of their parents in their younger days, who would always tear up the dance floor given the opportunity. She noticed Jackson and Pia's dancing was much more reserved and polite. Connor's energy was infectious and Pia laughed so much as she attempted to keep up with her brother that she was mightily relieved when the song was over and she could gather her breath. The band started on the next song, a different tempo, much slower and more romantic, and Ruby looked directly at her husband.

'Thanks, Jackson,' she said, before turning to meet Connor in an embrace.

Pia and Jackson were left alone together and she sensed he was about to move away off the dance floor when instinctively, giving in to the urge she'd been fighting, she grabbed hold of his body, placing one hand on his shoulder and the other on his waist.

'We should dance,' she said, laughing, knowing that he had no option but to agree. He could hardly reject her in front of all these people. His hands slipped around her back and she felt the pull of his strong body.

'Do you think this is a good idea?'

'Hey, what do you mean?' She looked up at him, concerned. 'You don't want to dance with me?'

'I'm not sure your boyfriend would approve.'

Daniel! Her stomach twisted with regret, and although she couldn't see him, she sensed Daniel's gaze upon them. Surely, he would understand her having one innocent dance with her boss, especially noticing the way in which Jackson was holding her now, awkwardly and at a distance, as though she might detonate in his arms. Pia sighed, thoughts rushing through her head. Daniel was a lovely guy, but he wasn't right for her – well, not as anything more than a friend. She would have to tell him. She would hate to lead him on unnecessarily, but tonight wasn't the time for those kinds of conversations.

'No, he's not my boyfriend,' she said now to Jackson as casually as she could muster, not wanting him to get the wrong idea either.

'Oh, I thought he was. But he is your guest today?'

She couldn't deny that. She nodded, shifting her hand on Jackson's waist, feeling the subtle adjustments of their bodies as they drew infinitesimally closer. A light scent of citrus fruits and masculinity reached her nostrils and she could sense the cut of his jawline up close to hers, so close in fact that she could imagine turning her face to meet his gaze, finding her lips upon his. An overwhelming swirl of desire rippled through her body. She shut her eyes tight, lost in thought for a moment, remembering how it used to be, reacquainting herself with the feel of his body, much broader and stronger now, and recalling the taste of Jackson's kisses. Back when they were teenagers there'd been no hesitation: they'd greedily given in to their desire for each other in a heartbeat, not thinking about the consequences. The only consequence for her was that she'd fallen in love and been left with a broken heart.

The music ended and Jackson dropped his hands to his side, his brown eyes smiling in the low light of the room, lingering on her face, reminding her of what it was that had attracted her to Jackson in the first place. Those gorgeous deep pools of eyes were enough to inveigle any teenage girl.

'All right, darling?'

The moment was shattered by Daniel's arrival. He placed a hand in the small of Pia's back where Jackson's hand had just rested, and she turned to look at Daniel, momentarily affronted. There was so much she was tempted to say, but she couldn't voice the words aloud, not in front of Jackson. Pia recoiled from Daniel's touch even though none of this was his fault; he couldn't have been expected to know how she was feeling.

'Daniel, let me introduce you to my boss, Jackson.'

She plastered on a smile. All she really wanted was for Daniel to leave so that she could pick up where she'd left off with Jackson, however unfair that seemed. Besides, she sensed the moment with Jackson was lost.

'Good to meet you,' he said to Daniel, with a tight smile.

'Great place you've got here.'

'Thanks.' Jackson paused long enough to indicate that he had no interest in continuing with the conversation. He turned to Pia. 'Look, I'm going to head off but enjoy the rest of the celebrations.'

She wanted to grab his wrist, tell him not to go, but already he was on the way out of the door, as a wave of disappointment and regret swept over her. If it wasn't for Daniel, standing at her side and looking at her expectantly, she would have run right after him.

30

It had been a truly special day; everyone's hearts were full of joy after having witnessed Connor and Ruby finally marry. The newlyweds left in a taxi just after midnight to be taken to a boutique hotel in a nearby village for an overnight stay before they headed off the next day for a four-night break on the Pembrokeshire coast. The last of the guests were leaving, piling into the waiting taxis, and Frank was waiting to lock up the barn after the last remaining stragglers had gone. Pia hung around until the very end to make sure all the revellers were safely on their way home. She and a few members of Ruby's family had already washed and cleared up, and swept the floor. Pia would wander over the following morning to make sure everything was as it should be.

'Pretty decent day, I'd say,' Daniel commented.

He took hold of Pia's arm and slipped it through his own, patting her hand, as they made their way back to the main house, with Pia uncertain who was holding who up. She hoped by the time they made it to the front of the manor, his taxi would have turned up, but as her gaze stretched to the end of the long driveway, there seemed to be no sign of it.

'What time did the taxi say they would be arriving?'

'I haven't booked it yet,' he said with an apologetic smile, squeezing her closely into his side. 'Any chance of a coffee round at yours?'

'Oh, I'm shattered, Daniel.' She'd already had a coffee at the barn, although Daniel had stuck to the beer. 'It's been such a long and lovely day. I was going to jump straight into bed.'

'You sure? I really don't want this evening to end,' he said, sounding disappointed. He wrapped his arms around her and leant in to kiss her for what she thought would be a quick peck on the cheek, but in fact turned into a full-on kiss on the lips, his tongue probing her mouth, his alcohol-soaked breath turning her stomach. She quickly pulled away, putting some distance between them. A few weeks ago she'd enjoyed canoodling with Daniel, it had been such a novelty spending some time alone with a good-looking guy, but something had shifted in her head and in her heart in recent weeks, but especially so today, and she'd quickly realised Daniel wasn't the man for her after all.

'Look, you call for your taxi and we'll grab a coffee while you're wait-ing.' She could hardly leave him hanging around outside the house until the taxi arrived and it would give her a welcome distraction to make some coffee. She wouldn't take him into her own flat, but she was sure Jackson wouldn't mind them using the main kitchen for a short while. With any luck he would have gone to bed.

'Lead the way,' said Daniel chirpily, his hands falling on her hips as though they were about to sashay their way through the house doing the conga. 'Cor, this house is pretty amazing, isn't it? What a great perk living in a place like this, although I guess it has its downsides, working for a guy like Jackson Moody.' He gave a low chuckle. 'He doesn't seem like a bundle of laughs.'

She didn't rise to the bait. It was hardly worth it. She'd already told him how much she enjoyed her new job and how Jackson was a great boss, so to hear him take a low swipe at Jackson after Daniel had enjoyed his hospitality all day just confirmed to her, if she'd needed any confirmation, that Daniel wasn't the man she'd first thought him to be. She certainly had no interest in pursuing a relationship with him after today. They walked towards the kitchen, but Pia stopped suddenly as she reached the thresh-old, and Daniel, who had been close up behind her, collided into her back, and laughed as he wrapped his arms around her chest to steady himself.

'Oh, you're here!' She immediately regretted her choice of words as soon as they tripped off her tongue, finding Jackson sitting at the kitchen table, poring over his laptop. Why wouldn't he be there? It was his home after all. Pia shook off Daniel's hold. 'We were just going to grab a coffee while...'

'You go right ahead. I was leaving anyway.' Jackson pulled closed the lid of his laptop and stood up, picked it up, gave a tight smile and walked out, his dark mood permeating the air. She couldn't help noticing how he didn't even look at Daniel and Pia wondered if she'd been too presumptuous inviting him into Jackson's house. In hindsight, perhaps she should have taken Daniel to her own flat after all.

'Jackson, there's no need for you to leave. Can I get you a coffee?' she called out after him, but he wasn't listening. Bertie got up from his position beneath the table where he'd been lying at Jackson's feet and came across to give Daniel a cursory sniff before settling down again, this time in front of the Aga.

As Pia flicked on the kettle and pulled out mugs from the cupboard, she listened out for Jackson's movements, wondering what he was doing. He didn't head upstairs to the master suite as she might have expected him to, but instead went to the office. No doubt putting his laptop away, she thought, mentally tracing his steps. Even after he'd emerged from there, he still didn't head upstairs towards his bedroom. What was he up to? If only she could go and find him and chat to him, check that he was okay and disassemble the day together, but there was no chance of that with Daniel on the scene. Pia handed him his mug of coffee, but her attention was definitely elsewhere, which was apparent when Daniel had to repeat his question.

'Why are you worried about him? He clearly doesn't like me being me here. That's all it is.'

'No, it's not that,' she snapped. Daniel knew nothing about Jackson so he should keep his opinions to himself. She just wished that taxi would hurry up and make an appearance.

When she heard the door to the boot room open, her chest filled with dread. There could be only one reason why Jackson was out there and where he might be heading at this time of night. When the door slammed shut, her worst fears were confirmed and it was only a matter of minutes before she heard the familiar throaty roar of his motorbike throbbing down the driveway. She peered out of the kitchen window until his tail-lights were out of sight, her stomach twisting with regret. Still there was no sign of Daniel's lift.

'Come here, Pia. We're alone now. Perfect. We've barely had any time to ourselves today.'

He walked towards her and she edged backwards until she was leaning against the worktop so that there was no escaping his full embrace. He reached up a hand to touch her face and pressed his lips against hers, his passion and fervour evident as his body pressed against her too. Suddenly she felt claustrophobic and she slipped out from under his hold.

'Stop, please, Daniel.' His crestfallen face gazed back at her. 'Look, I'm really sorry.' She took a breath, a heat rising in her cheeks. There would be no better moment. 'I'm very grateful for you coming along today. I really am. I think you're a very lovely guy—'

'But?' he interrupted her, his face suggesting that he knew exactly what was coming.

'But for me, I think any relationship for us going forward could only ever be on a friends basis. I am sorry, but I've realised I don't see you in a romantic light.'

'Savage,' said Daniel, wincing. 'Friend-zoned, eh?' From his sad expression, Pia actually felt sorry for him. He was a good-looking guy, friendly and would make a lovely partner for someone, only it wasn't her. She needed to stay strong. There was absolutely no point in stringing him along. 'What changed?'

'How do you mean?'

'Well, it seemed as though you liked me a few weeks ago when we first met, and then when we went on a date together.'

'I did, and I still do. It's just that I think we work much better as friends. I'm sorry if that's not what you want to hear.'

He took a seat, placing his mug on the table, examining the backs of his hands before he looked up at her. 'It's Jackson, isn't it?'

'What? No! What's this got to do with him?'

'I don't know, Pia. You tell me.' He admonished her with a glare. 'What I do know is that you seem very concerned about him. I noticed how you became very animated when he came across to the barn earlier, how you looked at him when you were dancing together. How you looked at him as though it was him you fancied and not me.'

'No!' Daniel was obviously hurting and wanting to find a reason why she was no longer interested in him, coming up with ridiculous explanations in the process. 'He's my boss, Daniel. I need to take an interest in him. It's my job.' Although as she said the words aloud, she knew she wasn't convincing anyone, not Daniel or herself.

'Whatever you say,' Daniel said with a resigned sigh. His gaze drifted out of the window as a car drew up outside. 'That looks like my taxi. I should make a move. I'll see you in a fortnight, though, at Steve's wedding?' He must have noticed her doubtful expression. 'It will be great fun. I promise you. I'll text you in a few days to organise the arrangements.' Before she had a chance to protest, his lips were pressed up against hers again and she gently pushed him away, citing the waiting taxi. She breathed a huge sigh of relief when she was able to see him out and close the door behind him. Disappointingly, he hadn't taken the hints she'd dropped. Never mind, she would make it perfectly clear when she texted him tomorrow that she wouldn't be seeing him again and couldn't accompany him to the wedding.

31

Pia stretched her arms high above her head and yawned extravagantly. She was exhausted, but her head was buzzing from everything that had happened over the last twenty-four hours. It had been a day filled with emotions: joy at seeing her brother married, sadness that her parents weren't there to witness it too, excitement at sharing such a special day with her friends and family, and regret that it hadn't worked out with Daniel in the way that they might both have initially wanted it to. Of course she was disappointed, but her overwhelming feeling, when she'd waved Daniel off in the taxi, was one of relief.

Part of her wanted to crawl into bed straight away, where she was certain she would fall asleep as soon as her head hit the pillow, but she was hoping she might see Jackson. What had possessed him to go off at this time of night? There would be all sorts of idiots on the road. Daniel had been right about one thing: she did worry about Jackson, but that was only because she sensed he was troubled and didn't have anyone to confide in.

With Bertie happily settled, curled up against the Aga, Pia sat down at the large oak table with a mug of tea and strained her ears to hear any approaching motorcycles. It wasn't long, though, before the excesses of the day got the better of her and she must have fallen asleep, her arms cradling her head on the table.

'Pia, what are you doing?'

The next thing she knew she was being shaken awake and she stirred groggily, her shoulders and neck aching from where she'd lain awkwardly across the table. She rubbed at her neck.

'You're back,' she said sleepily, feeling an almighty sense of relief at seeing Jackson standing there in the flesh. Through half-opened eyes, Jackson looked incredibly tall and broad in the leather jacket he now slipped off his shoulders. His black hair was dishevelled from where he'd worn his helmet and the dark shadow across his jawline lent him a wearied look.

'It's late. You should be in bed. Where's your friend?'

'He's gone. I sent him home. To be honest with you, I couldn't wait to get rid of him.' She let out a heartfelt sigh. 'I thought it would be nice to have a plus one today, but I would probably have had more fun on my own. Never mind, you learn from these things.'

'What, and you've just been sitting here, drowning your sorrows?'

'No, I was waiting up for you, Jackson. I was worried about you.'

'What?' He cast her a sideways glance. 'Why on earth would you be worried about me?' He bent down on his haunches to pet Bertie, who wagged his tail at the attention.

How could she possibly explain when she was struggling with her own feelings? She knew that she cared for him, a feeling she had no control over, but one that filled every inch of her being. All day he had been there, pushing into her thoughts, and she wasn't sure if it was because of the romanticism of the occasion or the fact that she sensed she'd made a deeper connection with Jackson today, but all she'd wanted to do was spend more one-on-one time with him. She hadn't imagined the way he'd looked at her when he'd complimented on her appearance or the chemistry that had sizzled between them when they'd danced together. Surely he'd felt it too? Or perhaps it *was* all in her imagination and just being in Jackson's vicinity took her back to being that teenage girl that was once so in love with him.

She shrugged, hesitating for a moment. 'You being out on that bike, in the dark. I guess... well, I suppose my mind went into overdrive.'

'Well, you know, Pia, I appreciate your concern, but really there's no need for you to worry. I've been riding bikes for years. I know probably better than anyone the dangers and I like to think I'm a pretty responsible rider.' He picked up her mug of untouched cold tea. 'Do you want me to make you another one of those?'

'I can do it.'

He held up a hand to stop her from getting up out of her seat, and he walked across to flick on the kettle, turning to appraise her as she glanced at her watch and groaned, realising how late it was. Now she felt foolish. It wasn't her place to allow her personal feelings to intrude on what was a working relationship. Living and working under the same roof as Jackson had created a false intimacy that had her believing she knew Jackson much better than she really did. It wasn't part of her job description to worry about Jason's personal safety.

'Going out on the bike, especially in the early hours when the roads are quiet, is my escape. It helps me forget.'

She tilted her head, looking at him, concerned. 'What is it that you're trying to forget?'

He came across and placed a mug of tea down next to her, then pulled out the chair opposite, his dark shining eyes coming to rest on her face. 'Nothing. And everything. When I'm on the bike, the only thing I'm thinking about is the ride, feeling the elements against my skin. The noise, the speed – it's energising, rejuvenating. Makes you feel as though you're really alive.'

She nodded, wondering if he was being strictly honest with her. What demons did he have inside his head that made him want to escape?

'How are you feeling about your dad being back on the scene?' she asked, hoping she wasn't overstepping the mark with her question, but it didn't seem to perturb Jackson.

He nodded. 'Yeah, it's good. As long as he and Ronnie stay apart from each other, it'll be absolutely fine.' He gave a wry smile. 'I mean, I'm not sure how long he'll actually hang around for this time.'

'Oh, but I thought he was back for good.'

'Well, that's what he tells me, but it wouldn't be the first time he's turned up, promising to stay, only for him to take off again.'

'That's tough.'

'Hey, it doesn't bother me these days. It was hard when I was a kid. Never knowing if they'd stick around and having to move between my mum's place and my aunt's, but I didn't know any different then. It was just how it was. Ronnie and my dad had a passionate and volatile relationship, helped in no small part by the booze and drugs, so it wasn't what you might call a conventional upbringing. They both had a bad case of wanderlust, and would often disappear for months at a time, usually separately. But you know, I can't hold grudges. Neither of them are getting any younger.'

Pia thought how different it sounded to her own childhood. Her family hadn't had a lot of money, but she and Connor had never been short of constant love and affection. What Pia remembered most of all was the laughter that rang around the house.

'And what about you? Did you not inherit the wanderlust from them?'

Jackson shrugged. 'I've done my fair bit of travelling, especially when I was working in the city. Travelling for business loses its appeal after a while. Staying in soulless hotel rooms, it can get pretty lonely. I'm glad I don't have to do that any more, but, you know, I'm happy where I am now. This is where I want to be.'

When he did that thing – and he'd done it before – where he locked his gaze on to hers, so that his eyes shone and a half-smile toyed at his lips, she wondered if there was something else he was thinking, something he wasn't saying aloud.

'I've never even been abroad,' she said, more to break the intensity of his scrutiny rather than anything else.

'Really?'

'Yeah.' She said it with a resigned sigh. 'I feel as though I missed out on quite a lot, staying at home to care for my parents, but I don't regret it in the slightest. I would do it all again in a heartbeat if I had to.' She meant it. What wouldn't she give to spend another day, or even an hour, with her mum and dad. So she may have missed out on many of the things most young people did in their twenties, like travelling, clubbing and going off to university, but, as she'd discovered, there wasn't just one way to live your life. 'I guess it's just a case of making up for lost time now.'

'Where would you go if you could go anywhere in the world?'

She felt her skin prickle with anticipation at the very idea. It was either that or Jackson's genuine interest in her that fuelled her excitement. 'Oh, I don't know. Maybe Paris, or Rome, or New York. Only for a holiday, though. I can't ever imagine wanting to move away from here.'

Jackson nodded and she had to wonder again what he might be thinking. 'I'm sure you'll get to all of those places one day, Pia.'

'Maybe,' she said wistfully. 'Jackson?'

'Yes.' His forearms were resting on the table, his fingers steepled together. He looked up and into her eyes again and she wondered if she might ever get used to the intensity of his stare and the effect it had on her whole being.

'Do you remember that last summer we spent together when we were teenagers before you left the village?'

'Of course I do,' he said, nodding, a smile on his face. 'Happy days.'

She didn't miss the glance he took at his watch, the way he picked up his empty mug as if he was getting ready to make a move. She didn't fill the silence, though, hoping he might explain what had happened, why he'd left so suddenly without so much as an explanation, leaving her in the lurch, forever wondering what had gone so utterly wrong with their relationship. But it was clear Jackson wouldn't answer any of those unasked questions or even take the opportunity to reminisce about those days. Instead, he pushed back his chair and picked up the empty mugs from the table, taking them across to the dishwasher.

'You must be exhausted after the day you've had. You should get to bed. I know I need to.'

'Yes, you're right. I'm shattered.' She stood up, following his lead, the intimacy of their late-night chat lost. Her weariness was tainted with frustration now. Whenever she felt she was growing closer to Jackson, he would pull away and she was reminded of the real nature of their relationship: boss and employee. Nothing more. Would they ever get beyond that? she wondered. One thing was for sure – he clearly didn't want to talk about the good old days, however much she might want to.

She went to walk out the kitchen, turning to look over her shoulder.

'Goodnight, Jackson. Thanks again for everything today. A day to remember, that's for sure.'

Within moments, Jackson was at her side and wrapped his big strong arms around her in a hug that was spontaneous, heartfelt and over before she'd even had time to consider what it meant.

'Goodnight, Pia,' he said, pulling away, taking small steps backwards, with that all-too-familiar look in his eye, and a soft smile on his face.

32

Tuesday morning and all the residents and workers at Primrose Hall gathered for the weekly house meeting over brunch. It had become a regular event soon after Pia joined the hall, with Jackson, Mateo and Frank in attendance. Ivy, Jackson's lovely housekeeper, was also there and she would prepare a full breakfast including fresh fruits, yoghurts and a fry-up for anyone who fancied one, with plenty of toast with marmalade and jam. It was a chance for everyone to chat informally about any issues or upcoming events at the hall. Ronnie wasn't officially invited, but she would always manage to find herself in the main kitchen at eleven o'clock on a Tuesday morning, and nobody seemed to mind.

Pia was enjoying a quiet moment, sipping on her coffee, flicking through the local newspaper.

'It's so sad what's happened to the village hall. They're saying it's going to be several months before the repairs of the roof are completed. And it's a possibility that the community library might not open again. It was in the small annexe to the side of the hall and it was under threat even before they closed because of funding issues. Now they're talking about extending the hall into the annexe so it's looking unlikely that it will ever open again.'

'Do that many people actually use it?' asked Jackson, pulling out a carton of orange juice from the fridge.

'I know that I did. It was a real lifeline to me when I was caring for my parents. I used to wander down there when I had some spare time and pick out five or six books, crime, romance, sagas, anything really and those novels, well, they helped me through some very difficult times. I could dive into those reads and escape to another world. It gave me a bit of a respite. I'd pick up some books for Mum as well. It's such a shame for those people who can't get into town to use the main library.'

'I've used it before too.' Ronnie helped herself to a succulent slice of watermelon from the centre of the table. 'Do you remember, Jackson, we used to pop in there after school? You loved those Goosebumps books and wanted to read them all. There were loads of them from what I can recall.' Jackson nodded as he pulled out a chair and joined the others at the table, while Ivy came over with a fresh round of toast. 'Anyway, I've been meaning to ask,' Ronnie continued. 'How did the wedding go on Saturday? I saw the bride and groom having some photographs taken; they looked very happy.'

'It couldn't have gone any better,' said Pia. 'It was such beautiful weather, which helped, but Connor and Ruby were so pleased with the venue. It was perfect for the reception – there was plenty of space and everyone could spill outside and enjoy the scenery. Mateo, everyone said how beautiful the grounds were. The photos are going to be amazing.'

'Oh, Mateo is just so talented,' Ronnie gushed, patting his hand on the table. Mateo blushed as he nodded with pride.

'I'm just glad we could help,' said Jackson.

'Do you know,' said Pia, 'we've already had several calls this week from people asking for more information about the venue or if they can come and have a look around, with a view to holding their weddings here. News obviously travels fast. I've had to tell them that we're not taking any bookings.'

'Really?' asked Ivy, sounding surprised. 'Why's that, then?'

'We're not going to be pursuing that line of business,' said Jackson emphatically, 'only because I think it could quite easily take over to become the sole focus of the business, which I really don't want it to do, so instead it's something we will offer as an exclusive experience. Besides, I really rather enjoy the peace and quiet of the hall. I don't think any of us would appreciate being overrun with visitors every weekend.'

'Definitely not,' said Frank. 'Wedding parties can be pretty rowdy. Luckily, the one we had at the weekend was very well behaved. They left the barn as clean and tidy as it was before the event.'

'I think it's a good idea to keep it exclusive,' said Ronnie. 'Although I do hope you'll let me hold my wedding here, Jackson.' Ronnie pursed her lips and widened her eyes innocently, laying a hand on Mateo's on the table.

'Oh, Ronnie!' Ivy clapped her hands together excitedly. 'Do you really have wedding plans? That's wonderful.'

Mateo turned to look at Ronnie, aghast.

'Well, nothing definite as yet,' Ronnie admitted, looking sheepish, 'but you never know, I'm always open to offers. So watch this space.' She threw her head back and howled, and the others sitting around the table couldn't help but join in with her infectious laughter.

'Do not look at me! I marry once already. I never do again.' Mateo made his position entirely clear.

'Well, just so as you know, anyone sitting around this table who wants to use the barn for their wedding or that of any family member, then of course you'd be more than welcome to. And that even includes you, Ronnie,' Jackson said with a grin. 'Although please let your poor intended husband have a say in the proceedings too, once you actually get to meet him, that is.' Ronnie looked suitably affronted but couldn't help smiling. 'Looking forward, the next big occasion here will be the classic car show at the end of June, along with the monthly open days that will take us through to the autumn so do help to spread the word if you can. We've already got a date in the diary for the Christmas carols, but I'm thinking it would be great to get something else on the calendar for the autumn, so if anyone has any good ideas on that front, then just shout.'

There were no suggestions from around the table until Pia piped up.

'The only thing I can think of is a book-related event. I've heard they're very popular. I might have an ulterior motive, though, because I've never actually been to one and I've always wanted to go; they sound like a lot of fun. You get to see different writers who come along to speak about their books and they have different panels, so you might get a group of crime authors discussing what makes a good villain, or you might get some romance writers discussing the importance of setting in their novels, that sort of thing. The stables would be a great place for the writers to set up and sell their books and the barn would be good for talks and panels.' Pia paused, seeing everyone else's bemused expressions. 'It was only a thought. I suppose it might not be everyone's cup of tea.'

'No, it sounds interesting. It's an area I know nothing about, so if you want to draw up a few proposals and put out a few feelers to see if it's something that would be of interest, then definitely, we can go for it.'

Pia liked the way Jackson listened to her ideas and didn't brush aside her suggestions. He trusted her judgement and she didn't want to abuse that trust by letting him down. She knew nothing about running a literary festival, but it was something she would definitely investigate. How hard could it be? There was a writers' group in town so she would start there, and already her excitement for the possible literary event was building inside.

'Right.' Jackson had finished his sausage sandwich and coffee and pushed back his chair at the table, casually crossing one leg over the other. 'Those posters and flyers you prepared for the classic car show, Pia – I thought I might drop off a few of those this morning, at the cafe in Primrose Woods and in the village. Do you want to come?'

'Yeah, great. We could take Bertie with us if we're just going into the village?'

'No, I want to go into town too; there's a few places I want to try so we'll leave Bertie at home this time and hop on the bike. It looks to be a beautiful day out there.'

'Sure,' she said with a big smile, doing a good job at masking her apprehension.

It had been a long time since she'd ridden pillion with Jackson so was it any wonder she was apprehensive? The last time, so many years ago now, had been on the back of his moped, and she remembered squealing with laughter as he took the bends in the local lanes at breakneck speed as she held on to his waist for dear life. Even now she could conjure up the exhilaration and excitement she'd felt at the time as she'd been thrown from side to side, doing her utmost not to lean the wrong way. These days, Jackson was so much more sensible and responsible, or at least that's what he told her, and she had to admit that as they rode steadily down the driveway of Primrose Hall, she felt the same sense of exhilaration she'd felt as a teenager. She was more than happy to put her entire trust into Jackson and his skills as a rider.

Riding along the country lanes surrounding Primrose Hall and the woods was just as thrilling now as it had been back then and, with her arms wrapped tightly around Jackson's body, she relished the sensation of the cool air whipping against her as the green and lush countryside rushed past. She was able to pick out all sorts of new vistas that she might never have noticed from the comfort of a car, but were easily visible from the vantage point at the rear of Jackson's bike.

They stopped off at the Treetops cafe, dropping off a couple of posters with Lizzie Baker, who promised to put one up in the cafe and one in the glass-covered noticeboard outside the visitors' centre.

'This look likes something Bill would enjoy. We'll definitely come along and I'll see if Katy, my daughter, and her family would like to come too.'

'Yes, do try and make it. It should be a fun day for all ages.' Pia knew that Lizzie was seeing Bill, Abbey's dad, and they were very happy together, according to Abbey, who was delighted that her dad had found happiness again with someone as lovely as Lizzie.

Jackson and Pia climbed back on the bike and took a ride to the village hall, where Connor and Ruby's wedding was supposed to have been held, but now the building was covered with scaffolding and had signs of 'No Entry' plastered over the doors. There was a notice on the board at the front explaining that the hall would be closed until further notice. Jackson took the opportunity to stick up one of his own posters on the same board.

'Are you allowed to do that?' Pia asked him.

'I'm not sure, but I can't see why not,' he said with a nonchalant shrug. 'Besides, I think it's the kind of thing some of the locals would be interested in. Don't you?'

She couldn't argue with that and Jackson had no qualms about sticking up his posters wherever he could, stopping to tie the notices onto telegraph poles and trees, as well as handing them into the doctor's surgery, the pharmacy and any shops that they passed. Confronted with Jackson in his leathers, his hair askew, his dark eyes shining attractively, Pia wasn't at all surprised that everyone he spoke to was more than happy to help him with his request. Jackson could be pretty persuasive when he wanted to be.

'I just want to call in and see Dad before we head back to the hall. Are you okay with that?' Spontaneously, he reached across and swept her hair back from her face, a gesture so gentle and touching that it made her tummy swirl.

'Of course,' she said, humbled that he'd asked her.

She was only doing her job but it had to be one of the best perks of her role. Spending memorable time alone with Jackson, riding pillion on a balmy early summer day, having the perfect excuse to wrap her arms around his strong torso. Back on the bike, she relished the sensations thrumming through her body as Jackson steered the machine along the country lanes.

A little while later, Jackson brought the bike to a stop in front of a row of terraced houses where Rex was sitting outside one of them on a kitchen chair, smoking a cigarette.

'Hello, son,' he said, standing up to greet them, his face beaming when he spotted Jackson. 'This is a lovely surprise. Hello again, Pia. I hope he's not scaring you half to death on that thing,' he said, gesturing with a nod to the bike.

Pia laughed and pulled off her helmet, shaking out her hair. 'Only a bit.'

'You know you really ought to give those things up, Dad,' Jackson said, as Rex put out his cigarette on the saucer he'd been using as an ashtray. 'They're bad for your health.'

'Give me a break,' Rex said good-naturedly. 'I've given up most things: the booze, women and some other stuff I won't mention now,' he said with a grimace in Pia's direction. 'I've got to have some pleasures in my life. I've cut right down on these things too. I'll give them up completely one of these days, I promise. Anyway, what are you two up to today?'

Jackson explained how they'd been spreading the word about the upcoming classic car event and Rex took a copy of the poster, reading it interestedly.

'Cars? Bikes? Auto jumble? You know, this sounds right up my street.'

'Well, where else did I get my love for all things mechanical from? That's the abiding memory I have of you: underneath an old banger, or in the garage beating out a dent from a car panel, or taking off on a ride on one of your own bikes.'

'Yep.' Rex nodded sagely. 'Perhaps I spent too much time on my motors rather than focusing on the important things.' He dropped his gaze to his fingers. 'Am I allowed to come along to this shindig, then?'

'Of course you are – that's if you'll still be living around here then?' Jackson threw the question out casually, but Pia suspected Jackson was fishing to know exactly what his dad's plans were. If he might up and leave, just as Jackson was getting invested in the relationship again.

'I've told you, Jackson. I'm back for good now. I'm not going anywhere. You're stuck with me whether you like it or not.'

'That's good to hear.' Jackson's relief was palpable, and Pia's heart twisted at his vulnerability. She wondered if Rex had noticed it too. 'You know you don't have to wait for an invitation to come and visit us at the hall, Dad? You're very welcome at any time. And if you need a lift, just drop me a text and I'll come and collect you on the bike.'

'Now that would be fun. That's a beauty, isn't it?' Rex wandered across to get a better look at the bike, and father and son were soon on their haunches, locked in conversation over engine sizes, fuel injectors and top speeds. Pia didn't mind in the slightest. She was happy to stand on the sidelines. It warmed her heart to see the pair of them bonding over a subject that was clearly a passion for them both. From what she'd gathered, Jackson had spent very little time with his dad growing up so to have him come back into his life at this point was an unexpected surprise and Pia really hoped they would be able to rebuild their relationship. If Jackson had been worried they might not have anything in common after all those years spent apart, then ten minutes this morning talking about bikes and cars had completely overturned that notion.

'I mean it, Dad,' said Jackson a little later when he climbed on the bike, as they got ready to ride home. 'You'll be welcome up at Primrose Hall any time.'

Rex gave Pia a hug before she put on her helmet and climbed on the back of the bike. Some people you take to immediately upon meeting them and Rex was definitely one of those people for Pia. Maybe it was because he seemed so utterly genuine and humble, or maybe it was because he reminded her so much of his son.

'Thanks, Jackson, although I don't want to upset Ronnie, not after last time. I'm not sure she was very pleased to see me. But then why I should be surprised about that after all these years, I don't know.' He laughed. 'She's just the same as she ever was, isn't she?' Rex commented, with a touch of admiration to his voice.

'Absolutely. She's just as forthright, opinionated and...' Jackson's mouth twisted as he tried to conjure up the right word '...loveable. But you know Ronnie – she's all bluster. She'll be fine once she's got used to the idea that you're back in town to stay.'

'I really hope you're right about that,' said Rex, chuckling. 'Or else we might have a few fireworks in store.'

* * *

When they returned to Primrose Hall, they made a slow approach up the driveway and Pia peered round Jackson's body to take in the sight of the magnificent house in front of them. It took her breath away. Every single time. Would she ever become used to its beauty? As she contemplated that thought, she noticed something else, a car parked askew near the side entrance to the kitchen. Her heart sank when she recognised the car and the man standing beside it. *Daniel!* What on earth was he doing here? Hadn't she made it clear enough in her text that she didn't want to see him again? Jackson must have realised who it was too because he brought the bike to a stop beside Daniel's car. Pia climbed off, hoping Jackson would do the same, but instead he made his excuses and sped off towards the garage. Left alone with Daniel, Pia took off her helmet and faced him.

'Daniel. What are you doing here?'

'It's great to see you too, Pia.' She could tell immediately by his tone and the way his arms were crossed in front of him that he was annoyed. 'Cool job you have here, swanning around on the back of a motorbike all day.'

'We have been working,' she said pointedly. Not that it was any of his business. 'I'm still working now,' she added more softly.

'Look, I'm sorry, Pia, just turning up like this, but I really wanted to see you. I've missed you.' His eyes were imploring now. All she wanted to do was get indoors and take off her jacket and boots, and make a cup of tea, but she wasn't going to invite Daniel inside. It really was the middle of her working day. 'I got your text.'

'Yes. I'm sorry, but I do think it's for the best.'

'The best? Huh! The best for who, though? You said you'd come to Steve's wedding with me. I already told Steve and the guys and they were looking forward to seeing you again. What am I supposed to tell them now? It's embarrassing.'

'I never wanted to make you feel bad, I promise.' She glanced all around her, hoping that someone might appear. Mateo or Frank or Ronnie. And where was Jackson exactly? She hoped he wouldn't take too long putting the bike away. 'How's Chloe?' she asked, desperate to get Daniel onto a subject that she thought might improve his mood.

'She's fine, but I'm not here to talk about Chloe.' He paced up and down, looking all around him too, clearly agitated, before returning to stand in front of her. 'Look.' He reached out and took her hand. 'Please come to the wedding with me. Just as friends. It will be a laugh. And I promise not to drink as much this time.' He grimaced and shrugged his shoulders

'No.' She shook her head and pulled away her hand. 'I don't want to, Daniel. I have to go; I really need to get back to work. I'm sorry it didn't work out between us.'

'Jesus Christ!' He threw his arms in the air as he kicked the gravel beneath his feet, sending a spray of small stones in the air, his outburst making her flinch. 'I actually thought you were different, Pia. We could have been so good together, but you didn't even give us a chance. Too hung up on that boss of yours, right? You know you're kidding yourself. Someone like that is never going to be interested in the likes of you.'

She turned away, heading for the door, bristling with anger. How dare he? Turning up at the hall knowing she would be working, making her feel uncomfortable.

'Don't walk away from me when I'm talking to you.' He grabbed hold of her wrist, this time with much more force, turning her to face him, his breathing heavy. 'Don't you think you owe me an explanation?'

She pushed him away, almost stumbling as she hurried to escape, her anger replaced with fear now.

'No, she doesn't.'

Relief flooded through Pia's body on hearing Jackson's voice as he appeared from around the back of the house.

'She really doesn't. You need to leave. Immediately. And don't come back. This is private property.' Jackson was calm and measured in his approach, but emphatic too.

'Ah right, I might have known. Here he is, your knight in shining armour to the rescue. Isn't that what you wanted, Pia? You're bloody welcome to her, mate!' He sneered, before jumping into his car, slamming the door and revving the engine as he scrunched the wheels across the gravel. Pia had never been so pleased to see the back of anyone before.

'Are you okay?' Jackson asked as the pair of them watched Daniel's departing car, making certain he left the grounds.

'Yeah, I'm fine,' she said, not realising until now that she'd been shaking. 'What an idiot he is.'

'Oh, yep. Absolutely. A prize idiot. Come on,' he said with a gentle smile. 'Let's get inside. I'll make us some tea.'

33

A couple of weeks later and Pia was down in the paddock with Little Star and Twinkle, giving them their regular pampering session. Their antics had been curbed somewhat by the new fencing and boundaries that Mateo had worked hard to put in place, but they still managed to get covered in dust and mud from larking about together. She found grooming the pair of them therapeutic. It gave her some much-needed thinking time, as she brushed Little Star's long straight tail with a dandy brush and some conditioning spray to keep out the knots. Whatever attention Little Star was getting, Twinkle made it known that he needed the exact same treatment too. They were a proper pair of divas, those two.

Pia's phone vibrated in the back pocket of her trousers and she took it out to take a look, relieved to see that it wasn't from Daniel.

Hey, Pia, how are you? Must be time for a coffee and a catch-up. What do you think? Let me know how you're fixed and we'll get something in the diary. Oh, and Wendy asked if you could pop in to the lodge and see her soon? There's something she needs to talk to you about. We could do both at the same time if that suits you better. Speak soon. Love Abbey xx

The trouble with working at Primrose Hall was that it was all-encompassing and it was easy to forget there was another world outside the gates. Pia's main focus was on doing her job to the best of her ability, keeping Jackson happy, looking out for Ronnie, Mateo and Frank – who all seemed to come to her if they had any problems – and then caring for Bertie, and Little Star and Twinkle too.

She felt a pang of guilt, realising she hadn't spoken to either Abbey or Wendy since the wedding, when she'd promised to contact them both in the following days. Being busy was no excuse. They were her friends who had supported her enough over the years. She needed to be there for them as well. With Simon back home, perhaps Pia was guilty of having taken a small backwards step as far as Wendy was concerned.

The conversation she'd had with Abbey at the wedding resounded in her head. Abbey had been telling Pia about her and Sam's wedding plans, which had been put on hold for the same reason as Connor and Ruby's had been relocated. Pia's heart had gone out to Abbey knowing how disappointed she must be, especially after her previously cancelled wedding debacle, but Pia now wondered if Abbey hadn't been putting out some feelers about the availability of Primrose Hall. Of course she had! Only Pia had been far too wrapped up in the celebrations of the day to realise at the time.

Although Jackson had said no more weddings for the foreseeable future, Pia felt sure he would look upon Abbey and Sam's as one of those special cases. They were local, he'd met them both already and Jackson owed Sam a favour for all those occasions when he'd rescued Little Star and Twinkle from the woods. It was a brilliant idea. She'd speak to Jackson once she was finished here to run the idea past him.

As for Wendy, there was only one reason why she would be specifically asking Pia to visit her at the lodge. A black and white spotty reason. Pia sighed, a pain tugging at her heart. Ever since Simon had come home, she'd been anticipating with dread the moment when he announced that he wanted to take Bertie back into his own care. It wasn't that Pia had any reason to complain. She'd always known looking after Bertie would only be a temporary arrangement, but she could never have anticipated how much more she would come to love and depend on that daft dog. How would she ever manage without him?

It was something she could only put off for so long and not addressing the situation would just prolong the agony. After she'd spoken to Jackson, she would reply to Abbey and arrange a time to pop over to the lodge.

'Oh, guys,' she said, wrapping one arm around Twinkle and the other over Little Star. 'What will we do without Bertie?' She gave a wry smile. She wasn't sure Twinkle would necessarily miss Bertie – they were usually involved in a stand-off, keeping a respectful distance away from each other – but Little Star loved his canine friend. And what about everyone else at the hall? They all loved Bertie too, especially Jackson. The house just wouldn't be the same without Bertie's sunny personality about the place. 'Right, I can't hang around here with you two all day. You actually look quite respectable, so try and keep yourselves clean if that's at all possible.' She chuckled, knowing she'd have more chance of them clearing out the shelter. 'Behave! And I'll see you later.'

Walking back to the hall, Pia didn't take any notice of the unfamiliar car that was parked outside, having first reassured herself that it didn't at least belong to Daniel. Her head was filled with thoughts of Bertie and his impending departure. She definitely needed a big hug with him – that's if he was in a huggable mood today. Who knew where he might be. He'd certainly made himself at home at the hall, and would just tag along with whoever he fancied on any particular day. Last time she'd seen him he'd been hanging out with Ivy in the kitchen where she'd been cleaning out the fridge. Pia didn't like to cast aspersions but she suspected Ivy might be popping him treats, like slices of ham and cubes of cheese, when no one was looking, despite Pia telling her not to give in to those imploringly soulful brown eyes.

'Hey, Jackson, do you have a moment? I need to speak to you about weddings.'

As she walked into the office, Pia spotted Jackson sitting in his chair, in his usual position, with his legs up on the table and his ankles crossed, looking deep in thought. She only noticed when it was too late that he had a visitor.

'Oh, I'm sorry!' Her feet welded to the spot. 'I didn't realise you were busy.'

Pia's gaze shifted between Jackson and his visitor. She didn't need any introductions; she knew exactly who it was sitting opposite her boss. She only wished she hadn't walked in on their meeting. Would it be rude to turn around and walk straight back out again? However big the temptation, she knew she couldn't.

Jackson jumped up out of his seat.

'Tara, meet Pia, my new assistant, and Pia, this is Tara—' He stopped abruptly, but there was really no need for him to fill in the blanks. Pia had worked it all out already.

'Hey, it's great to meet you.' Tara sprang up from her chair and held out a hand to Pia, who surreptitiously wiped her hand on her trousers, hoping Tara wouldn't notice. She hadn't washed her hands since she'd groomed the animals, and suspected she might have a whiff of the farmyard about her. In contrast, Tara looked every bit as glamorous as Pia had known she would be, if all those photos were to be believed. If anything, Tara was even more gorgeous in the flesh. Her straight, long, blonde hair hung in a mane over her shoulders, her skin was clear and bright, and her teeth were a natural brilliant white. She was effortlessly put together too in a pair of cream wide-legged trousers and a matching buttoned-up cardigan.

Pia felt positively dowdy in comparison. At least Pia didn't need to wonder about Bertie's whereabouts any more. She might have known he'd be schmoozing up to Tara. The pair of them complemented each other fabulously, looking like something from a high-fashion magazine cover: sophisticated, regal and elegant.

'Although good luck with talking to Jackson about weddings. It's not exactly your favourite subject, is it, darling?' Tara flashed him a smile, but it was the dagger-like pain that came from hearing that one little word that caught Pia totally by surprise. *Darling!* It sounded far too intimate to Pia's ears and she could only wonder what exactly Tara was doing here. Had Jackson known she was coming? Had he invited her?

Pia plastered on a big smile to match Tara's, although she wasn't certain that either of their smiles were genuine. Pia noticed the non-too-subtle dig behind Tara's comment.

'We had a wedding party here the other week – my brother and his wife, actually, it was such a brilliant day.' *Stop wittering on*, she chided herself. 'I just wanted to chat to you about something that's cropped up, Jackson, but it's not urgent. It can wait.'

'Really?' Tara turned to him. 'That's great to hear. I always told you it would be a fantastic venue for weddings, didn't I? Although I don't think you were ever terribly keen on the idea. I'm glad you've managed to talk him around, Pia. You clearly succeeded where I failed,' she said, laughing.

Pia nodded, looking at Jackson for a bit of moral support, but his gaze had drifted out of the window. Pia had the distinct impression she'd walked in on an intimate and personal conversation. One thing was for sure: there was an awkward atmosphere in the room and Pia knew her presence was only adding to it.

'Eugh, no.' Tara looked down at her beautifully tailored trousers. 'I'm covered in hairs,' she said, looking accusingly from Bertie to Pia as she grimaced, picking at the tell-tale signs of Bertie's over-familiarity on her long legs.

'Well, I've just remembered that there's something I need to do, in the barn.' It was the first thing that popped into Pia's mind. 'Can I fix you a drink, a coffee or a soft drink, before I go?'

'No, it's fine. Don't worry. I can always help myself. I know where everything is,' Tara said, her laughter tinkling around the room.

'Come on, Bertie. You need to come with me.'

As Pia walked out of the office, saying her goodbyes to Tara, she sighed, relieved to be distancing herself from the situation. She was still puzzled, though, about what exactly Tara was doing here. Were she and Jackson going to give their relationship another try, and how exactly would that impact on Pia's position at the hall? Would there still be a job for her here, and even if there was, would Pia want to stay to witness Jackson falling back in love with another woman?

34

'Ooh, this is a treat! To what do I owe the pleasure? Why don't you have a seat and I'll fix us a drink. Will rose lemonade do?'

'Sounds perfect,' said Pia, grateful to sit down in one of the loungers in front of Ronnie's camper van. At this particular moment, she could definitely see the appeal of jumping behind the driver's seat and heading off into the distance, never to return again. Her head was full of conflicting thoughts and she was surprised by how much Tara's sudden appearance had unsettled her. Even if Tara and Jackson were not planning on getting back together, it made her wonder how she would cope if Jackson should ever meet someone that he wanted to move into the master suite at Primrose Hall. It was bound to happen at some point. Perhaps her first thought about this being a stop-gap position until something more suitable came up had been the right one.

'What's the matter, sweetheart?' Ronnie said, handing her a glass. She was nothing if not perceptive.

'Just one of those days.' Pia gave a heartfelt sigh. 'I'm worried about losing Bertie. I think I told you that his original owner is back in the country, and I suspect he will want to have him home again soon. Wendy, my friend, has asked me to pop in to see her and I just know that's what it will be about.'

'Oh no! We can't have that! We'll all be bereft if Bertie has to go. He's one of the family now. Perhaps it won't come to that,' said Ronnie hopefully.

Pia crossed her fingers in the air.

'Perhaps, but I'm not holding out a lot of hope.' Every time she thought about it, she was filled with sadness.

'Well, you know if Bertie has to go, I'm sure Jackson would be happy to get another dog here. He seems to have enjoyed having him about the place; the two of them have really bonded. And I reckon we should always have a Primrose Hall house dog now.'

Pia gave a tight smile, realising in that moment that Ronnie didn't understand at all. She was only trying to be supportive, but there was no way that Bertie was replaceable. Simply getting another dog would never fill the gap that his departure would leave behind.

'Mind you, I suppose another dog wouldn't be the same as having Bertie, would it?' Ronnie said, as if she'd actually given it some thought and had come to the same conclusion as Pia. 'It's like men. You can't simply replace one with another. Lord knows, I've tried!' Her distinctive chuckle rang out around them. 'Some men, like dogs I guess, carve out a special place in your heart.'

Wasn't that the truth, mused Pia, with a wry smile. She took a sip of the refreshing lemonade.

'Anyway, how's life with you, Ronnie?'

'Oh, up and down. I was doing fine until that silly sod turned up again.'

'You mean Rex?'

'Yep, I know you'll tell me off for being silly, but Rex being back on the scene has totally unsettled me. It's brought up a whole raft of bad feelings that I don't know how to deal with. I can't say anything to Jackson because he'll say I'm being overdramatic. So what can I do? I know Rex is his dad and, believe me, I do want them to have some kind of relationship together, but I'm not sure I want Rex back in my life, in any shape or form, after all this time.'

'I don't think you're being silly at all. It's never easy when you come face to face with your past like that, but what you had with Rex was a long time ago now, Ronnie. I expect you've changed and I bet Rex has too. If he is going to be hanging around, then the likelihood is that you're going to be bumping into him more often, so the pair of you will have to find a way of managing the situation.'

'Hmmm, I'll try,' said Ronnie with a sweet smile. 'But I can't promise that we'll be able to be civil towards each other. The trouble is, in the heat of the moment, when I come face to face with Rex, all reason escapes me. Sometimes just being in the same space as him, looking at his familiar face with that same old ridiculous smile, and hearing that deep, gravelly voice is enough to infuriate me on its own.' She paused, lost in her own thoughts for a while. 'And delight me at the same time,' she added wistfully. 'He's still a very handsome man.'

'He really is, and Jackson looks just like him, I think.'

'He does. They're two peas out of the same pod. Talking of which, what's he up to this afternoon, then?'

'Oh, he's got a visitor. Tara's here. I thought I'd give them a bit of space.'

'Really?' Ronnie's face lit up with curiosity. 'What's she doing here, then?'

Pia shook her head, wishing she knew the answer.

'I don't know. I didn't realise she was coming.' She played with her fingertips, wondering if they were still chatting and how it was going, if the two of them were about to emerge and announce that they were back together again.

'You like him, don't you?'

'What?' She'd been so lost in thought she wasn't sure she'd heard Ronnie correctly. She looked up into the older woman's hazel eyes, which were observing her closely.

'Jackson. You like him, don't you?' Pia was about to protest, but Ronnie waved away her words before she'd even had a chance to voice them. 'It's all right. I won't say a word. Your secret is safe with me.' She chuckled. 'I've seen the way you look at him. It's the same way I used to look at his father. Even now when I see Rex, something stirs deep inside me.'

'Jackson's been very good to me.' It was as much as Pia was prepared to admit. She was much more comfortable talking about Ronnie's love life. 'Why are you even allowing Rex to get beneath your skin again? I thought you and Mateo were enjoying each other's company these days?'

'We are, but only as friends. Mateo is a lovely man, but he is still very much in love with his late wife and I've never been very good at playing second fiddle to anyone. And anyway, I think I'd be far too demanding for him. He wants an easy time at this stage of his life and who can blame him, but I still feel as though I've got an awful lot of life to live and hopefully I might meet someone to share my next adventures. Someone who is exciting, adventurous and passionate. Someone like Rex.' There was a wistful note to her voice. 'I don't think I ever really got over him.'

Pia reached out a hand and squeezed Ronnie's arm. 'That's sad.'

It wasn't what Pia needed to hear. She didn't want to still be haunted by Jackson in years to come, looking back on her first love as the one who got away. Maybe for her own mental health she needed to take a step away now, while she still wasn't totally invested emotionally in Jackson. Although maybe it was even too late for that. Her relationship with Daniel hadn't worked out, but there would be other people out there that she might meet and form a connection with, although she wasn't going to do that all the time she was ensconced at Primrose Hall. If Tara would be coming back to the house, Pia wasn't sure how much longer she would want to stay on the scene.

'But you and Jackson?' Ronnie was looking at her, her head tilted to one side as though waiting for an answer to her previous question. 'Come on, you can tell me.'

'Yes, well, obviously, I like Jackson,' Pia said now, trying to brazen it out. 'He's my boss, and we do work really well together, but that's all there is to it.'

Ronnie nodded her head sagely, a smile resting on her lips. 'You don't have to convince me, love. It's whether or not you can convince yourself – that's the most important thing. Let me ask you one thing. How would you feel if Tara were to move back into the house, then?'

'Do you think she will?' Pia said, jumping on Ronnie's words, her dismay at that idea evident on her face.

Ronnie shrugged. 'I don't know. I was just wondering, that was all.'

Pia thought for a moment. She'd been wondering the same thing, knowing instinctively that she wouldn't be able to hang around to watch Jackson make a future with another woman. And Ronnie had been right:

Pia's feelings for Jackson were so much more than a boss–employee relationship, so much more than just old friends.

'I'm not sure I could bear it, Ronnie,' she said in barely more than a whisper.

'I thought not,' she said, clasping Pia's hands from across the table.

There was no denying the irrefutable truth that Pia was in love with Jackson and probably always had been from the very first time that she'd met him. Now she was faced with the unwelcome possibility that she might have to say goodbye soon to the two most important men in her world, Jackson and Bertie, and the thought of that simply broke her heart.

35

'Good morning!'

Pia wasn't sure it was a good morning. She climbed out of her bed just after six o'clock, aware of a sense of dread lodged in her chest. The first thing she did was to quickly dash into the main kitchen, on the pretext of getting a bottle of water from the fridge. She was hugely relieved that no one was around and, having a quick look over her shoulder to double-check she was really alone, she stood up on her tiptoes to peer out of the sash windows and then breathed a huge sigh of relief. *Thank goodness!* There was no sign of Tara's car. After visiting Ronnie late yesterday afternoon, Pia had retired to her room for the night, so she'd had no idea if Tara had stayed until late or even stayed over. She was glad to discover that she hadn't. Unless, of course, Tara had gone home only to collect her belongings for a return to Primrose Hall.

After she'd showered and dressed, Pia headed over to Primrose Woods with Bertie. It was a beautiful morning with the sun filtering through the trees, throwing patterns over the ground. She was more determined than ever to enjoy her early morning adventures with her not-so-faithful hound, not knowing when their last walk together might be before Bertie was returned to his rightful home. She could come and walk over in the woods on her own, but she wasn't sure she would want to. It just wouldn't be the same without Bertie at her side.

Back at the hall, she fed the dog, who was then more than happy to sprawl out against the double doors in the office, soaking up the shafts of lights from the sun, while Pia opened up her laptop and set to work on her to-do list. Her main job for today was to finalise the entries for the upcoming car show, and to send out exhibitors' information packs for everyone attending. With thirty-two cars and fifteen bikes signed up already, it was going to be a small and exclusive event, but Jackson, who was incredibly excited and enthusiastic for the day, was confident that word would spread and next year's event, for which the date was already in the calendar, would be even bigger and better. Along with the auto jumble being held in the barn, the stables would be open as well with each of the units already booked out to different small businesses. There would definitely be something of interest for everyone of all ages.

Now, Pia looked up at Jackson, who came bearing a coffee, made just as she liked it, milky with a dusting of chocolate on top.

'Thank you,' she said, grateful for his kindness, as she looked up into his eyes for any signs of emotion there.

'How are you, then?' he asked jauntily, perching on the edge of her desk, definitely far too close for comfort. How was she supposed to concentrate on her screen when she had Jackson's fresh-out-of-the-shower scent wafting beneath her nose? Something, or maybe someone, had put him in a good mood today.

'Good, thanks. I'm just running through the schedule and the timings for the car show. I'll email over the programme to you when it's done.'

'Honestly, Pia, I remember when I first interviewed you and you tried to convince me that you were unqualified for this job and just look at you now. You've really made this role your own. You do realise you'd be able to walk into any executive PA role now, if you wanted to?' He flashed her that wide smile that warmed her insides and she blushed at the compliment. Until she stopped to consider what he'd actually said. Was he hinting that she might be looking for a new job soon?

'Now what was it you wanted to talk to me about? Something about weddings, I think?'

It had seemed such a good idea yesterday, before Tara had appeared on the scene. Now she was struck by a pang of self-consciousness, wondering if she was about to overstep the mark. Jackson had mentioned several times already that he wasn't keen on holding too many weddings at the hall, and here she was about to suggest another one, for her friend.

'Actually, I'm not sure it's important now...' She hesitated and Jackson raised an eyebrow by way of invitation for her to go on. 'You know my friends Abbey and Sam, the ranger who works at Primrose Woods, well, they're in the same boat as Connor and Ruby. They had their wedding booked for the end of August at the village hall, but obviously it's been cancelled. I feel really bad for her because she's already got one abandoned wedding under her belt.' Seeing Jackson's confused expression, she elaborated. 'Oh, that was to her ex who she'd been with for years. She only discovered he was a lying douchebag a few weeks before the wedding and had to call it off.'

'Poor girl,' said Jackson.

'Exactly! It's not that she's asked about using the barn at all, but I just thought with the pair of them being local, and her being one of my oldest friends...' Her words trailed away.

'Absolutely. Let's put the invitation out there. I like Sam. He's a great guy. He's helped me out a few times with Little Star and Twinkle when they've taken impromptu visits over to the woods, so I'd be more than happy to host them here.'

'Really? Thanks, Jackson,' she said, feeling immensely relieved and grateful to him, even though his trousered thigh was still perilously close. Clearly the energy she felt charging between them went unnoticed by Jackson or else he might have helped by putting some distance between them. 'I'm seeing Abbey later today so I'll have a chat to her about it.'

'Great. Anyway, how are you really doing, Pia? Ronnie mentioned something about you being a bit low yesterday.' Jackson laid a hand on her shoulder and she felt the resulting vibrations reach her toes.

What exactly had Ronnie been telling him? She hoped it wasn't anything about Tara or Ronnie's suspicions that Pia might have feelings for Jackson. *How embarrassing*, but then she shouldn't really be surprised at

Ronnie's inability to keep a confidence. Seeing the momentary panic on her face, Jackson clarified what he meant.

'I understand we might be saying goodbye to Bertie soon?'

Of course, Bertie! And while that was obviously a very worrying situation, for the briefest moment Pia felt a sense of relief that Jackson hadn't been talking about anything else.

'Yep, I'm going to visit Wendy later today as well; she's asked to see me, and I expect it's to do with Bertie going home to Simon. I'm trying to mentally prepare myself for that possibility, but I know it's not going to be easy. I'm going to miss that goofy dog so much.'

'Is there anything I can do to help? What if we offered to give some financial compensation to Simon in exchange for keeping Bertie permanently?'

'It isn't about the money, Jackson,' Pia snapped. 'Bertie's not a commodity. It's about the love you have for an animal and that never leaves you. Simon and Wendy adore that dog just as much as we all do here.' How could he talk about money at a time like this? Is that how he solved all his other problems, simply by throwing money at them? Life wasn't as simple as that. She sighed, feeling tears prickling at her eyes. 'At least we know that he will be going to a good home, and maybe Simon will grant me visitation rights,' she said, trying to lighten the mood for her own benefit.

'Fair enough,' he said, looking suitably chastised. 'Look, will you come and speak to me later after you've seen Wendy and Abbey? There's something I want to talk to you about and probably best done over dinner. I'll do us a couple of steaks – how does that sound?'

'Okay,' she said, sighing inwardly, wondering what it was that he couldn't tell her now and having the distinct impression that today was going to be a day for difficult conversations.

36

'Pia, how lovely to see you!' Abbey greeted her warmly, like the old friends they were. 'Good timing. Tea and cakes have just been served in the lounge so I'll get someone to bring us through a selection. I've been wanting to have a debrief with you ever since the wedding. Wasn't it an amazing day?'

'It really was and I was just so relieved that Connor and Ruby had the sort of celebration they wanted and deserved. They're back from their honeymoon in Wales now and still buzzing about it all.'

'Jackson really did come to the rescue there. How's it going with your gorgeous ex? He seems like a pretty cool, laidback guy.'

'He is. We've not had any major fallings-out yet. Well, apart from the time when he threatened to send Little Star and Twinkle away because of their escape antics. I mean, honestly. I had to put him straight on that one!'

'Too true. They were the stars of the Christmas event last year – you couldn't possibly get rid of them, and we were with little Rosie when she chose the animals' names. Honestly, she was so proud, bless her. That was another really lovely touch from Jackson.'

'Yes.' Pia pressed her lips together, nodding. He was good at the big gestures, but she had to wonder about his motivation behind these acts of kindness and why he felt so compelled to give back to the local community.

'Do we have to talk about Jackson?' she said, shaking the thoughts away. 'He already takes up too much of my headspace as it is.'

'Does he? Oh, Pia! What about Daniel, though? Is he not taking your mind off Jackson?'

'No, that was the plan, but it didn't work out that way. He wasn't the guy I thought he was.' She sighed, opting not to tell Abbey the finer details. Those could wait until they had an evening out together. 'I decided it wasn't fair to carry on seeing him when my heart wasn't in it.'

'When you heart is lost in another direction, maybe?' Abbey said while raising an eyebrow. 'I can understand it, though. Jackson's very good-looking, and he's rich and charming to boot. A pretty lethal combination, I'd say.'

Wasn't that the truth? Was Pia infatuated by the idea of Jackson and everything he represented rather than the man himself? She didn't think so. She knew him of old and appreciated his soft centre beneath the sometimes brusque exterior. His vulnerability made her heart melt, but she also admired his practicality, how he was always keen to find a solution to any problem and how he showed kindness to her, the rest of the staff and his family.

'Do you think there's any chance that you two will get together? I mean, you were a couple once before.'

'I know, but that was when we were kids and Jackson's never really mentioned that time, not since I've been working for him. I get the feeling he wants to keep the past in the past, which is fair enough. It's probably for the best if we keep our relationship on a professional footing.' She gave a rueful smile. 'Besides, Tara was back at the house yesterday so I'm not sure what's going on there, if they might be getting back together.'

'Oh, really?' Abbey and Pia shared a look of understanding. 'Well, Tara seemed very nice when we met her. I'm sure you'd get on well together.'

Perhaps she would. It was what everyone told her, but if Pia was being absolutely honest with herself, she wasn't sure she would want to work alongside Tara, not when she'd had a taste of having Jackson all to herself.

'Anyway, tell me, how are things with you and Sam?' Pia was keen to change the subject. Thinking about Jackson only tied her mind up in knots. 'It's such a shame about your wedding; you must be so disappointed.'

'I know, right?' Abbey sighed heavily and put her hands up to her hair, releasing it from its restrictive band, shaking her head so that her lovely auburn waves fell onto her shoulders. 'I'm honestly starting to believe that I'm not destined to be married. Twice now my wedding has been cancelled, admittedly to two different men, but I'm wondering if perhaps someone somewhere is trying to tell me something.' Abbey gave a wry smile. 'It'll be fine, we'll set another date when we know the hall will be open again.'

'It's just really bad luck, but you know, sometimes these things happen for a reason…?'

Abbey's face furrowed with confusion.

'I was talking to Jackson, telling him what had happened, and I thought, well, we both thought, that the barn at Primrose Hall might work for your wedding? Only if you're interested, of course,' Pia added. 'You might have your heart set on the village hall…'

'Are you kidding? I didn't think you were renting out the barn for weddings. I'm sure I heard Jackson saying something to that effect. That's why I never brought up the possibility with you, although I'd be lying if I said I hadn't thought about the idea.'

'That's true. We're not opening it up to the general public. Jackson wants to keep the barn available for other events and opportunities that may crop up, but for friends and family, or people from the local area, then he's more than happy to host the occasional exclusive wedding.' Pia turned over her palms to the sky as though presenting a fait accompli.

Slowly realisation dawned on Abbey's face as she took in the full implication of what Pia was saying.

'Really? Are you sure?'

'Absolutely!' Pia nodded, smiling at Abbey's excited response. 'And it means your wedding can go ahead on the date as planned.'

'That's amazing. Sam and I were saying how lucky Ruby and Connor were to have their wedding at the barn, never believing for one moment that we might be able to use it too. You don't know how much this will mean to Sam. His job at Primrose Woods is his life, so to be able to marry next door, in those surroundings, will mean the world to him.'

'Great, I'm pleased. Have a chat with him about it and then give me a call in the next few days and we can start making some plans.'

Abbey pushed back her chair and went round to hug her friend tight. 'Honestly, I knew there was a reason why you've been my friend for all these years. Thanks for looking out for me, Pia. It means the world. And girls' night out soon to celebrate?'

'Definitely,' said Pia, laughing. 'Honestly, I'm becoming an expert on weddings, so you'll be in very safe hands.'

A little later, when they'd finished catching up, Abbey took Pia along to Wendy's room, and Wendy's face lit up to see them both.

'Abbey, have you told Pia my news yet? Come and sit down, Pia.'

'No, I haven't. I thought I'd let you do that.' Whatever news it was, it was clearly good news as Wendy's face was beaming. 'Look, I've still got a few bits to finish up in the office so I'll leave you two to it,' said Abbey, 'but I'll see you soon, Pia, and thanks again.'

'She's a lovely girl, that one. It's no surprise to me that the two of you are friends. Anyway, Abbey's been helping me the last couple of days; we've been talking things through and we've decided that I'm going to become a permanent resident here at the lodge. What do you think about that?'

'Really?' Pia took a seat in the chair beside Wendy's. 'Well, that's very good news. If you're happy with the arrangement, then I'm happy too.'

'Yes, I really am. I've talked it through with Simon as well. He had suggested going to live with him somewhere, selling the cottage and us buying a place together, but do you know, I'm really quite settled here now. Besides, I would never want to be a burden to him. He's got his own life to lead. I've got this lovely room here and I can join in with as many or as few activities as I want to. I think it's the ideal solution. Knowing you are only round the corner is a bonus as well.'

'I'm pleased for you, Wendy. Really I am. It's a big relief all round. And don't worry, I'll be calling in all the time. I'd miss our regular catch-ups if I didn't.' Pia jumped up from her seat and hugged Wendy tight. She could tell from just looking at Wendy that a huge weight had been lifted from her shoulders. There was a lightness and excitement about her that radiated from her, reminding Pia of the old Wendy she'd once known and always loved.

'Anyway, the other reason I needed to speak to you was about Bertie.' Pia detected the subtle shift in her friend's voice, her tone more serious now. She'd known this conversation was coming, but it didn't make it any easier. She steeled herself, determined not to cry, but already she felt a huge swell of emotion form at the back of her throat. She pressed her lips together, not wanting to make Wendy feel any worse than she probably already did. Wendy took hold of Pia's hand.

'You know how grateful Simon and I are to you for taking Bertie on and looking after him so well. Even before I had my fall, you took him out every day.'

'It was no hardship, really. I've always enjoyed our walks together.'

'I know you have, sweetheart, but now with Simon home I guess you've been expecting things to change.'

'Well, of course. We always knew that I was only helping you out until a better solution came along – we said that right from the start.'

'Yes, well, you know how much Simon loves that dog. He missed him so much while he was working abroad and seeing the pair of them reunited at the wedding lifted my heart. And Simon's too. Honestly, he spoke about it all the way home, how he was certain Bertie remembered him.'

'I'm sure he did,' said Pia with as much enthusiasm as she could muster. 'He's such a clever dog.' She could hardly say what she really thought, that Bertie was likely to go off with any Tom, Dick or Harry that paid him the necessary attention.

'The thing is, it's very upsetting for Simon, but he's realised that he's not going to be able to take Bertie back, as he would have wanted to.'

'I'm sorry...?'

'I know, I know. The thing is, because of Simon's new business interests it means he's going to be travelling up and down the country several times a week. As it's only him at home it would mean Bertie being left alone most days. I know there are doggy day care services, but it's not the same and not always convenient. In the old days I would have taken Bertie myself, but of course that's simply not possible now. What he needs is a good, reliable home where he's loved and cared for.' Wendy tilted her head to the side, a smile appearing on her lips. 'I mean Bertie, obviously, not Simon. Although thinking about it, Simon could probably do with the same thing but that's another story entirely! What I'm trying to ask in my roundabout way is whether or not you'd be prepared to have Bertie on a permanent basis? Neither of us like the idea of having to find him a new family who wouldn't know his funny little ways. We've seen how happy he is with you and he has the most marvellous playground at Primrose Hall.'

'Wendy, are you mad?'

Wendy's face dropped at Pia's reaction. 'Oh, I know it must seem a cheek, when you've got your own busy life to lead, and I appreciate that you have Jackson to consider too and his lovely house.' Wendy gave a shake of her head. 'All those muddy footprints... But I just wondered, well, we both wondered, if there's any way you could see...'

'Oh, Wendy!' For the second time in a few minutes, Pia leapt out of her chair and wrapped Wendy in a hug, kissing her gleefully. 'You don't understand. The answer is yes! Yes, yes and yes. I've been dreading the moment when I would have to say goodbye to Bertie; everyone at the hall has. Our daily walks have become part of my routine and he's the best buddy ever. Honestly, I tell him all my problems and he's such a good listener too! He really does give the best advice in the world.' Pia hugged herself with a small squee. 'I couldn't imagine how I would ever get by without him now.'

Wendy's face relaxed into one of understanding. 'And you think Jackson will be happy having Bertie on board as a permanent member of staff at Primrose Hall?'

'Honestly, Wendy, he'll be over the moon,' she said, smiling as a sudden thought popped into her head, dampening her smile. What about Tara? If she was coming back to the hall, what might she have to say about Bertie being in the office, getting under her feet and moulting all over her gorgeous designer clothes?

37

'You look happy!'

Pia returned to the hall just after six in the evening to find Jackson sitting at the kitchen table, enjoying a gin and tonic. He looked across with a smile to greet her and at the same time Bertie came bounding across the room, tail wagging furiously, and her heart swelled with love as she got down on the floor and Bertie attacked her with a barrage of kisses.

'I am,' she said, laughing as she attempted to steady herself under Bertie's onslaught. She'd not been able to stop smiling ever since she'd left the lodge.

'Good. Do you want one?' Jackson asked, holding his glass up to the air, before springing up out of his chair.

'Yes please,' she said. Why wouldn't she be happy after the news she'd received from Wendy this evening? Coming home to Jackson and Bertie always lifted her heart too, although she could hardly say that aloud to Jackson. It wasn't a regular occurrence, but she loved these occasions when they shared a drink together after a day's work, talking casually about everything and nothing. There was something intimate about being together, chatting about common goals over a glass of something. She couldn't imagine a time when she wouldn't be here, sitting at the kitchen table, but then whether she stayed here for any length of time wasn't down entirely to her.

'Anyway, good news! We can all breathe again now. The meeting with Wendy went much better than I expected. She actually asked if I wouldn't mind looking after Bertie on a permanent basis.'

'Really?'

'Can you believe it? Apparently, Simon's new working arrangements mean he'll be doing a lot of travelling so he's not really in a position to take Bertie back, as much as he might like to.'

'Thank Christ for that. I was already making plans to stage a hijack to get Bertie back to the hall if necessary.'

Pia laughed, relieved by Jackson's positive response.

'Here you go,' he said, placing a glass in front of her. He rested a hand on her shoulder and gave it a gentle squeeze, and she looked up into those dark, beguiling eyes, feeling lost there. 'Isn't that the best news ever? Are you hungry?'

'Aren't I always?' she said with a smile. 'Can I do anything to help?'

'Nope, it's all under control.'

Wasn't that exactly the way Jackson liked it? Calling the shots, being in control, doing things his way. She didn't have a problem with that. He was her boss after all, and she was there to support him, but she knew that he could be quite ruthless in his business and personal relationships if things didn't go his way. She was impatient to know about Tara, and the nature of her visit yesterday, but she would just have to wait it out until Jackson deemed it necessary to tell her.

Now she watched as he quickly peeled potatoes and put them on to boil for a few minutes, before then slicing and putting them into a pan of butter and olive oil, along with some garlic and fresh rosemary, to gently sauté. The delicious aromas wafting in her direction made her tummy rumble.

'So, tell me about our book festival,' Jackson said over his shoulder.

'Well, the planning is still in its early stages, but I've fixed the date for the last weekend in September. I've been in touch with a couple of local writing groups and the response has been really positive. One of the members is a very successful romance writer and she's agreed to come along and talk about her series of books, on both days. And then we have a crime writer and a historical fiction writer who have signed up too. I'm hoping to get a few more authors along as well. I'm also organising some story-telling sessions for the children and some workshop sessions where they'll be able to have a go at writing stories as part of a group.'

'That sounds great.'

'Honestly, Jackson, I'm so excited about it. I really can't wait.'

'Well, you know, if there's anything else you need to talk through or something I can help with, then you only need to ask.'

A little while later they sat down to eat the steaks, sauté potatoes and green beans. Simple food, but cooked beautifully and complemented by a smooth, mellow red wine. Pia didn't feel self-conscious eating in front of Jackson; it was only when the conversation stilled and their eyes met across the table, lingering there for a moment too long, that she felt a heat rush to her cheeks.

'Have you heard any more from Daniel?'

'No, thank goodness! I think he may finally have got the message. I'm sorry about all that.'

'You've nothing to apologise for. The guy was an idiot. You deserve so much better than someone like him.'

'Thanks,' she said, dropping her gaze, only annoyed that Jackson would presume to know what was good for her. 'I've clearly got rotten taste in men.'

She noticed the almost imperceptible quirk of his eyebrow, the curl of his mouth.

'And you got to meet Tara at last,' he said casually, pushing his plate to one side and sitting back in his chair, arms folded.

'Yes.' And then, only to fill the awkward silence, she added, 'She seems nice.'

'Yes, she is,' he said, his eyes locking on to hers, appraising her reaction. 'I hope it wasn't too uncomfortable for you?'

'Not at all,' she said disingenuously. 'I just thought I'd leave you in peace to talk, that's all. Did you know she was coming?'

'No. She just "popped by",' he said, making quote marks in the air. 'Not that we're really in popping-by distance from Tara, but I think she just wanted to see how we were doing. I think she was slightly put out that actually we're doing quite well.'

'Ah, I see,' she said, feeling uncomfortable talking about Tara for fear her words could be misconstrued.

'I just wanted to explain the situation with Tara in case you were wondering what was going on.'

Pia shrugged. 'It's not really any of my business.'

'Well, it might be if you were under the misapprehension that we were getting back together again.'

'So does that mean you're not, then?' she asked, rather too eagerly.

'No, Tara wanted us to give it another go, but it's not going to happen. Yesterday was a one-off.'

Pia glanced away, hoping her utter relief wasn't visible, but feeling a pang of sympathy for Tara all the same. Pia had been on the end of a broken heart at the hands of Jackson once and she knew how utterly miserable that felt.

'Okay, well, thanks for letting me know, although obviously your personal life is nothing to do with me.'

'Are you sure about that, Pia?' There it was again, her name lingering on his tongue, as though he was caressing it over in his mouth.

'Yes, absolutely. I'm here to work for you, and I'm very grateful that you have given me the opportunity to do that, but what's going on in your personal life is for you alone. I don't really need to know about that.' She let out a forced laugh, hoping she didn't sound rude, but really what was she supposed to say in the circumstances?

'Let me clear these plates,' she said, jumping up and leaning across the table to collect the dirty crockery.

'I'll help,' said Jackson, and as he stood up and leant over from the opposite direction they collided over the table, bumping into each other with a jolt. 'Oh, sorry – here, let me take those.'

Jackson took the dirty crockery over to the worktop, placing it beside the dishwasher before turning to face her.

'Look, all I was trying to say was that I really value you being here. You're such an integral part of the team now and I would hate to lose you. And Bertie, of course, too. Hell, especially Bertie,' he said with a grin. 'But not nearly as much as you, Pia.' At that moment Bertie was nudging Jackson's hand with his nose in the hope that he might get the tiny sliver of steak left over from Pia's plate, and Jackson immediately gave in to his demands. 'I think it's important that we have these conversations because obviously, working so closely together, these things will impact on you. If there's anything you're not happy about or if you have any concerns then please come and talk to me so that we can see if we can find a way to sort them.'

It was as though Jackson could read her mind. Pia had been worried about Tara's reappearance and what it might mean for Pia's future at the hall, but now Jackson had explained she felt so much better. Could he really be that perceptive or had someone, namely Ronnie, been feeding him tales?

'Sure, that makes sense,' she said, trying for nonchalance, but not really achieving it. She put the dirty plates in the dishwasher, washed up the frying pan and put away the condiments in the pantry. There was only so much clearing away she could do, especially when the atmosphere in the kitchen had grown heady and intense.

'Are you done?' said Jackson, when she finally turned to face him and there was literally nothing left for her to do.

'I think so. I like to be useful. You did make dinner, after all. Thank you, it was utterly delicious, but...' She could hear the words rattling inanely off her tongue. 'I should probably go...'

'Why? We haven't had our desserts yet. Come here.' He beckoned her over to his waiting arms. There'd been plenty of friendly hugs between them before so there could be no harm in one more, surely. The way he looked at her, though, his gaze appraising her body and her face, felt more intense tonight and made her insides curl with anticipation. She stepped into his arms, not pausing to consider whether this would be the best career move of her life. It was too late for those kind of considerations. His arms around her felt strong and comforting and all too seductive. When he tipped up her chin with his finger, his face came within touching distance of her own, his lips far too tempting to ignore. She closed her eyes and felt the gorgeous sensation of his mouth upon hers, sending shooting stars along every vein in her body.

38

'You kissed me!' she said, more in surprise than indignation.

'I did.' Jackson observed her, his brow furrowed.

'You can't do that!'

'I can't? You didn't want me to do that?'

'No! Well, yes, but...' She extracted herself from his hold, fanning herself with her hand to cool the burning temperature soaring around her body. Her head was a mud swamp of emotions. 'I work for you, Jackson. We have to keep our relationship professional or else this will all end in disaster. I really don't want to lose my job.'

'You're not going to lose your job, Pia,' he said softly. 'I've told you how important your contribution is to the hall. I don't want you going anywhere – do you understand me? Honestly, I'd be lost without you now, in more ways than one.' He tipped up her chin again and she felt like her teenage self, so intoxicated by Jackson's presence. 'I can't help it if I want to kiss you. I wanted to do it on the first day we met up again, at the Treetops Cafe. You don't know how much self-control it took for me not to wrap you in my arms and kiss you passionately. I couldn't, though. I didn't want you running in the opposite direction. I've wanted to kiss you every day since.'

Oh god! Could that really be true? Or was this Jackson at his persuasive best?

'Is that the only reason you gave me the job? Has this been some kind of elaborate seduction ploy?'

He laughed, his dark brown eyes shining fondly.

'Absolutely not. What kind of a man do you take me for?' He took a step backwards, placing his hands on his hips, looking suitably affronted. 'I wanted you to have the job because you were the... um... on—the absolutely best applicant for the position.'

'Hey, hang on a minute.' She'd heard his hesitation and had a moment of dawning realisation. 'How many applications did you have exactly for the role?'

He scrunched up his eyes as if trying to recall. 'I don't remember, but...'

'Oh my god! It's true. I was the only one to apply, wasn't I?' she said, sounding outraged.

'Um...'

'Don't lie to me, Jackson.'

He pressed his lips together and shrugged. 'Okay, but that didn't make a jot of difference, I promise you. You were still absolutely the best person for the job. I mean, just look what you've done here. The difference you've made. You are the heart of Primrose Hall, ask Frank or Mateo or Ronnie, and I'd never want that to change.'

They fell quiet, gazing reproachfully at each other, Pia trying to make sense of what Jackson was telling her.

'I don't have plans to go anywhere. I love being at Primrose Hall. With you and the rest of the team. I feel as though I've found my home here.'

'You have, Pia. For as long as you want it to be. Look, I apologise for kissing you. I kind of thought... I'm sorry.' He raked a hand through his hair, looking vulnerable and sexy at the same time. 'I presumed too much. It will not happen again. I promise you.'

She looked across at him, her bottom lip curling involuntarily as she walked across and into his arms, feeling the pull of his embrace. She looked up at him, running a hand along his jawline.

'Oh, Jackson, please stop talking and kiss me again.'

* * *

Jackson did exactly as he was told several times over during the course of the rest of the evening. She was flushed from desire and her skin tingled from the sensation of his stubble brushing against her face. His kisses and caresses were every bit as magical as she remembered them to be. It was as though all the missing years had fallen away, and they were back to being carefree teenagers, madly in love again. Only that particular story didn't have a happy ending. The niggling thoughts were whirling round and round in her head. What did it mean for their relationship now? Would it be another passionate romance destined to come to a dramatic and sudden halt?

'What happened to us, Jackson?' she asked. It was over a decade ago now, but still she needed some answers or else she would never be able to move on.

'How do you mean?' He caressed a hand along her cheek, looking intently into her eyes.

'When we were kids. I was so madly in love with you. We made so many plans together. I thought you loved me.'

'I did love you. I think there's a part of me that's always loved you. That's probably why none of my other relationships have worked out since.'

'So, what did I do so wrong? One moment you were there promising me a future and then the next moment you were gone without any explanation whatsoever. What you did to me was positively cruel, Jackson. You could have told me instead of leaving me not knowing what the hell had happened.'

'Oh, Pia.' He wrapped his arms around her shoulders. 'You didn't do anything wrong. It wasn't about you at all. It was all about me. Is it too late for me to say I'm sorry?'

'No, never,' she said contemplatively, 'but I still don't understand what happened. I need to know. You were the first guy I ever slept with. That was so very special to me.' She gave a bashful smile and shrugged. 'You're the only guy I've ever slept with – can you actually believe that? See what you did to me?'

'Really?' His face was filled with kindness as he stroked the hair behind her ears. 'Oh jeez. I can't apologise enough. Sit down, Pia.' He pulled out one of the kitchen chairs for her and another for himself. He sat down and dropped his head into his hands. 'I don't like talking about that time, but here goes nothing.' He took a deep breath and Pia could tell from his reticence just how difficult this was for him. 'Do you remember Ryan Bradshaw?'

Her brow creased as she tried to place the name. 'The name definitely rings a bell but I can't remember who he was.'

'He was a friend of mine. We hung out together on our bikes. We spent a lot of time together that last summer. Then he died.'

'Oh my goodness!' Her hand flew to her mouth. 'Yes. Ryan Bradshaw. I remember that now.' She'd never put two and two together before. 'A motorcycle accident, wasn't it? I had no idea you two were good friends, though.'

'Yep.' He nodded. 'I was with him the night he died.'

'That's terrible.' She reached over and grabbed Jackson's wrist, knowing how hard this must be for him. 'You were there when the accident happened, then?'

'No, but I'd been with him all night long, drinking cider, racing round the lanes and over the fields, generally causing a nuisance of ourselves.' He shook his head sadly. 'It seemed like huge fun at the time. We just didn't care. We did exactly what we wanted to do and sod the consequences.' His mouth twisted with regret. 'At the end of the evening he went home; he lived in Wishwell so he went in the opposite direction to me. I only found out the next day that he'd lost control on one of the bends and had died.'

Pia gasped. 'That's so sad.'

'It really is. It's never left me. I still think about him now every time I go out on the bike and drive those lanes. Why him and not me, Pia?'

'You can't think like that.' She took hold of his hand and squeezed it tight.

'But it's true. If we hadn't been drinking that night, if we hadn't been tearing up the roads, if we hadn't been stupid arrogant kids then Ryan's death might so easily have been avoided.'

'You don't know that. It was a terrible accident. That's all. A real tragedy, but it wasn't your fault, Jackson.'

'That's why I took off. I'm sorry but I didn't stop to think how you might be feeling. That's not to say I didn't think about you in the following months and years, because I did, quite often actually, but after the accident I just couldn't cope with being around here any more, and facing all the reminders of Ryan and his death. Listening to the gossip and witnessing his parents' grief. It was too much.'

'You know you could have confided in me.'

'I realise that now, but at the time I just had to get away. I tried to bury that trauma but I know now that you can't escape the past however much you might want to. It was only a couple of years ago when I was referred for some therapy that I actually came to terms with what had happened. It was one of the reasons I was so keen to come back here. I wanted to make amends.'

All this time and Pia had believed that she must have done something to upset Jackson, or that he'd simply fallen out of love with her, when in fact he'd been running away from his own demons. She felt a huge swell of love and sympathy for the young man he'd been back then and the thoughtful, kind man he was today.

'I'm really pleased you did come back, or else we might never have met up again.'

'Exactly.' His eyes shone as he looked at her. 'It was the best thing I ever did. I came home to see my aunt when she was dying and being back in the village made me realise that I couldn't keep running. It hadn't helped in all those years I'd been away. The feelings of guilt and remorse stayed with me. Marie urged me to speak to someone about the accident and after she died, that's when I sought help. I decided that I wanted to reach out to Ryan's parents, to explain what had happened, so I wrote them a letter, apologising for my part in his death, telling them how much I missed him, and how I wished it had been me who had died that night, and not him. I'm not sure I was expecting a response, but his mum got in touch the very next day to say how much my letter had meant to them and that I should go and visit them. I was so apprehensive, thinking they would bombard me with questions and berate me for my part in Ryan's death, but they couldn't have been lovelier or kinder. When his mum hugged me tight it helped to lift all those bad feelings I'd been carrying around with me for so long. We all cried, of course, but we laughed as well, and talked for ages

about Ryan.' Jackson nodded as though reliving that meeting. 'It was definitely cathartic for us all.'

Pia had tears in her eyes as she listened to Jackson's story.

'Thanks for listening, Pia, and for not judging me. It means the world
to be able to talk to you about what happened. I hope with time you'll be
able to forgive me.'

She felt a huge swell of emotion rise up in her chest.

'Don't be daft, Jackson,' she said, kissing him on the bridge of his nose
and wrapping him in her arms. 'I already have.'

39

'Would you do something for me?' Pia asked Jackson.

They'd sat and chatted for ages and Pia had felt so humbled that Jackson had opened up his heart to her. It was as though all the intervening years had slipped away and that the connection they'd felt as teenagers had been restored. Pia had a much deeper understanding and affection for the man sitting in front of her now.

'Anything. I suppose I do have a bit of making up to do,' he said, tracing a finger around her chin as her mouth twisted in a smile.

'That's what I thought,' she said, grinning. 'In that case, you'll come in the hot tub with me?'

Jackson groaned. 'What, now?'

Pia nodded enthusiastically.

'Anything but that! Aren't we comfy enough in here? Look at Bertie. He's fast asleep by the Aga; he won't want to go outside.'

'Yes, he will. Come on, it will be fun. And it's such a lovely evening, we'll be able to watch the stars. There's some trunks in the cupboard in the office if you need some!' she said with a cheeky expression, before rushing off to get changed, as Bertie duly jumped up, excited by the sudden activity.

Despite his protestations, Pia knew that Jackson wouldn't say no to her. How could he when he'd admitted himself that he had some making up to do? Not that she thought that was true in the slightest. He didn't owe her anything, not now he'd apologised and told her the whole story. She felt so much better for knowing what Jackson had been through.

In her turquoise swimsuit, clutching a big fluffy towel, she stepped out of the door of her flat to find Jackson waiting for her, dressed in only black swim shorts, and at the same time their eyes lit up to see each other.

'See, I told you this was a good idea, didn't I?' Pia said, laughing, as Jackson reached for her waist and pulled her in for a kiss, their hands exploring each other's naked skin. Jackson's body was strong and taut, the muscles of his abdomen clearly defined with the tattoos on his chest and arms complementing the contours of his body.

'Come on, let's do this, or else I'll want to turn you right around and take you straight back to your bedroom.'

Outside, they held hands as they took tentative steps into the hot tub and Pia gasped as the warm water washed over her legs.

'Didn't I tell you this was amazing?'

They sat beside each other, still holding hands, their legs intertwined as they looked over the darkened landscape, the fairy lights over the wooden pergola providing soft pools of light. Their conversation was only interrupted by their inability to stop kissing each other. Suddenly Jackson pulled away.

'You know I meant every word that I said?'

Pia looked into his dark eyes, which grew ever more captivating the longer she peered into them, and tilted her head.

'That I've probably been in love with you ever since we first got together. I thought about you often over the years and when you came back into my life so unexpectedly, I couldn't believe my luck. Seeing you again, at the Treetops Cafe, brought all those emotions flooding back and I knew I couldn't lose you for a second time. I messed up once; I didn't want to do it again.'

Pia smiled, hardly believing what she was hearing. 'I felt the same, and I was so worried about working for you, thinking you were still with Tara, and wondering how my poor heart would cope seeing you with another woman. But I was desperate for a job,' she said, laughing, breaking the intensity of the moment.

'There's only every been one woman for me, Pia. I promise you. I love you, girl.'

'I love you too, Jackson.'

Jackson leant into Pia and kissed her passionately, his hands running over her soft curves, sending sensations of delight rippling through her entire body. His fingers ran around the edges of her swimsuit, and she felt her desire increasing with his every moment, until a sudden and all-too-familiar noise interrupted them and made them both sit straight up.

'Oh, look at you two in there, having a wonderful time. It's so magical under the night sky. Doesn't it look inviting, Mateo? Do you mind if we join you?'

'Yes,' said Jackson emphatically, while at the exact same time, Pia said, 'No, not at all,' before she laughed, digging Jackson in the ribs.

'No! I not want to go in tub. I must go to bed.'

'Oh, Mateo, where is your sense of adventure?' said Ronnie. 'It will be fun and romantic.'

'No, I go to bed. Right now. I not want romance. Goodnight to you all.'

'Well, he doesn't know what he's missing,' Ronnie said, chuckling, when Mateo had left. 'You will wait for me, won't you,' she said to Jackson and Pia, 'while I go and get changed. Should I bring a bottle of your nice rosé with me for us to share as well?' Ronnie's eyes lit up expectantly.

'Perfect,' said Jackson, grimacing, before closing his eyes and sliding fully beneath the water, while Pia looked on, giggling.

40

'Come and have a look in here.' Pia led Abbey and Sam into the stables to the very end unit, which was filled with a selection of books. 'Ta-da! Our very own book exchange. What do you think? The idea is that you can borrow a book or a few if you'd like, and then you can return them when you're finished with them, and drop off any of your old books that you don't want any more.'

'It's brilliant,' said Abbey, looking impressed.

'Isn't it? It will be open every day when the stables are open and I'm hoping people will get to know it's here and will want to use it. It's a resource for the local community as well, while the repairs are carried out on the library at the village hall. We're also organising a book festival in the autumn, which you'll have to come along to.'

'Definitely. Just let me know the details and I'll be there.'

Pia was warmed by how her friends and people in the local community had rallied round to support the events at Primrose Hall and today was no exception.

The car and bike show at Primrose Hall had brought in the crowds and everyone seemed to be enjoying themselves, mooching around looking at the vintage cars and motorbikes. There was something for everyone as, along with the auto jumble, there were the craft stalls in the stables and a number of other general stalls outside selling leather goods, cheeses and locally brewed beers.

'Where is Jackson, then?' Sam asked, his gaze trying to pick out Jackson's distinctive figure amongst the throng of visitors. 'I wanted to have a word with him if possible.'

'Last time I saw him he was down at the bikes with his dad. I'm sure you'll find him over there somewhere.'

'You look happy,' said Abbey, once Sam had wandered off.

'I am. I'm just relieved that we've had such a good turnout. I really didn't know how many people to expect but Jackson assured me that people would come. Who knew old cars and bikes would be so popular? I'm really pleased for him, though; this was the event that he's really been looking forward to.'

'It's brilliant. You two are a great team, aren't you?' said Abbey, a glint in her eye.

'We really are,' said Pia, widening her eyes and sticking her tongue out of the corner of her mouth.

Abbey knew Pia well enough by now to know what that gleeful expression meant. 'Hey, really? Are you two together now, then?'

Pia nodded, unable to stop the wide smile from spreading across her face. 'We are, but we're keeping a low profile at the moment. Just finding our way and seeing how things go. But I'm really happy, Abbey.'

'I can tell! That's the best news, Pia. I'm so pleased for you both. You seem so good together. And don't worry, your secret is safe with me. Although I do hope Jackson will be your plus one at our wedding? There's only a couple of months to go now.'

'I know, the date's in the diary. It's so exciting. And Jackson will definitely be my plus one even if he doesn't know it yet,' she said, laughing.

Abbey was joined by some friends: Lizzie from the cafe with her partner, Bill, her daughter, Katy, and Katy's husband, Brad, with their small children, Rosie and Pip, who were undeniably cute. Rhi, who used to work at the Three Feathers in Wishwell, was there too with her boyfriend, Luke, so Pia said her hellos and goodbyes, and went off in search of Jackson.

'Ooh-ooh, Pia.' She turned round at the sound of her name and her face lit up to see Ronnie heading in her direction.

'Well, well, just look at you. You look absolutely stunning in that dress, Ronnie!'

'What, this old thing?' Ronnie said, raising her eyebrows cheekily, but Pia wasn't fooled. She knew that it was a new purchase bought specially for the occasion. The yellow gingham print looked lovely against Ronnie's tanned skin and her hair was newly coiffed, making her look years younger than her actual age. Ronnie slipped her arm through Pia's.

'Have you seen Rex at all?' She feigned nonchalance. 'I wonder if he'll be here today. I shall do my utmost to avoid him if he is,' she said haughtily, but her sparkling hazel eyes didn't stay still; they were searching out the entire area in the hope of spotting Rex.

'I've already seen him. I think he's with Jackson. They've been talking engines. I was just heading that way. Are you coming with me?'

'Well, I suppose if I have to,' said Ronnie, pursing her lips.

The pair of them walked together over to the main arena, chatting all the while.

'Hello, you two, how's it going down here?' Pia called when she found Jackson caught in a huddle of guys, including Rex, examining a huge motorbike.

'Hey, you!' He jumped up from his haunches and came across and kissed Pia fulsomely on the lips.

Pia laughed as she scrunched her shoulders, his kisses sending goosebumps all over her body. 'I thought we were supposed to be keeping this to ourselves for a while.'

'I can't see any point, can you? I love you and I don't care who knows it. Besides, Ronnie knows now so that means the whole world will know sooner or later.'

Pia laughed. 'Hey, I will never grow tired of hearing you say that. I love you too.' Okay, so maybe she'd loved Jackson even before she'd started her job at the hall, but every moment she spent with him just increased the depth of her feeling for this man.

Rex turned and spotted her too and came across for a hug.

'Hello, lovely, how are you? What a great show you've put on here,' he said, looking all around him. Then he must have spotted Ronnie standing to the side because he glanced at her and then quickly did a double take.

'Hiya, Ronnie, you okay? You look pretty gorgeous today, but then you always did scrub up well.'

Ronnie visibly puffed up with pride. 'I'm surprised you noticed, Rex.'

'How could I not?' he said with the same winning smile that Jackson used with such devastating effect upon Pia. It was obviously something in the Moody genes, and Pia could tell just by looking at Ronnie that it had a similar impact on her.

'I was just going to get an ice cream. Anyone fancy one?' asked Rex. Both Pia and Jackson declined the offer, and Ronnie turned the other way, as though she thought he couldn't possibly be talking to her. 'Ronnie?' he prompted.

'Yes?' she said, looking up coyly from under her darkened eyelashes.

'Would you like me to treat you to an ice cream?'

'Oh, I don't know, um, well, I suppose if you're having one, I could,' she said, uncharacteristically coyly.

'Come on, then. I know you always loved a raspberry ripple back in the day, didn't you?'

'I did,' she said, laughing, her skin turning pink, as though she was a teenage girl again.

Jackson and Pia stood hand in hand, watching Rex and Ronnie as they walked across to the ice-cream van, and Ronnie slipped her arm through Rex's.

'Look at those two getting on so well. Do you think there might be a softening on both of their parts?'

'Oh, believe you me, it won't last,' said Jackson, laughing. 'They'll probably be hurling abuse at each other by the time they've got to the end of their ice-cream cones.'

'I'm not so sure about that. Something tells me there might be love in the air with those two. Have you seen the way they look at each other?'

'What? When they're not trying to kill each other, you mean. I don't know, Pia. I'm not sure I could cope with the drama of my parents getting back together.'

'Well, they're both much older and wiser these days. Mellower, even. Shall we give them the benefit of the doubt?'

Jackson rolled his eyes and laughed, not sharing Pia's optimism. 'It's been such a great day and that's down to all your hard work. Thanks for everything you've done.'

'It was very much a team effort, wasn't it, with Frank and Mateo and Ivy as well? We're a pretty good team, don't you think?'

'We are. And this is only the beginning. We've got Abbey and Sam's wedding to look forward to, the book festival coming up in the autumn and then the Christmas carols too. I can't wait for that. We could probably do with getting a couple more events in the diary too. Maybe Halloween or Bonfire Night? What do you reckon?'

'Let me get my thinking cap on and I'll come up with a few ideas.'

Jackson pulled Pia into his side and tipped her chin up with his finger, his dark brown eyes always so seductive as his full lips landed on her mouth and she succumbed so willingly to his intense and delicious kisses, the sensations reaching her fingers and toes. Suddenly she was oblivious to the hubbub around them.

'I feel so lucky that I've found you again, Pia,' he said, when they came up for air. 'And this time I'm never going to let you go. You don't know how happy you've made me, being here, such a good friend to me, as well as being the woman I'm so madly in love with.'

If it was anything like the way she felt towards him then she knew exactly what he meant. She was the lucky one. In the space of a few months her whole life had been turned on its head and she'd found a happiness at Primrose Hall that she never thought possible.

'Just don't go breaking my heart!' he said, kissing her, gently this time, on her lips.

'I promise you, I've got no intention of ever doing that. You're never getting rid of me now.'

At that moment, at Pia's side, Bertie gave an insistent bark, demanding attention after he'd been ignored for the last few minutes.

'Yes, Bertie, I know,' said Jackson, dropping his hand to pet the dog. 'You've carved a special place in my heart too.'

Pia's heart swarmed with happiness as she took in the beauty of the landscape around them, a sight that would never grow old. Jackson was absolutely right. This really was just the beginning. There were many more adventures still to come at Primrose Hall and she couldn't wait to discover what their future together held in store for them both.

ACKNOWLEDGMENTS

Thank you for reading my book! I really hope you enjoyed your visit to Primrose Hall and getting to know Pia and Jackson.

I'm having so much fun writing this series of books set in the beautiful surroundings of Primrose Woods. The characters have become my friends and I'm so pleased that readers seem to view them in the same light too.

I have to thank my amazing publisher Boldwood Books for all their help and support. They are such a dynamic team who work tirelessly at producing, promoting and selling my books with such enthusiasm and creativity. Thank you, Amanda, Claire, Nia and the entire Boldwood crew.

Thanks, in particular, to the ever cheerful and hugely efficient Jenna Houston for all your help on the marketing side. You really are a star! A special thanks too to my lovely editor, Sarah Ritherdon, whose editorial insights are always spot on and who somehow manages to help me transform my first draft into a bright, shiny and polished new book. Every single time!

A big thank you to Rachel at Rachel Random Resources for organising the blog tours and to all the bloggers who take part. I'm so thankful to you all for reading my books, writing such detailed reviews and helping to spread the word.

Ellie – so much love and thanks! I am very happy you have discovered the wonderful world of romance and our conversations about heroes and tropes and, everything in-between, are so stimulating and helpful, and have encouraged me to look at my writing in a completely new light. I feel so lucky to have the benefit of your instincts and mainly useful suggestions (!) and I'm eternally grateful for your enduring support, love and laughter.

Nick, Tom and Amber – well, I just couldn't do it without you!

Finally, thank you to every single reader who has picked up one of my books, and read and enjoyed my stories. Your support makes it all worthwhile.

Much love

Jill xx

MORE FROM JILL STEEPLES

We hope you enjoyed reading *Dreams Come True at Primrose Hall*. If you did, please leave a review.

If you'd like to gift a copy, this book is also available as an ebook, large print, hardback, digital audio download and audiobook CD.

Sign up to Jill Steeples' mailing list for news, competitions and updates on future books.

https://bit.ly/JillSteeplesNews

Explore more feel-good love stories from Jill Steeples...

ABOUT THE AUTHOR

Jill Steeples is the author of many successful women's fiction titles – most recently the Dog and Duck series - all set in the close communities of picturesque English villages. She lives in Bedfordshire.

Visit Jill Steeples's website: https://www.jillsteeples.co.uk

Follow Jill on social media:

twitter.com/jillesteeples

facebook.com/jillsteepleswriter

instagram.com/jill.steeples

Boldwood

Boldwood Books is an award-winning fiction publishing company seeking out the best stories from around the world.

Find out more at www.boldwoodbooks.com

Join our reader community for brilliant books, competitions and offers!

Follow us
@BoldwoodBooks
@BookandTonic

Sign up to our weekly deals newsletter

https://bit.ly/BoldwoodBNewsletter

Ingram Content Group UK Ltd.
Milton Keynes UK
UKHW041140150323
418368UK00006B/12

9 781802 807110